THE CHOSEN: BOOK 2

REIGN OF ASH

MEG ANNE

This book is a work of fiction. The names, characters, places, and incidents are products of the author's imagination or have been used fictitiously and are not to be construed as real. Any resemblance to persons, living or dead, actual events, locales, or organizations is entirely coincidental.

Cover Design © Lori Follett of HellYes.design

Editing: Hanleigh Bradley

For the men in my life that taught me distance don't mean $#!+
Real love endures zip codes, time zones and lifetimes.
Grandpa, Dad, and Gabe you are the proof.

THE CHOSEN: BOOK 2

REIGN OF ASH

ELYSIA

Grey Spire

Etillion

Talyria

Vyruul

The Queen's Aerie

Caederan

Endoshan

Emerald Ocean

Kiri's Palace

Tigaera

Daejara

The Mother's Tears

Sylverlands

Sea of Mist

Kaspar's Catacombs

Baul

Holbrooke Estate

Broken Vale

Forest of Whispers

Ebon Isle

PROLOGUE

*G*illian could feel the weight of her mistress's stare and allowed her eyes to dart up to the woman on the throne. She had many titles, but Gillian knew her best as mother. At least, she had. Once.

There was nothing left of the mother Gillian had once known in the woman sitting above her. In truth, it felt like there was a chasm that separated the once kind, if only mildly affectionate woman who raised her from this aloof and cold-hearted queen. Now instead of mother, she was simply referred to as Mistress by Gillian and Rowena by those too stupid to know what was good for them. Or those that had a death wish.

As the last Damaskiri, she was both Helena's predecessor and a woman believed dead by the people she once ruled. She was a Queen in hiding, biding her time until she could strike against her enemies and reclaim her rightful place amongst the Chosen.

Rowena leaned back slowly, her eyes never drifting from the red-haired girl kneeling before her. Sitting as she was, she was the personification of queenly grace, her posture perfect and unflinching. She was stunning in a cold and frightening way. Her face was currently schooled into an expressionless mask; her ice-blue gaze glacial as she stared. Her colorless blonde hair was pulled up into an elaborate mess of braids and surrounded by the glittering and twisting spikes of metal that comprised her crown. A fitted black satin dress encased her lithe body, the severity of its color only enhancing the luminosity of her skin. Rowena tilted her head to the side, the movement deliberate and calculating, a predator assessing its prey. The silence lengthened and became uncomfortable until Gillian finally shifted nervously, her skirts rustling as they moved against the ground.

There was a metallic tinkling as Rowena's fingers tapped a steady beat on the dark arm of her throne. Gillian's green eyes widened, noting the sharp-clawed tips of the rings which adorned each of the slender fingers on mother's right hand. She forced herself to look away, shifting her focus back to the stone floor. After another long moment of strained silence, Gillian bowed her head lower, allowing a waterfall of copper curls to spill over her shoulder and obscure her face. The protection from Rowena's scrutiny was welcomed, even if only imagined. That icy gaze missed nothing.

"The prisoner?" Rowena finally asked, her voice as expressionless as her face and as weighted as her stare.

Gillian felt her shoulders stiffen as she relayed the latest report, "Still under the effects of the *Bella Morte*, Mistress."

"You were careless in your dosage." It was both a statement and judgment, the words leaving absolutely no room for doubt; she would be punished for her transgression. Gillian swallowed thickly. Her mistress's punishments were unfailingly harsh and varied. One thing Gillian had come to expect was that she would never see it coming.

"I do not believe he is lost to the dreaming, Mistress." Gillian winced, hearing the quavering in her voice.

"You do not *believe*?" The question was a harsh crack. Gillian found herself grinding her teeth before she could respond.

"He is not showing any side effects besides the hallucinations," she amended.

"Other than remaining in a drugged stupor since his arrival," Rowena contradicted caustically.

"Yes, Mistress. It is as you say," Gillian meekly agreed.

"You had better hope that he wakes, and soon. For your brother's sake, if not your own. Micha's remaining days on this earth are a direct result of your success..." She paused for one endless moment before adding contemptuously, "or your failure." The words were savage but measured, the threat delivered as matter-of-factly as one might discuss the weather.

Fear scratched down her spine and Gillian could feel her body break into a sweat, despite the chill in the room. Before she could respond further she was dismissed, Rowena standing and exiting from one of the doors in the back of the cavernous room.

Gillian did not move immediately, not trusting her limbs to support her or that her mother would not be back. While she waited, she let her eyes bounce from the arched windows and soaring ceilings back to the throne of twisting metal sitting in the center of the dais. After it was clear Rowena would not be returning, Gillian stood and made her way to the door. Her legs trembled as she exited the room but she made it to the safety of the corridor before slumping against the stone wall. Her eyes fluttered closed as her heart raced and a thought tinged with desperation raced through her. *One moment. I just need one moment.* Gillian struggled to calm her heartbeat. Eventually, she peeled herself off of the wall and took a final, shuddering breath as she continued her journey to the prisoner.

He would wake; she would see to it. She would bring his mind back to his body even if it required her to take him to the brink of death to do so. There was no room for failure. Micha's life depended on it. No matter how much she enjoyed her plaything, Micha's life was worth infinitely more to her than stolen moments in a prison cell. One way or the other, it was time for Von to wake up.

CHAPTER ONE

*H*elena sat beside the fountain, a picture of quiet devastation. She could no longer see her reflection rippling in the water's pristine surface. She also couldn't remember the last time she moved, or even hazard a guess as to how long she'd been sitting there. Despite her statue-like stillness, the serenity was only an illusion. Every night since Von's capture she had sought out a place where she could be alone to search for some sense of their bond, some spark that would help guide her to him. And just as it had been every night since she started her search, there was only a vast and endless darkness.

Helena flinched violently as a warm hand brushed against her icy shoulder. She spun around, teeth bared in a feral snarl until she recognized the green eyes studying her with concern.

"You forgot your cloak again," Darrin murmured gently, offering her the deep purple garment lined with sable fur.

"Oh, thank you," she rasped, her voice raw with disuse. Her stiff fingers tried to take the cloak but could not bend enough to grasp it before Darrin let go. It fell clumsily to the floor. She sat unmoving; her eyes, which tracked its progress to the ground, were the only sign she was aware of what had happened.

"Here, let me," he offered finally when she made no move to pick it up. He lifted and deftly wrapped the warm fabric around her shoulders. Helena shivered as its warmth seeped into her skin.

"What time is it?" she asked, her words coming slowly as she struggled to come back to the present.

"It's getting late, and you missed the evening meal. Again." His voice held none of the gentle rebuke she was used to hearing. In its absence, there was only worry.

She had not been taking very good care of herself and it showed. Her aqua eyes, usually shining with light, were bruised and dull. She had missed more meals than she ate and had gotten little, if any, sleep. The sleep she had managed to get had been fraught with nightmares, which only added to the haunted look in her eyes. The lack of food and quality sleep, combined with a headache which had only grown in intensity since Von's disappearance, left her looking decidedly haggard.

Von would be so disappointed in her if he saw her walking through the corridors of his home like a ghost of the woman he loved. She could almost hear his deep growl echoing in her mind: *"What do you think you're doing, Mate? That body belongs to me; take better care of it."*

The wave of longing that slammed through her at even that paltry imitation of him had tears blurring her eyes. She swallowed the emotion back down and gave herself a mental shake. She could not go on like this for much longer; both her body and her heart would give out on her soon. If not for her own sake, she could at least try to take better care of herself for him. She had vowed to find him and destroy his captors after all. She could hardly make good on the promise to avenge him if she was too weak to do more than sit there and scowl menacingly. The mental image caused a barely discernable smile to flit across her lips before quickly fading.

Helena blinked back the last of the tears and really looked at Darrin for the first time. "Do you think there's something left for me to eat?"

Relief flooded his face at the request, "Yes, Kiri. I believe we can scrounge something up for you."

6

She nodded once and stood, ready to follow him back into the manor. They had reached the Holbrooke Estate only a day after discovering Gillian's betrayal. Helena winced as she remembered her first meal with Von's family.

THE CIRCLE SAT around a massive oak table that was colored and pitted with age. The room was bright, lit both by the fire roaring beside them, and by soft balls of light which floated above them. Helena had been given a place of honor at the head of the table, although the sneers Von's father, Darius, wore whenever she caught him looking at her did much to undermine the display of hospitality. Margo, Von's mother, was much kinder. She had welcomed the group with warm hugs and wept silently when she had learnt what had become of her eldest son. Von's younger brother Nial had not been feeling well and was unable to come and greet the group, although he had sent his apologies for his absence and promised to meet with them soon.

Helena had moved through the introductions numbly, allowing Timmins to explain what had happened. All of the fury and promises of vengeance had burned out of her, leaving only a fragile shell in its place. Well, that was not strictly true; her wrath continued to simmer along the surface of her magic, but it was leashed by the lack of a target. Without it to fuel her, she was left with little to buffer her against the storm of emotions raging within. Guilt. Fear. Sorrow. All were relentless as they continued to crash against the inner barriers of her mind.

She couldn't recall much of the short tour they were given as Margo led them to their rooms. Despite being at the base of a mountain the manor was warm. It had wide halls and vaulted ceilings that created a sense of openness and flow from room to room. There were also large windows in every room so that the beauty of Daejara was incorporated throughout their home. It often seemed as though they were sitting outside, although the fact that they were sheltered from the biting winds was certainly a welcome reprieve.

The dining hall sat to the east of the home, overlooking the view of the massive cliffs and sparkling blue ocean below. Helena had never seen the sea before, but there was something about the roar of the crashing waves that called to her. Perhaps, if she could get away from the prying eyes of the Circle, she would take Starshine out over the water to get a better look.

Thinking of Starshine had her remembering her last night with Von under the stars. The feeling of his warm hands running along the length of her back. The scrape of his teeth as he ran them over the cords of muscle in her neck before biting down gently, and then licking his way back to her ear to trail sweet kisses down to her lips.

She felt her lower lip quiver at the memory. Her desire for her Mate was quickly overshadowed by her grief at his absence, and at the way things had been left between them. It was her fault he had been taken. If she had not been so stupid and believed Gillian's lies... if she had not trusted the harlot in the first place... if only she could tell Von how sorry she was, and how much she loved him.

The sniffling brought her out of her memories. She looked around the table with wide eyes, shock quickly replaced by mortification as she watched each person sob. Serena had her head buried in Ronan's neck, while the warrior hastily wiped at his eyes. Darrin had his head bowed over his plate, shoulders shaking with tears. Timmins was blowing his nose while Joquil dabbed at his dripping eyes. Margo and Darius clung to each other, their cries echoing loudly in the spacious room.

Kragen's eyes were dry but despondent, anguish cutting deep lines in his usually smiling face. "I much prefer the days you would have us seeking out dark corners to fumble beneath a maid's skirts to this, Kiri," he muttered.

Helena blinked and let out a startled bark of laughter. That was all it took to break the spell; the men and women parroted Kragen's sentiment as their tears were swiftly replaced with watery laughter.

"You and I both, Sword." While her smile didn't quite reach her eyes, the gentle teasing had worked. She was no longer drowning in her misery and was able to get through the evening without further incident.

"PERHAPS I WILL ACTUALLY MAKE it through a meal without embarrassing myself," she murmured, heartened by the fact she would be eating in relative solitude.

Darrin chuckled beside her, "No one blames you, Helena."

She sighed, "No, I know that... it would just be nice to have my feelings be a little less," she paused searching for the right word, "contagious."

He placed his hand lightly on her shoulder, "One would only have to look at your eyes to know what you were feeling."

She blinked up at him before smiling sadly, "I haven't been doing a very good job of being a leader these past weeks, have I? I've been too busy wallowing."

Darrin made a dismissive sound, not bothering to answer.

Helena squared her shoulders and said with forced determination, "Well, no more of that. It's time I got back to my training. Will you let Ronan know I would like to work with him in the morning? And tell Joquil I'd like to continue with our lessons as well."

Darrin's eyes widened in surprise before he nodded quickly, "Of course."

I really must be pathetic these days if that was enough to shock him, she thought dejectedly.

"Oh," she added aloud, "And I would like to set aside some time to see Nial. He was the entire reason for this trip, at least originally. I would like to see what I can do to help him."

"Are you sure you're strong enough for something like that?" Darrin's question mirrored her own concerns.

Helena shrugged as they rounded the corner and walked into the kitchen, "Honestly, I have no idea, but until I see what I'm dealing with, it's too hard to say one way or the other."

Helena had met Nial only briefly. She had taken one look at his dark hair and those familiar gray eyes and practically put down roots in the floor. The similarity between him and his brother had been enough to have her heart lodge in her throat. She had stood there like a slack-jawed fool, staring at him with hopeful longing. It had taken a few moments for her to recover enough to stumble through an apology, her cheeks a blazing pink. Nial had kindly waved it off, smiling as he adjusted the soft blue blanket in his lap.

Once her heartbeat had returned to its normal pace, she realized there were a number of subtle differences between the brothers. To start, Nial's voice lacked Von's deep growl and his gray eyes were more a stormy gray-blue than silver. Helena had also noticed that his wavy dark hair was much shorter than Von's. Even so, it hurt to look at him, the visual reminder of what she had lost was more than she could bear, and she had limited her interactions with him. Yet another reason she had avoided so many meals. *Coward. No more hiding, Helena*, she chided herself. *Von deserves better than this.*

Darrin moved across the room, opening a chilled cabinet to gather the leftovers from the evening meal. She watched him open up various containers before selecting one that appeared to be full of a vegetable stew and another full of a fluffy white substance.

"Potatoes," Darrin said in answer to her lifted brow.

Helena's stomach growled as the smell of the food hit her nose.

Darrin laughed loudly, his eyes crinkling with mirth as he said, "Well, I guess I don't need to ask if that sounds good to you."

She stuck out her tongue in response as he quickly dished out large portions of each.

"Can you manage reheating these?" he gestured toward her hands. "I'm not certain where anything is in here or I would offer to do it myself."

Helena nodded and stepped over to him, her fingers running over the smooth surface of the large wooden counter as she did. Grasping the dish, she closed her eyes and called the smallest tendril of magic to her. She felt the heat of Fire quickly rush to the surface, and found herself making soothing noises to gentle the rush. She released her magic entirely once the spicy steam was wafting up to her face.

Darrin let out a low whistle, "Such a convenient talent."

Helena nodded in agreement, accepting the spoon he was holding out to her. She dug in greedily and immediately let out a startled yelp as her eyes began to water. Her hand was pressed over her mouth while she blinked back tears.

Darrin howled with laughter beside her, "Alright, perhaps it's not as convenient as I thought if you make it too hot to eat."

She glared at him, "You're lucky I'm too hungry to dump this on you."

He held up two hands and stepped back, "Merely an observation, Kiri."

She rolled her eyes, "Standing on formality will not protect you, Shield."

He lifted a shoulder while his smile grew, "You can't blame me for trying, Hellion."

She winked at him, before taking another spoonful of the stew and making a show of blowing on it. His laughter died down and he stood across from her, watching her silently.

She lifted her brow. "What?" she asked, her mouth full of stew and the word coming out garbled.

He just shook his head, a small smile playing about his lips, "It's just nice to see you looking happy, Helena."

She swallowed and looked down into her bowl before speaking, "I miss him, Darrin."

"I know," he said gravely.

She shook her head slowly, "No, I don't think you do." Her aqua eyes blazed brightly as they met his before continuing, "I feel as though a piece of me is missing. It's not something as obvious as a limb, but I feel just as crippled. Nothing feels right without him here. I'm so lost..." she trailed off, averting her gaze as she did, her voice thick with emotion.

"We will find him, Helena. Do not lose hope."

He watched a small tremor work its way through her body, her fingers gripping the spoon in her hand more tightly. When she looked back up, there were hints of the swirling iridescence in her eyes and

11

her voice resonated as though spoken in harmony, "I haven't and I won't."

Darrin nodded, his shoulders relaxing at the small appearance of her power. "Good. Now eat up."

Helena made a face but continued to work her way through the meal until it was mostly gone. Taking the bowl from her, he made quick work of rinsing it out and setting it to dry with the others.

"Feeling better?" he asked, his voice too inquisitive to be casual.

She nodded, smiling ruefully, "Yes, mother."

Darrin laughed, and pulled her into him, hugging her tightly, "We are going to get through this; you'll see." The words were soft as he rested his cheek atop her head.

"I know," she said just as softly, her words muffled by his chest. She clung to him as they stood in silence, willing his promises to come true.

CHAPTER TWO

"Harder, Helena," Ronan boomed as she swung the heavy training stick into the dummy.

"I'm swinging it as hard as I can, asshole," she panted as she lifted it again, her muscles screaming in protest. They had begun their workout with the dawn, and hours later she was well past the point of tolerating the Acting Commander's instruction.

"My granny could hit that sack of feathers harder than you," he taunted.

She growled low in her throat before swinging the stick for all she was worth. The dummy exploded with a satisfying thwack; gray and white feathers rained down upon them.

"Satisfied?" she asked, smiling up at him as she dropped her weapon to the ground.

"Now now, there's no need to whip your cock out and start waving it around. It's highly unladylike."

"Whipping my—" Helena sputtered.

Ronan's shoulders were shaking with laughter as he watched her face turn pink with indignation. "I'm just teasing you, Kiri."

"I would be happy to get the measuring stick out if you'd like. In fact, that sounds like a great idea. We can have all your men line up and drop their pants right here," Serena purred as she pulled feathers out of his braid.

"The Mother's tits you will!" Ronan growled before pressing a swift kiss against her smiling lips and muttering, "Minx."

Helena merely shook her head as she watched the couple; yearning for Von flared swift and hot through her at the sight of their easy embrace.

"Tough morning?" Serena asked lightly, violet eyes studying her friend with concern.

Helena grunted.

Blonde brows lifted in amusement as Serena replied, "Oh, I see."

Ronan's hand ran down Serena's back to curl around her waist, "That's enough for today. We lost a lot of progress in the last couple of weeks, but we should be able to make up for it quickly, so long as you continue to take care of yourself."

Her cheeks flamed at the gentle reprimand, but she nodded, still struggling to catch her breath.

"Just you two this morning?" Serena inquired, as her eyes scanned the small courtyard they had used for their practice.

Ronan nodded, the morning sun glinting against his scar and causing it to stand out in sharp relief against his cheek. "We wanted to test her limits today. It has been awhile since our last session, so I needed to establish her baseline and determine where we need to focus in order to rebuild her strength and stamina."

Helena whimpered when she realized she would not have Von to help ease the ache from her muscles this time. Her heart constricted painfully in her chest. Everything had become a constant reminder of his absence. Feeling the weight of their twin stares upon her, she straightened her shoulders and stood with her hands on her hips, attempting to convey a haughty confidence she did not entirely feel.

"Are you sure you still want to meet with Nial this morning?"

Helena nodded once.

"We can push it back. I'm sure he'll—" Serena ventured but was cut off.

"No, I've waited far too long as it is. I should have met with him by now. I just... wasn't ready."

Ronan leaned down and kissed Serena's forehead, "I will leave you two ladies to your morning. Helena," he turned to look at her sternly, "do not push yourself so hard that you cannot practice tomorrow. That's an order."

He turned and strode away before he could see the ball of Water she had manifested in the palm of her hand. Serena could hardly suppress her giggles as Helena let it fly straight into the back of Ronan's head. The large man stopped and turned slowly, his brows lowered menacingly over ice-blue eyes.

Helena bit down on her lip as she fought back her own laughter.

Ronan lifted a finger and pointed it at her face. "You," he said deliberately, "are very lucky."

Helena raised both brows in surprise, "And why's that?"

"If I wasn't so damn happy to hear you laughing again, I'd make you pay for that bit of cheekiness. As it stands, I'm just glad to have my friend back." He blew her a kiss and continued with his leisurely stroll to the manor.

Serena wrapped her arm around Helena, "For what it's worth, so am I."

Helena rested her head on her friend's shoulder, saying in a voice tinged with sadness, "I'm trying."

"We know, dearest," Serena replied matter-of-factly, giving her a tight squeeze before leaning down to sniff her delicately. "Perhaps you should bathe before we go up to meet the youngest Holbrooke. The poor lad has suffered enough already; he doesn't need to be assaulted by your ripe stench."

Helena sputtered with laughter as she shoved Serena, who landed on the ground in an undignified heap.

Serena was a picture of astonishment as she gaped up at Helena. "Alright, I deserved that," she said between breathless bouts of laughter.

Helena wore a self-satisfied smile as she offered Serena a hand to help her stand, "Yes. Yes, you did."

BATHED AND CHANGED into a dove gray gown, Helena met Serena in her suite's sitting area as she quickly braided her damp hair. Her rooms were large and airy, and much lovelier than Helena had anticipated given Von's description of life in Daejara after the ban. The focal point of the room was a hearth that was as tall as she was on the western side, the wall surrounding it comprised of large gray stones. The rest of the room was painted a soft lilac where it was not covered by colorful tapestries. The floor consisted of long, dark wooden planks that peeked out beneath the various plush rugs that littered the room. Also within the room was a massive four-poster bed, its golden coverings matching the heavy curtains currently pulled back from the floor-to-ceiling windows that opened onto a balcony overlooking the sea. The strategically placed furniture was made from the same dark wood as the floor and included a large bookcase, writing desk, and vanity. There were a few chairs and one low bench set up beside a glass table where Serena currently sat sipping tea.

Helena did a quick twirl, and asked dryly, "Do I pass inspection, Commander?"

Serena laughed at her use of the Daejaran title and offered a mocking nod, "You'll do, warrior."

Helena rolled her eyes, chuckling. She could not deny that her practice with Ronan had done much to ease some of the weight she had been carrying within her. It had felt good to whack that training dummy, imagining Gillian's smug smile on its face as she did. She had found release in running and pushing herself until she was ready to collapse. At the very least, it had given her something to *do*. She was so tired of feeling impotent. It had also given her something to focus on and allowed her to finally block the flurry of thoughts running on a never-ending loop inside her mind. For that alone, she was almost giddy about continuing her training tomorrow. Although, she was certain her muscles would be arguing with that sentiment come the morning.

There was a soft knock at the door before a flaxen head peered around the side, "Are you ready for me to take you up, Kiri?" Effie, the maid, asked in her sweet voice.

Effie looked deceptively young, probably because she was such a tiny thing. Her proportions were more doll-like than those of a woman well into her twenties. Her long blonde curls fell down her back and framed an elfish face with wide sky-blue eyes and long sooty lashes. She had a smattering of freckles across a slightly upturned nose and perfectly pouty lips that were almost always smiling. Helena had liked her instantly.

"Yes, thank you, Effie," she said with a smile that actually reached her aqua eyes.

Effie blushed and bobbed a quick curtsey before stepping back into the hallway.

"She's not used to people taking notice of her," Serena commented under her breath as she placed her empty cup on the table and stood to walk toward the door.

"I'm familiar with the feeling," Helena responded wryly.

Serena snickered softly, "I'm sure you are."

The stares and whispers had been almost constant since crossing the border, although people were finally polite enough not to blatantly comment on the shimmering iridescent rings around her pupils. Kragen had enjoyed a good laugh the first time Helena threatened to break the finger of the next person that tried to poke her in the eye. By the seventh, he was offering to do it for her.

"Everyone is just curious about their new Kiri," Serena offered as they exited her room.

"Lucky me," Helena muttered, her words dripping with sarcasm.

Serena snorted, "At least they ceased asking you to perform bits of magic for them."

"Because *that* went well," Helena retorted, ears burning as she recalled her failed attempt to make a teddy bear dance for a young boy in one of the villages. All she had meant to do was make it twirl about a little. Instead, the thing had exploded leaving stuffing and bits of fur floating in its wake. The boy had burst into tears and hid in his mother's skirts. His mother had been kind, but Helena was mortified. Kragen and Ronan had teased her ruthlessly for days after.

She still couldn't seem to find the level of control required to use her magic in the simplest of ways. At least, not consistently. The harder she tried, the more unwieldy it became. Lately, it felt more like she was trying to wrestle with a wild beast rather than simply coax a small wave of magic. Large magic was no issue, or it hadn't been so far. Helena had a growing suspicion that Von's kidnapping was playing some part in her struggle for control. When she'd broached the topic with Joquil, he'd brushed away her concerns stating that there was no record of a Mate's proximity having any effect on a Kiri's magic.

Effie escorted them expeditiously through the halls until they reached a quiet corner in the northeastern part of the manor. Helena could hear waves crashing in the distance as Effie gave the large wooden door a perfunctory knock.

"Come in," a deep male voice called from inside.

Effie opened the door, standing aside to let the ladies enter before her. Once they passed through the doorway, she made a small curtsey and shut the door, leaving the ladies alone with Nial. Helena was prepared this time, steeling herself against the despair that threatened to wash through her at the sight of Von's brother. There was a boyish charm to him and intelligence shone brightly in those familiar gray-blue eyes. He flashed her a broad grin, his eyes crinkling with good humor.

"Hello again, Kiri," he said by way of welcome.

Helena made her way toward his overladen table. It was littered with open books and parchment and looked ready to collapse at the hint of a stiff breeze. She eyed the open window warily as she approached him.

"Forgive me for not standing," he quipped.

She rolled her eyes, her lips quirking despite herself. "Ever the comedian, I see. And call me Helena, please, we are family now, after all," she murmured warmly. Noting the ink stains on his fingers and the pages filled with lines of precise notes, she added, "I'm not interrupting your studies, am I?"

He was quick to shake his head, "Not at all." As he turned to address Serena, who was standing just behind her, his eyes opened wide and his nostrils flared.

Helena's eyebrows furrowed as she looked from Nial to Serena. Serena's face had drained of color, her eyes unblinking as she stared at the man seated before her, mesmerized. Helena coughed discreetly, causing both of them to blink rapidly and straighten.

Nial held out his hand to Serena, "I don't believe we've met. I'm Nial."

"Serena," the warrior said in the softest voice Helena had ever heard her use. She placed her hand in his, jumping when he leaned down to kiss the back of it. As soon as he let her go, she stepped hurriedly back, her cheeks and chest splotched with pink and her violet eyes glazed.

Curious at her reaction, Helena asked, "You two have never met? I thought you and Ronan had known Von since you were children."

Serena gave a start at the mention of her lover's name. She blinked and shook her head, dragging her eyes from Nial back to Helena. "No, Kiri, neither Ronan nor I have had reason to visit the Holbrooke home before now. We always stayed in the barracks, or visited our own families, when Von would make his infrequent trips home."

"More's the pity," Nial said in a low, honey-coated voice. Serena blushed, her eyes darting to the floor.

Helena froze. The tone of his voice so like his brothers in that moment, she felt her own cheeks flush. Letting out a jagged breath, she refocused, reminding herself that she had a job to do. *Interesting*, Helena thought, studying the two. If she didn't know better, she would say that Serena was as infatuated with Nial as he obviously was with her. Helena knew she was wholly committed to Ronan though, so it didn't quite add up. *Something is definitely going on here*, Helena decided, determining to get to the bottom of it, eventually.

"I'm sure Von explained in his letters to you why I wanted to visit..." Helena interjected, trying to get their conversation back on track.

Nial nodded, his eyes continuing to examine the tall blonde beside her as he asked, "Do you really think you'll be able to help me?"

Helena shrugged, "I certainly hope so." She didn't think now was the appropriate time to mention that she had never attempted something of this magnitude before.

Nial moved his hands from the table to his sides and pushed himself back. Helena noted the wheels attached to his chair with surprise, "What a clever idea!"

Nial grinned up at her. "I may not be able to do many of the things my brother can, but at least this way I don't need to be completely dependent upon the help of others to get about."

Helena was more than a little impressed as she returned his smile, "You came up with this?"

"I did."

"Brilliant!" she exclaimed, eyeing Nial with more interest.

"Just because my body has limitations, does not mean that my mind does," he joked.

"I never thought for a moment that it did," Helena said sincerely. Nial offered her another warm smile before wheeling himself over to his bed. She was just about to offer to help him when he placed both palms on the bed and pushed himself up, twisting in the air to land with a soft plop. Helena blinked, trying to cover her astonishment. She really shouldn't be so shocked; he had obviously learned how to do much on his own, especially if those muscles flexing and bunching as he maneuvered his chair were any indication. This man did not seem at all like the crippled brother Von had described to her so long ago.

"I suppose you'll need to see the legs," Nial asked tightly, lifting one of his dark brows.

Helena's expression softened, "Yes, seeing the extent of your injuries would best allow me to understand how to undo the damage."

He nodded, his lips twisting into a frown as he warned, "It's not a pleasant sight, Kiri."

She shrugged, "I'm not easily frightened." As he worked his pants down his legs, she lifted the blanket that had fallen to the floor and held it up to offer him a modicum of privacy. She heard the gentle rustling of fabric before he let out a low grunt.

"I'm ready."

Helena set the blanket onto the vacated chair and tried to keep her face in a calm mask as she took in the twisted limbs. She heard Serena gasp behind her, Nial's ears turning red at the sound. His shoulders were stiff and his lips flat as she reached out a cool hand to run down the length of the leg. He grimaced, flinching at the contact.

"You can feel that?" she asked neutrally.

He bit down on his lip and nodded, "Yes. My legs are quite sensitive actually."

"That's a good sign. The nerves cannot have been completely damaged. That should assist with the healing," Helena offered as she continued her inspection.

That's probably the only good sign, she thought while trying to keep her expression neutral. His legs had been broken in multiple places; the skin was discolored and thick with scars from where his bones had pierced his skin when they broke. It was clear that the bones had never been properly reset. Both kneecaps appeared as though they had been completely shattered. His limbs were utterly mangled, only marginally resembling the shape they were supposed to be. *How could someone ever survive this kind of pain?*

Her aqua eyes glittered as she looked back up at Nial's face. There was a new level of admiration and respect in them. This was a man who had looked adversity straight in the eye and didn't back down an inch. He could teach her a thing or two in that regard.

Nial was staring straight ahead, bracing himself for what he was sure would be bad news.

"It might take me a few tries. I am still learning, but if you don't mind... I would like to try," she said softly, her hand coming to rest over his closed fist.

He looked up at her in surprise, "Really?"

She nodded, her smile soft.

"Yes," he cleared his throat, "I am more than willing."

Helena moved to sit beside him, apologizing with her eyes when the movement made him wince. Nial's anticipation of further pain gave her a moment of pause and her hands trembled slightly in her lap. His eyes were clenched shut and he was breathing quickly through his nose. Her instinct had always seemed to guide her before; she sincerely hoped it wouldn't let her down now. She didn't think her heart could stand the disappointment of another failure, let alone witnessing devastation in those blue-gray eyes.

Mother guide me, she fervently prayed as she placed her hands on either side of his left leg. Helena took a deep breath to begin the process of centering herself before diving into the pool of her magic. As always, her magic was waiting for her; its smooth surface rippling in greeting as she began to draw it into herself. She used it first to enhance her senses, allowing her eyes to see through his skin and into the muscles and bones beneath. Brushing her fingers down the length of his leg, she moved slowly, allowing her fingers to act as magnets that guided the bones back into place. She continued to move them, each wiggle an attempt to untangle the muscles that had knotted around the broken bones. As she moved, she also pushed her magic into his body, shielding him from the agony such adjustments would cause.

Helena lost track of time, working down his leg a number of times before switching to the other. She could feel her own body start to shake, her magic draining her even more quickly than usual given the way she had failed to take care of herself. There was a hand on her shoulder and she heard Serena's voice calling from a distance, "That's enough for today, Kiri."

Ignoring the voice, Helena continued to knit the bones back together, her fingers moving as though they were placing pieces of a puzzle.

"Helena," her friend finally snapped, shaking her.

She blinked, trying to refocus on the physical world, her hold on her magic slipping until it settled back into her inner reservoir. Still blinking, she looked into Nial's awed face. "Did I do it?" she asked, her voice hoarse.

Tears filled his eyes as he threw himself on her, wrapping her in his grateful embrace. Startled, she looked over his head at Serena, who had tears streaming down her cheeks. She untangled herself gingerly, not wanting to jostle him. When she looked down at his legs, she let out her own awestruck gasp. Where two grotesque imitations of human limbs had lain previously, there were now two perfectly sculpted legs. The skin was soft and responsive beneath her fingers, his toes twitching as she ran a finger down the arch of his foot.

"Can you try to bend it?" she asked, her voice still a gentle rasp.

Nial's face twisted in concentration as he tried to repair the link between his mind and the muscles he had not used for almost twenty years. Before long, both knees were bent and his feet were flat on the bed.

Serena cheered as he swept his legs over the side of the bed, Helena moving to offer assistance as he attempted to stand. He swayed slightly, trying to adjust to the feeling of standing again. When he straightened to his full height, he was almost as tall as Von. Helena wrapped her arm around his waist, helping him take his first teetering steps since he was a child, her own eyes filled with tears.

"How do you feel?" Serena whispered, her eyes bright with yet more unshed tears.

"A little weak," Nial admitted.

Helena helped him sit back down, "That's to be expected. While the muscles have healed, it will likely take time for you to regain full strength in them."

"You can train with Helena in the mornings. While she learns how to use weapons, you can work on building up your own strength again," Serena offered.

Nial's smile was blinding as he looked up at her, "Thank you, Helena, from the bottom of my heart thank you. I will never be able to thank you enough for what you have done for me."

Helena rolled her eyes at his dramatics but was grinning as he continued effusively, "You have given me something I long ago stopped believing was possible. Not only that, but in my wildest dreams, I never imagined that there was a possibility I would recover completely. You've truly gifted me with a second chance at life."

23

"It seems to me you were doing just fine, even without the use of your legs, Nial."

Nial's eyes seemed to glow as his stare moved to Serena, "There are certain things a man needs full use of his body for, at least if he wishes to do them properly."

For the second time ever, at least to Helena's knowledge, Serena blushed. Although this time, as Serena looked away she was biting back a smile.

CHAPTER THREE

*H*elena curled up in an armchair; her body and mind were so fatigued she could do little more than sit there while she half-listened to the men speaking around her. Things had been progressing, at least on the trade front. The merchants she'd brought with her from Elysia had made the connections necessary to establish new trade lines and set up shops in the central market. As for the rest of them, their new mission was less about diplomacy and more about rescue.

They had gathered in the library to discuss their next steps, but Helena couldn't find the energy to participate in the conversation. Her Circle had been relentless as they chased down leads that might take them to Von. Time and time again they returned empty-handed. The problem was that there was simply no trace of Gillian or Von; they had literally vanished from the camp, leaving no trail for the others to follow.

Kragen and Ronan had taken charge of the Holbrooke's garrison, sending riders off in every direction to see if anyone had seen them, but Helena knew it was futile. After learning of the Kaelpas stones and how they could instantaneously transport one or more people across the realm, she knew it wouldn't be as simple as searching a nearby town. No, this would require smoking the she-rat out of her hidey hole. *If only there was someone that could at least point us in the right direction*, she thought desperately.

"What if we send for Micha?" Kragen suggested in his deep rumble.

Helena's ears perked up at the question. "You think he might know where his sister went?" she asked from her chair. The men spun toward her, seeming to have forgotten she had been sitting there.

"It's a possibility worth considering, Kiri. They are twins and share a linked history. It seems unlikely they would have many secrets between them," Kragen responded.

Helena chewed on her bottom lip, thinking about the playful man who had been one of her first friends in the Capital, as well as one of her suitors. "Could he have been part of it?" she asked no one in particular.

"I highly doubt Gillian was acting alone, although I'm not certain Micha is involved," Timmins answered thoughtfully.

"At the very least, he should be informed of his sister's actions. His reaction to the information could be highly illuminating. If his friendship with Helena is genuine, perhaps he would be willing to help us locate his sister," Darrin added.

"You mean turn against her," Helena clarified dryly, her tone indicating the likelihood of that possibility.

"I don't hear you coming up with any ideas," he muttered darkly as his arms crossed his chest.

She lifted a brow at his insolence but left the comment unchallenged. There was a creak as the door to the library opened, Effie stepping in with a tray loaded with fruit, cheese and a selection of dried meats.

"I thought you all might like a snack," she said by way of explanation, setting the tray upon the table.

"Thank you, Effie. It was very kind of you to think of us," Helena said, making no move toward the food. The others all stepped eagerly to the table, loading up plates with their treats until the tray was almost bare.

"Would you like me to make you a plate, Kiri?" Effie asked, her voice a gentle chastisement for the men who had not thought to leave anything for Helena. For all that she tried to remain unobtrusive, the girl's pointed words brought the men to a halt.

Helena's eyes twinkled with laughter as they paused in their eating to look comically from their plates to her empty hands. Darrin's ears turned bright red and he quickly offered his plate to her. Kragen, Helena noted, merely shoved another piece of cheese into his mouth and winked.

"Nice try," she said sarcastically, rolling her eyes at Darrin before looking back at the maid and shaking her head, "Thank you, Effie, but I'm fine."

"You missed the afternoon meal while you were with Lord Nial," she countered. Again, while delicately delivered, her reproach was a direct hit.

Helena laughed, "I much prefer when you are focused on the others."

The girl's lips pursed with laughter, but she knew she had made her point and felt no need to comment further.

Helena let out a deep sigh, relenting, "Fine, a little something to eat would be most welcome."

"How is it that she can boss you around, but we cannot?" Darrin asked in annoyed disbelief, watching Helena accept her plate.

"Because I like her more than you," Helena teased.

Effie blushed at the compliment and moved to start clearing off the table.

Kragen cuffed Darrin on the back of his head, "Rein in your pride, Shield. It doesn't matter who gives her food, just be happy she's eating and stop asking stupid questions."

"Especially when she spent most of the day channeling a great deal of power," Joquil added sagely, as he crunched neatly on a cracker.

Helena shook her head as she bit into a piece of cheese, its tangy flavor making her stomach growl in approval. Effie smirked at the sound.

"Are you certain you aren't gifted with Spirit, Effie? It seems like you are a bit of a mind reader," Helena joked before taking another small bite.

Effie shook her head, blonde curls dancing as she did, "No, Kiri, simply observant. I am ungifted, but I grew up listening to my Gran tell me stories about the Masters of Prophecy."

The girl's words unlocked a memory in Helena's mind. She looked up at Timmins, her brows furrowing as she recalled his story about her prophecy. "Timmins, that night around the campfire you said that the prophesied one would be born to an ungifted woman and would be marked with the sign of the Mother—"

"That's not the way my Gran told it," Effie interjected, Helena's attention making her more confident than usual.

"What do you mean?" Timmins asked looking sharply at the maid. Helena could see that he did not appreciate being told by a mere slip of a girl that he had gotten his facts wrong.

Effie's eyes rounded as she turned toward the Advisor, "I didn't mean…"

Timmins waved her off, "What did your Gran say?" His question was more demand than inquiry.

"Well… Gran always said that there was much the Chosen had forgotten about the Mother and her Mate and that… that the prophecy regarding the Mother of Shadows was a warning," the girl finished tentatively.

All four men were looking at her unblinkingly, Effie's shoulders rolling in as she tried to make herself smaller under the joint scrutiny. She turned beseeching blue eyes to Helena, looking ready to bolt.

Helena's face was filled with understanding as she encouraged in a soft voice, "Please continue, Effie."

Swallowing audibly, the girl tried to muster her courage before beginning again, "Well, the prophecy *was* about two queens marked by the Mother, but it never referred to a physical marking. They would be twins of her gift, but not of her power. The first of them would be known as the Corruptor, the one who would be filled with resentment at what the Mother did not give her. She would corrupt her gift to gain greater ability. The second would be known as the Vessel, the one blessed to be a true recipient of the Mother's power. Upon learning of the Vessel, the Corruptor would seek to destroy her, seeing her as the ultimate sign of the Mother's rejection. With each act, her corruption would pull her further away from the Mother's gift, meaning that she will never be able to truly comprehend the full price of her actions."

Effie licked her lips, her quavering voice gaining strength as she continued, "The Vessel, responding to the threat, would stop at nothing to protect those she safeguarded. But her power would be raw, still untested, and if left unbound it would be her and the Chosen's undoing. The Mother's gift always comes with a price and that price demands balance; just as the Mother had her Mate so too would the Vessel. He would carry the other half of her soul, holding a part of her power within himself as it would be too much for her to contain on her own. If for any reason, the bond never fully matured between the Vessel and her Mate, the Vessel would undergo the Fracturing, so called because her mind would shatter and she would be lost to the madness of her magic. Once Fractured she would unleash the full extent of the Mother's power on the Chosen without knowledge or understanding of what she did. She would become a Mother of Shadows, as much a slave to her magic as all those that served her."

There was no sound in the library as the girl finished her retelling, save Helena's shallow gasps of breath. Out of everything she had just heard, the reason for the Corruptor's betrayal stood out in sharp relief; she hadn't found her Mate. Sensing Helena's panic before the suitors had declared themselves, Timmins had assured her that a Mate had always been found. *Had he lied?*

She turned her bewildered aqua eyes to Timmins who appeared to shrink under the unasked question. Embarrassment colored his cheeks and he sheepishly shrugged his shoulders. He knew what had caught her attention and felt guilty for having been found out. Helena scowled at the realization. *What other little white lies had he fed her in the name of keeping her calm?*

Joquil spoke before she could give voice to the accusation. "But we checked; when Helena was born she had the Mother's star on the base of her skull…" Joquil trailed off.

29

Timmins tore his eyes from her and picked up the question where Joquil left off, "If the prophecy does not refer to a physical marking, then how are we to know who it refers to?"

"By the bonding of the Vessel to her Mate," Effie said, seeming surprised that they did not know this. "While Chosen can find their mates, such a bond is nowhere near as strong as that of a Kiri and her Mate, and even that connection pales in comparison to the bond that the Vessel will forge with her Mate. They will know true fusion, their powers feeding and growing with one another until they achieve a total binding, their souls forever entwined and strengthened by the other. Neither will die so long as the other still breathes. They will take their final breaths together, returning to the Mother as one. That is, of course, if they complete the binding. If the bond is rejected, or simply does not achieve its completion, both will be at the mercy of the Fracturing."

The words of the explanation crashed into Helena as their true meaning crystalized and began to shriek within her mind. "The Trial of the Kiri," she whispered, blanching. If what the girl said was true, her and Von's separation was more serious than any of them realized.

"If what you say is true," Timmins question mirroring Helena's thoughts, "why is there no mention of this in any of the histories that have been passed down from Circle to Circle?"

Effie shrugged, "I was simply telling you the story that my Gran told me when I was young. She always said that no one knew what the prophecy really meant, or when it would come into being. So long as a Damaskiri never allowed herself to be fully corrupted, there would never be a reason for the Vessel to rise. Everything would be contingent upon that final choice."

"So what of the Corruptor, how are we to know who the prophecy speaks of without the marks to rely on?" Darrin interjected.

Effie raised a brow and pressed her lips together, as though trying to hide a smile, before stating, "I am not sure, but I suppose it would be obvious, given the prophecy's warning of her betrayal."

Darrin scowled at her logic and turned away from the group while the men shared disturbed glances. Eventually, Kragen's deep voice asked, "Is your Gran still here, child?"

Effie shook her head, "No, sir. My Gran left a few years ago to live with her friends in the Baelian Forest."

Kragen brows rose in surprise, "She went to Bael? Do the tribes still live amongst the jungle beasts there?"

"I do not know, sir. I've never been. She did leave me instructions on how to reach her, if I ever had need to. Should I..." she looked around before finishing her question, "Should I try to reach her?"

"I think it would be very wise for us to speak with this Gran of yours, and perhaps with those friends of hers as well, especially if they are who I am starting to believe they might be," Joquil answered.

"And what of Micha?" Darrin asked, facing the group again.

"Send for him," Kragen said. "He could still be useful in determining where his sister is hiding. In the meantime, Effie, you will write to your Gran and see if we might be able to visit her."

Effie nodded moving to do so at once. Before she reached the door, she stopped, pausing in front of Helena, "I'm sorry, Kiri. I did not know my words would upset you so."

Helena reached out a hand and placed it gently on the girl's arm. "There's no reason to apologize, Effie. You might have very well given us a piece of the puzzle we so desperately needed."

Smiling with relief, she fled from the room. Helena looked up at her Circle after the door closed.

"This changes everything," Joquil declared.

"This changes nothing," Helena countered.

"How can you possibly say that?" Darrin challenged, his green eyes narrowing.

She lifted a hand to silence him, "Our mission has not changed. Finding Von is still our priority. It is perhaps even more crucial now than before because if her story is true... well, you heard her. If we are not able to complete our binding, it would be the end of us all."

The men were grim as they stared at her. Closing her eyes, she begged, *Please, dear Mother, please let me find him in time.*

IT WAS LATE when Effie opened the door to Helena's room. She noted the hearth and the fire that had turned to smoldering embers with a flicker of concern. Using that as an excuse, she stepped inside, turning to close the heavy door with a soft click. That complete, she let herself take a few more tentative steps, scanning the dim room as she did. Still, she did not see Helena.

Effie had just opened her mouth to call out her name when she noticed the figure half hidden behind the heavy curtains. Helena was staring out the window, the moon illuminating her with its blue glow, her eyes unblinking as they stared out into the night.

"Is everything all right, Kiri?" Effie asked in a whisper-soft voice. Helena turned her head slowly, eyes blinking owlishly as she tried to place the girl's face. It took a moment for clarity to arrive.

She smiled sheepishly, her eyes sad as she asked, "Have you ever had a night where you had to stay awake to greet the dawn?" She turned her face back toward the sky as she continued, "A night where you could no longer be certain about the promise of a rising sun?" Helena sighed before adding even more quietly, "A night that felt so long and you felt so helpless, that you actually needed the safety of the sunlight, just to help you believe that all was not lost?" Despite the grief etched in every word, her voice was hollow, as though she was consciously trying to keep her emotions at bay.

The maid's lips turned down in an empathetic frown as she processed the questions. "I don't know if I have ever quite felt that hopeless, Kiri, but I've never lost someone who I cared about in the way that you have. For what it's worth, I'm sure that wherever he is, Von's out there looking up at the sky wishing he was here with you too."

Helena's answering smile was wistful.

"Are you sure there isn't anything I can get you?" the girl asked, desperate to wipe the despondency out of those aqua eyes. She had only known the Kiri a short time, but it was impossible not to feel her own heart breaking, just a little, as she watched her fight to hold onto her hope as another day passed without word of her Mate.

Helena shook her head, "No, thank you. I'm just going to stay here and stargaze awhile longer. It was sweet of you to come up and check on me, Effie."

The girl nodded, still frowning as she walked out of the dim room.

HELENA FELT a little of the tension ebb when she heard the door click shut. The mask she had been wearing these last couple of days was hard to maintain. She had stopped her nightly vigils by the fountain and had ensured that she made it to every meal on time. She had even made a conscious effort to get to know Von's family. Helena was trying, she really was, but the empty space in her mind where Von's voice used to be was cutting more deeply each day.

She had never felt this kind of loneliness before, not even after her mother had passed away. There had been a time when she had been little and Miriam had traveled to a neighboring village to help a new mother with the birth of her first child. Helena had been distraught, too young to understand why her mother was leaving her. It had been the first time they had ever been separated and she had been inconsolable, crying for hours after Miriam left.

Once the sun had gone down, Helena had gotten it into her head that she was going to go find her. Anderson caught her running down the dirt road just as the sun had set in the sky. After asking where she thought she was going, Anderson had sat her on his knee and solemnly pointed at the sky.

"Do you see that star, little bug?" he asked.

Helena had wiped dirt-smeared hands across her wet cheeks and nodded slowly as she continued to sniffle.

"That's the Mother's star. You can see it from wherever you are in Tigaera. Do you know what that means?"

Helena shook her head, her tears slowing as curiosity took over.

"That means that the Great Mother is watchin' over your Mama right now. So you don't need to feel lonely, little bug. So long as the Great Mother has her in her sights, your Mama ain't far at all. She'll be tuckin' you in right and proper again soon, but for now, you'll keep old Anderson company until she gets home. Is that okay with you?" he asked in that same grave tone, peering into her tear-stained face with his kind green eyes.

Helena sniffed back the last of the tears, "Doesn't Darrin take care of you, Papa Anderson?"

Anderson winked at her and ruffled his hand through her tangled curls, "You keep tellin' him that, little bug. You just keep on tellin' him that."

Helena covered her mouth as she giggled into her small hand.

"There now, there's my girl. I missed that pretty smile."

Helena grinned up at him, beaming with the full glory of her newly gap-toothed smile.

"When you smile at me like that, little bug, you're like my own personal ball of sunshine."

Helena threw her arms around his neck and squeezed with all the strength in her six-year-old body, tears long forgotten.

Anderson stood with her slight weight in his arms, pretending to stagger as he groaned with mock strain. "My little bug has been growing again. Pretty soon you'll be a real lady and you won't want to come hear my stories anymore."

"Don't be silly, Papa! You have the best stories," Helena assured him as he started walking toward his small cottage. "Will you tell me the one about the lost Kiri?"

"Again?" Anderson asked, feigning surprise.

"Please Papa Anderson!" she begged, "It's my favorite!"

He pretended to consider it, thick gray brows furrowing, "Well, alright, if you insist little bug. Can you help me remember how it starts?" Helena enthusiastically began to recount the story as Anderson carried her back inside, his low voice eventually joining in with hers.

It was not lost on Helena that the story she had so loved to hear when she had been younger had ended up being about her. But as with many things looked upon with age-wizened eyes, she no longer felt the same when recalling that story. There was no flutter of delight when thinking about where the lost Kiri could be, nor about the idea of the Mother's star.

As much as she wished that the Mother was watching over Von, she knew that he wasn't out there staring up at a star in the night sky thinking of her doing the same. No, Helena was certain that wherever Von was he was definitely not looking at stars. If he was, she would be able to feel him instead of the bottomless silence that had taken up residence inside her, taken up residence in the space that had been his and his alone. Wherever he was, if Von had been able to contact her he would have done so by now, which meant that something must be preventing him from doing so. If that was the case, Helena was going to need a not so small miracle in order to find him.

So she stood there, head pressed against the cool stone as she stared out into the night sky, praying that the Mother would grant her another day and another chance at finding some answers.

CHAPTER FOUR

The mist swirled around him, making it impossible to discern anything past the stretch of his arm. Sometimes he would hear voices calling him, but when he tried to chase after them, all he would find was more of the dense fog. Von continued to wander aimlessly, searching for something that would help him escape this place. He had lost all track of time and had no recollection of how he got here.

The only thing that had been constant was the overwhelming feeling that he was forgetting something. It was as though he had lost something and desperately needed to find it, but he didn't know what that something was and the harder he tried to recall what it was, the more confused he became. His thoughts and memories were slipping away like grains of sand slipping through his fingers. All he knew was the swirling fog.

"Von!" a childlike voice called from somewhere within the mist.

He spun, gray eyes scanning the horizon for the source of the voice.

"Come catch me!" the voice taunted, seeming to come from further away.

Von took a few tentative steps forward, startled when the mist parted to reveal a grassy knoll that hinted at familiarity. He blinked a few times, his eyes squinting against the harsh light of the sun which shone down from a cloudless blue sky.

"Betcha can't reach me before I get to the stables!" the small boy called to him over his shoulder as he ran down the hill toward a sprawling manor home. He had a mop of dark hair that was blown back as his arms and legs pumped furiously.

He was not aware of making a conscious decision to chase after the boy before he was already running; his legs felt much shorter than they had only moments before. Von looked down, surprise flaring brightly before fading almost immediately. Gone were legs that were thickly corded with muscle and his hands were no longer calloused or battle-scarred. He was no longer a man in a man's body, but a boy merely on the cusp of manhood.

There was no time to wonder at the change, the urgency to catch the boy spurred him into action. Even stunted, Von's legs made easy work of the distance between them, and he was upon the boy within a few heartbeats. The stormy eyes grew wide when they noted how close he had gotten. The boy's tongue darted out, his eyes narrowed in concentration as he pushed with all he had to try and clear the remaining distance between himself and the wooden stables only a few lengths away.

Despite the unfamiliar pang in his chest at the sight of the boy, Von felt no mercy and easily overcame him, hand slapping against the wood in clear victory. The boy skidded to a stop a hairsbreadth before he would have crashed into the side of the stables. He was scowling in disappointment, face flushed from the exertion.

Now that they were closer, Von could study the boy more carefully. He was no more than seven and small with dark hair that was thick with waves. His blue-gray eyes were so large that they seemed to take up the entirety of his face and were currently staring up at him with something akin to worship shining in their depths. Before Von had a chance to say anything, the boy's lips twisted back in a disappointed grimace, "I almost had you that time!"

Von's hand moved on its own accord, ruffling the mop of hair as an unfamiliar voice said, "You'll catch me one day, Squirt." Von took a mental pause, trying to catalogue the differences in his voice. It was not so much unfamiliar as long forgotten. It was still his voice, but lacking the deep inflection and growl that had developed over the years. It was warm, unburdened, and still ringing with the innocence of one more boy than man.

His hand started to shake and a sense of foreboding shot through him as the core part of himself, the part that was still Von, the man, realized what he was seeing. "Nial," he said in a strangled voice.

The boy looked up at him from the side of his eye, tongue slipping back out as though weighing his next words.

"Nial!" he shouted, wrapping the boy in a bone-crushing hug.

"Get off me," his brother grunted, trying, unsuccessfully, to push away from his brother's uncommon display of affection, even though it secretly made him warm with happiness to receive the attention.

"Let's go look at the new horse father brought home!" Nial declared, already making a move in that direction.

Von's hand lurched out and caught the back of his brother's shirt, pulling him up short, "No!"

Dark brows lowered over bright eyes, "Stop treating me like a baby. I can ride just as well as you can!"

Terror raced through Von at the words. His own lips had mouthed them as his brother spoke. He had witnessed this scene before; he had not only witnessed it, he had lived through and barely survived it. Perhaps this was his chance to do it over, to change the outcome and save his brother from a lifetime of agony.

Nial struggled against Von's hold, finally slipping from the tight grip by wriggling his way out of the rough-spun shirt.

"Nial!" Von shouted as the boy hurried away from him and rounded the corner into the stables. The stable boys were nowhere to be found, likely off having a quick lunch before returning to their afternoon chores.

Despite his speed, Von did not make it into the stables in time. His brother had already thrown himself atop the black stallion, too excited to notice the eyes that swirled with madness at his unwelcome presence.

"Nial," Von said, his voice trembling with fear despite trying to speak calmly, "get down from there. If you want to ride, we'll get the pony ready for you."

His brother's cheeks flushed with wounded pride, "I'm too big for the pony! 'Sides I'm an excellent rider, you told me so yourself!"

"Yes, Squirt, you are an excellent rider, but that horse has no love for any rider. He's not ready for *you*," Von's voice broke on the last word, cracking with his anxiety as he tried to coax his brother from the horse.

"He lets you ride him," the voice was small, the words petulant.

Von nodded slowly, daring to step closer to the horse as he said, "Yes, but just barely. The beast fought me every step of the way. Let's get you down from there and I will let you ride Kismet." Kismet was Von's new wolf and he had refused, until now, to let his brother get anywhere near him.

He could see the debate warring in his brother's eyes but knew he had lost when the small shoulders straightened with determination. "I can do this, Von. You just watch," and with that, the boy kicked into the stallion's sides.

The horse reared, snorting angrily before kicking open the fence in front of him and tearing off out of the stables.

Von saw his brother's eyes widen in panic; his small mouth opened on a soundless scream as he held on for all he was worth. Von's fingers scrambled clumsily as they tried to grasp the reigns, but it was too late. The stallion was enraged and using his anger to fuel his speed.

Before he could mount and chase after his brother he heard the screams. Running at full speed, his heart pounding somewhere in the vicinity of his throat, Von rounded the corner just in time to watch his brother go flying from the back of the horse. He looked like a ragdoll, his limbs flailing bonelessly until he crumpled into a heap dangerously close to the stallion's hooves.

Nial cried out, one of his arms and both of his legs bent at awkward angles. Von swallowed back his fear, charging forward to try and get to his brother before the horse noticed him. He felt like he was running against water, each step harder and slower than the last. He knew what was going to happen and he was desperate to try and stop it from happening again.

He opened his mouth to shout his brother's name as the stallion reared again. Nial's eyes were showing white as they rounded with fear. He was motionless as a stain began to grow in his tan trousers. A tear rolled down his young face, shame and fear colliding as the seconds slowed to hours. An entire lifetime passed in those handful of seconds. Nial's frightened eyes found his brother's, the panic tearing into him like a brand as he reached his one good arm out helplessly. He wouldn't reach him in time. He would fail.

The stallion's hooves came down, and with a sickening crack and a scream, his brother fell back to the ground, unconscious. Von reached his side only moments later, the stallion running toward the forest and away from the small human that had set him off. The sight of blood and bone jutting out from his brother's twisted limbs had Von bending over and retching. His whole body cramping as his stomach emptied again and again. As he knelt there beside his brother's broken body, the mist began to swirl and overtake him.

It was then he knew with certainty where he had been trapped all this time. The Mother was finally punishing him for his sins. He was in hell.

CHAPTER FIVE

*H*elena wiped the sweat from her brow, appreciating the cool breeze that licked at her hot skin. Kragen had joined her training this morning and Ronan pulled no punches as he set them against one another. Serena had kept her promise and was working with Nial a short distance away. Ronan spent the better part of the morning throwing the two confused glances when he thought no one was looking. Helena didn't blame him; she was just as busy trying to decipher the shy smiles on their faces.

Helena's attention moved back to Nial, wondering how he was still standing when her own muscles were limp with fatigue. She was hoping no one noticed that the tree she was leaning against was all that was keeping her upright; the last thing she wanted was for the men to cluck at her like oversized mother hens. Luckily the others were too busy trying to pretend they weren't staring at each other to give her any notice. It was nice, not being the center of attention for once. Helena was more than happy to use her rediscovered invisibility to watch the rest of them.

Nial was red-faced and panting as he struggled through the stretches meant to build the strength in his legs. *Perhaps it is only his desire to impress his trainer that had him pushing himself so hard*, she mused. He caught her gaze and lifted a questioning brow. *So much for being invisible*, she thought with a chagrined shrug. He shook his head at her, his lips quirking with his own smile as he refocused on the woman barking orders at him. He blew Serena a kiss and said something that had her blushing but was far too soft for Helena to hear from her spot beneath the tree. An unexpected ring of steel met her ears and had her shifting her own focus back to the others.

Twisting slightly, she watched Ronan and Kragen attack each other, or at least it appeared to be an attack, although she was still fairly certain they were only practicing. Kragen and Ronan were both dual wielding axes, the weapons spinning and flying through the air as they reinforced the moves with their magic. Both were exceptional warriors, but Ronan was hacking away at Kragen like a man possessed. The latter was clearly on the defensive as he ducked away from the deadly metal. Helena tried to bite back an amused smile as she realized Ronan's performance was for the benefit of the lithe blonde across the clearing. Her friend had obviously grown tired of being ignored by his lover.

The men had removed their shirts and sweat was already dripping down their bare chests. The purely female part of her appreciated the swell and flex of their impressive muscles, but the tired trainee was only interested in how much longer it would be before they were done showing off and she would be dismissed. She plucked at the shirt sticking to her skin, wishing it wouldn't have been inappropriate for her to remove it as well. Helena snorted as she imagined the reaction that move would get her, especially if her Mate had been there to witness it. She could almost hear his voice purring down the bond, *"If you're in such a hurry to get naked for me, Mate, I don't mind an audience."* Helena fanned at her face, hot now for a different reason.

Serena and Nial joined her, jolting her out of her wistful daydream. Before she could say anything Serena let out a low whistle, "The only thing that gets me hotter than watching a man work his weapon, is watching a sweaty, half-naked one." The frank sexual appraisal in her voice had Nial's shoulders stiffening and his usual easygoing smile vanishing. Sensing his discomfort at her words, Serena's eyes scanned

44

his face before clouding over. Frowning, she looked away and remained silent.

"There is something impressive about watching someone who is a master of their craft," Helena added neutrally.

Nial relaxed at her words, but refused to meet her gaze, focusing instead on the warriors in front of him. Helena let out a little huff, annoyed that male egos were such fragile things, even as she felt a flicker of sympathy for his obvious desire to prove to Serena that he was as much of a man as the others.

"Kiri!" Joquil's voice rang out as he entered their practice area.

"Over here, Joquil!" she called, pushing off of the tree and automatically bracing herself for bad news. He had never sought her out during one of her practice sessions before. She could only imagine that his doing so now was an indication of something urgent.

"Micha has arrived, my lady," Joquil's face and voice remained impassive, but Helena heard a low grunt as the two men behind her ceased their sparring.

"It would appear that practice is over for today," Serena commented lightly.

Helena nodded distractedly, her anxiety at what the meeting would reveal causing shivers to race down her neck and arms. In response, the wind whipped through the trees causing leaves to rain down upon them.

Joquil's expression did not change as he brushed a few leaves from his head and shoulders. Helena couldn't help but appreciate that he was as unflappable as ever, his steadfastness doing much to ease her nerves.

"Where would you like to meet him, Kiri?" Joquil asked patiently.

Helena thought for a moment, before declaring, "Have him meet me by the fountain in an hour. I will wash up and change."

There were grumbling protests behind her, but Helena ignored them. "Will you have Effie set up a small picnic for us? Micha was my friend before all of this occurred. I would like to maintain that pretense, if it even is a pretense, to prevent us from giving away our hand sooner than strictly necessary."

Joquil nodded, approval warm in his amber eyes as he said, "It shall be as you say." With that, he turned and walked unhurriedly back the way he came.

Helena sighed as Micha's laughing green eyes swam into her mind. For as much as she wanted answers, there was a part of her that was greatly dreading this encounter. She didn't want her memories of him tainted by finding out he was involved in his sister's scheme.

Serena rubbed her back soothingly before smacking her soundly on her butt, "Move it, Kiri."

Helena stuck out her tongue, chuckling as she made her way back into the manor. Kragen fell into step beside her, his silent strength bolstering her courage. No matter what the meeting revealed, she would not be facing it alone. On impulse, she wrapped her arms around his sweaty torso and squeezed. Shock at the unexpected embrace had him standing still until he recovered and lifted her into his own bone-crushing hug. He pressed a sloppy kiss to her forehead, his laughter vibrating in his chest when she squealed and started wiping the slobber off on his equally sweaty shoulder.

"Unhand me you brute!" she crowed, her laughter ringing down the halls.

Curious faces peered around corners and stuck out of doorways to see what had the usually reserved Kiri making such a racket. At the end of the hallway, Margo and Effie stood, watching the scene unfolding before them. Margo had her hand pressed against her lips, eyes shining brightly with her mirth. Effie's eyes were wide and her mouth had fallen open in shock as she watched the tattooed warrior start to tickle her. Evidently, they were not expecting to see such a playful side from their new ruler and her Sword. Especially not after she had done little more than mope about their home the last few weeks. It was clear they did not know how to react to the sight.

"Traitors!" she cried at them, realizing her error when the color drained from their faces. These were the people that had been declared traitors and suffered for centuries because of it. Thinking quickly to try and recover the jovial atmosphere she shouted, breathless with her laughter, "If you won't punish Sir Sweats-a-Lot, I guess I will!"

The crowd had grown in size, although Kragen had not stopped or slowed as he walked down the corridors leading to her rooms. She could feel their collective intake of breath as they waited to see what she would do.

She called her magic forth, feeling it ripple in its excitement to be set free. Around her she could feel her curls waving in the air, lifted in a wind only they could feel. Her skin was pulsing with the flood of her magic rushing to the surface, and she could see she was starting to emit a soft glow as it grew in power.

Deciding to pay him back in kind, she planted her hands on the sides of his ribs, the only place her hands could really reach given the way his arms were banded about her. Calling Fire, Air and Water, she shot her magic into the surface of his skin. He froze, eyes snapping wide in surprise as her magic took over. He let her go with a yelp, squirming while his hands tried to slap away the playful balls of electricity that were moving across his body.

All around them gasps of delight rang out. She was using tiny sparks of lightning to tickle him. There were no painful shocks, only the warm buzz of energy causing his muscles to spasm as he tried to twist away from their relentless assault.

"You are a cruel mistress," he tried to pout while laughing.

Taking pity on him, she pulled her magic back. At least, she tried to. Some of the magic did flow back into her, while other sparks shot out landing in the crowd. Suddenly the gasps of delight were turning into shocked chuckles. Some were wiping tears of laughter from their eyes as others wriggled and twisted under the dance of her magic. It had no mercy as it sought its own form of revenge, moving from victim to helpless victim, tickling and tormenting, until one by one the sparkling balls of light reunited with her.

Whispers broke out as they stared at her in her un-dampened form, her magic, simmering just below the surface, still making her glow. Her eyes were shining iridescent pools as she spoke in a voice that echoed in harmony with itself, "Serves you right for standing there laughing at me." They could tell by her smile that she was not offended. Any that had not already fallen in love with her because of her devotion to Von and his people, or how she had healed Nial, did so then and there.

HELENA WAS STILL SNICKERING when she made her way back to the fountain, and to Micha. Effie could barely suppress her reaction to the display of Helena's magic and had been caught staring at her in awe three times before Helena finally dismissed the girl so that she could finish dressing in peace. She could hear the whispers and giggles as she passed people in the halls, a small smile tugging at her lips in response.

It had been a good morning. Unexpected, but much needed. There was a lightness within her that left her feeling almost buoyant after so many nights of being weighted down with a growing sense of helplessness. It felt good to laugh, to let go of her fear just long enough to relax with her friends. She knew it would be fleeting. The feeling would likely dissipate completely by the time she finished with Micha, but it was even more precious and necessary because of that. No matter what happened, she could not afford to let go of her ability to laugh. Laughter was a symptom of hope. Without the presence of one, there was generally a lack of the other. Losing it would mean that Gillian had won, and she could not bear to give her that kind of power. Not with so much at stake.

With renewed purpose, Helena entered the small garden. Micha was standing with his back to the entrance, his hands clasped behind his back. She watched his fingers fidget, the only indication of his nerves.

"Mother's blessings to you, Micha," she said softly.

He spun, a smile blooming across his face in greeting. He threw open his arms already stepping toward her.

If he's an actor, he's a very good one, a warning voice murmured in her mind. Helena's smile felt forced as she walked into his embrace. He pulled her close and she caught a whiff of the spicy cinnamon scent she had grown to associate with him. The familiarity had her muscles relaxing enough to return his hug.

Micha stepped back, his hands warm against the sides of her arms. "I must say, I was shocked when I received your summons, but it will be nice to see my sister again. Where is she by the way?" he asked, his smile still firmly in place as his eyes looked past her in search of his twin.

Helena felt her eyes narrow in suspicion but kept her voice even as she said, "She's out at the moment, so I'm afraid she won't be joining us for lunch today. You aren't too disappointed that you're stuck with just me for company, are you?"

Micha's laugh was warm, "Not even remotely, Kiri. Although, I find it hard to believe any in your Circle, especially your Mate, would willingly let you go anywhere by yourself."

Helena's answering laugh was genuine, his observation was not far off the mark, and she knew that Darrin, Kragen, Ronan and Serena were all tucked just out of sight. The only reason Timmins and Joquil had not joined in was because they were busy pouring over the tomes that had arrived early that morning from the Palace archives. They were searching for anything that would corroborate Effie's retelling of the prophecy.

She pretended to pout, laughter still evident in her voice as she said, "I'm not completely helpless, thank you very much."

Micha let go of her arms completely and stepped back, "I did not mean to imply that you were. I still fondly remember the way you handled the crowd during your welcoming ceremony."

Helena's smile grew as she remembered her instinctive reaction to defend Von only moments after meeting him. "Yes," she said wryly, "I suppose that was fairly memorable."

Micha laughed at her, "Just a bit."

Helena motioned for Micha to take a seat at the table Effie had set up for them, "Would you like to eat?"

Micha rubbed his flat stomach as he gave her a wide grin, "You have no idea how much I'm looking forward to a real meal. As exciting as travel is, there's little you can do to make camp food edible."

Helena's smile turned sympathetic, "You aren't wrong, my friend."

They each took a spot at the small wrought-iron table. There were two plates, a pitcher of deep red juice and two crystal goblets waiting for them. Her stomach twisted in protest, nerves making it hard to appreciate the food on her plate.

"Kiri—" Micha started.

"Helena, please," she corrected automatically, cutting off whatever he was about to ask.

He smiled up at her, before turning his attention back to his plate. "Helena, as much as I love a good holiday, and as flattered as I am that you summoned me, not to mention that you are seeing fit to personally entertain me, I can't pretend to understand why it is you felt the need to bring me here."

Helena waited for him to take a bite before responding, "To be frank, Micha, it concerns your sister."

He dropped his fork, his face draining of color as he worked to swallow his mouthful. "Gillian? What's wrong with her?" he finally asked in a voice full of concern.

Helena's lips pursed as she tried to work through her phrasing. Truth be told, she was completely winging it. "It's not so much that something is wrong *with* her..." she trailed off. *Although being a traitorous, backstabbing bitch is certainly an unbecoming quality in a friend,* she silently seethed.

"Helena," her name was a plea for information.

Helena filled her glass with the juice, taking a quick sip before she tried again. "Gillian has betrayed us," she said simply.

"Betrayed you?" he gaped, his voice a hoarse croak. The tips of his cheeks and ears turned a bright shade of pink, "Now see here –"

"No, you see here!" she snapped, her hand clenched around the goblet causing it to crack as her nails lengthened into sharp black claws. Bright red drops seeped through the fissures in the crystal looking like drops of blood as they splattered on the table.

Micha blanched at the sight.

"Your *sister*," she hissed, "has abducted my Mate."

Micha's lips opened and closed as he tried, and failed, to respond.

He looked like a gaping fish, and Helena found herself holding back inappropriate laughter at the thought.

"And you brought me here as a hostage? To try and get her to trade him for me?"

Helena blinked in surprise. Truly the thought hadn't even crossed her mind, but hearing him suggest it now she definitely saw the appeal.

"No," she said after a few heartbeats.

Micha wiped at the sweat on his brow, the food sitting forgotten before them.

"Then – then you mean to kill me?" he asked, his voice now a high-pitched whine.

Helena's brows came together as she stared at him in shock, "Kill you?" she sputtered, equal parts offended and shocked. "Who in the Mother's name do you think I am, Micha? Did you *do* something requiring your execution?" Her words had taken on a feral quality, her voice dangerously soft.

His eyes flicked down to the sharp claws that were raking across the top of the table before he stammered, "N-n-no, Kiri."

"Then what reason could I possibly have to kill you?" she genuinely wondered as she tilted her head inquisitively to the side. "Perhaps you had better stop giving me ideas, Micha, and let me explain."

He nodded mutely, his cheeks and ears the only color remaining on his terrified face.

"I want to know where she's taken him. You are the closest person to her. Tell me, Micha, why would your sister be so foolish as to declare war on me in this way? What could possibly motivate such idiotic behavior? She has to know I will find her, and when I do…" she trailed off, letting his imagination fill in the blanks.

She didn't think it possible, but he became even paler. She could see his pulse flicker beneath the thin skin of his neck, his eyes fluttering as though he was fighting to remain conscious.

He swallowed and licked his lips, "I don't know, Kiri, I swear! I cannot believe she would come up with such a scheme on her own."

"What would cause her to do so?"

He shook his head, "I – I'm not sure."

Helena slumped back in her chair, the claws retracting back beneath her skin. His terror was too genuine to be an act. He had no idea of his sister's schemes or her whereabouts. "Can you not hazard any guess where she might be hiding?" she finally asked, her voice returning to its normal tone.

Sensing the change in her, Micha relaxed a bit in his seat. She could see the sweat stains under his arms and felt herself frowning in sympathy. She hadn't intended to get quite so carried away, although it had felt damned good giving into her anger now that it had a target. If only momentarily and not the right one.

"If I had to guess, Kiri. I would say perhaps she has returned to our mother's land. She was born in the mountains of Vyruul. It's fairly isolated, almost impossible to find unless you have been there before. She would feel safe there, if she was trying to hide."

Excitement prickled beneath her skin. Finally, a direction.

"You will take us there." It was not a question.

Micha nodded, "Yes, you have to believe me, Kiri. I want to help. I want to find her, whatever caused her to do this, it cannot be good. She needs me, I am certain of it."

"I cannot promise you any leniency when it comes to her, Micha. Do not ask me to." The words were fierce.

He swallowed again, "I know, Kiri. But please, will you at least let me talk to her when we find her? Before you..." he struggled to continue his sentence.

"Condemn her?" Helena offered ruthlessly.

Micha blinked and nodded, fully curling into himself as the realization that his sister was a dead woman sank in.

"I am not without mercy, Micha," she said taking pity on him, "But she took what's mine. She pretended to be my friend while plotting against me and leading an army of abominations to our camp. She was the cause of countless, meaningless deaths. *Children's* deaths, Micha. She cannot be allowed to go unpunished, no matter the reason for her actions."

His green eyes widened with horror at the recounting of his sister's crimes. It was bad enough that she had taken Von, but he had no idea that her treachery had run so deep. When he spoke again his voice was deep with conviction, "I will help you find her, Helena. And when we do, I will not interfere when you pronounce her sentence. She has earned her punishment; I only ask to speak with her before any sentence is carried out."

Helena nodded; it was a small enough request, and not one she felt inclined to deny him.

Her Circle peeled away from the shadows in which they were hiding. It was Darrin who spoke first, "When do we leave, Kiri?"

Helena shook her head, "We don't, at least, not right away. We are not prepared for what we might find when we get there. You," she turned to Ronan, "will work with him," she gestured toward Micha who started at the appearance of her men. "Come up with our strategy for when we arrive, as well as various contingency plans. We will not underestimate her again."

Ronan nodded and she turned her attention back toward Kragen and Darrin, "You two will work with Effie. We should have a response from her Gran soon. We will go to Bael as planned and meet with the Masters of Prophecy. I am sure there is much they will be able to tell us that could help with our plans for Vyruul."

Again the men only nodded. Her eyes found Serena's smiling face. Helena could feel the approval radiating from her in waves.

"Now, if you all will excuse me," Helena stood and let out the low whistle that would summon her Talyrian. She had been itching to get away from the manor for a while now. She could not imagine a better time to go for a ride.

Starshine was there within moments, as if she had already anticipated her mistress's need of her. She flapped her majestic gray wings as she landed, the earth trembling slightly as her massive paws met the ground. Helena's hands were already buried in the velvety white fur at her neck as she leaned in to whisper in the beast's ear, "Take me away from here, Starshine. I want to chase the stars with you for a while."

The Talyrian let out a soft roar of approval, small wisps of smoke flaring from her nostrils as she bent low enough for Helena to mount her.

Helena eyed her friends with amusement. Her Circle had grown accustomed to the sight of Starshine and were not as terrified of her as they had once been. Starshine was still fiercely possessive of her though, and the Talyrian did not hesitate to stake her claim by shooting jets of flame at whoever dared approach Helena without her permission. Von was really the only person that Starshine seemed to tolerate without question, likely because Helena had declared him as her Mate, a position the Talyrian understood.

Micha, on the other hand, had never seen a Talyrian and could not stop blinking as he stared at the massive white feline and her leathery gray wings tipped with deadly talons. He looked like he was about to piss himself, and Helena felt a small flicker of pity at all that she had made him endure in such a short period of time.

With a small wave, she pressed her legs into the Talyrian's sides and was almost immediately flung into the air. Helena wrapped her arms more tightly around Starshine's neck as they soared toward the sparkling blue of the sea. Her laughter bubbled up as the feeling of joy that always seemed to accompany flying overtook her. For the second time that day she felt real stirrings of hope.

I will find you, my love. Wait for me; I am coming. She shot the words down the yawning emptiness of their bond, knowing in her heart that even if he could not hear the words, a part of him would know she had not given up her search.

CHAPTER SIX

*G*illian stood outside the door, her heart continuing to race within the confines of her chest. It was not that she dreaded what she would find when she entered. At least, not in the sense that she would be surrounded by human filth or have to observe evidence of sadistic torture as one would in most dungeons. In fact, dungeon was a rather misleading term. Von was being kept in a cell that was decorated as lavishly as any of the guest suites on the upper floors. The only distinctions being that he was tied to the bed and there was only one spelled entrance into the room, the door behind which Gillian currently cowered.

No, bearing witness to the cruelties of being a prisoner was not what held her steps. As it was, she rather enjoyed blood play under the right circumstances. What had her heart fluttering like a captive bird was the possibility that he would be awake, especially if he remembered how she had manipulated both him and his Mate. Conscious and coherent were two words she did not want to have to use when describing her prisoner.

She knew she was no match for Von's strength or temper once he woke. Even had she been able to shift into a form that would give her a chance to overpower him, his magic still vastly surpassed her own. And that was assuming she was at her full power... which she was not.

Every new shape pushed at the limitations of her magic and she wasn't sure how many more she could add to her repertoire. Humans were by far the biggest drain on her magic. Triply so if it was a specific person she was shifting into. There were just too many minutiae to replicate if she didn't want to be exposed as an imposter. She had only ever attempted a human shift a handful of times prior to Von's capture, hating the sense of hangover that the heavy use of magic caused once she shifted back. Here she was weeks later and she was still feeling sluggish after her latest attempt.

Since she could not rely on her magic to protect her, her only hope was that she would be there when the first vestiges of the drug wore off. That would be the only way she and her mother would have enough time to act. They would have to work quickly in those initial moments before he regained his full abilities if they wished to retain the upper hand.

Rowena had not seen fit to enlighten Gillian regarding her grand plans for Von, although Gillian anticipated he was to be her finest conquest yet. She did not envy him the title. Being the focus of Rowena's attention was daunting, to say the least. Gillian would be happy enough if she could just fade into the ether of her mother's mind never to be thought of again. Unfortunately, she knew the likelihood of that was less than slim. Her mother enjoyed her playthings too much to give one up so easily.

Helping her mother had seemed simple enough when she was first approached with the plan. Granted, she had been overcome with shock at the time, having just learned that her mother was still alive after weeks of mourning her death. There were no words that could adequately depict the degree of stupefaction she had felt when her mother had first spoken to her through the mirror.

One night just as she had blown out the last of the candles to go to sleep, she heard an icy voice whispering her name. Gillian had thought she was imagining things until she saw the figure cloaked in thick fog take shape in her mirror. When Rowena had told her what she needed to do in order to keep herself and her brother alive, she had not hesitated to acquiesce. Frankly, she hadn't been capable of doing more than nod her head in mute agreement let alone consider the option of refusal.

It was all theoretical at first. She would befriend the new Damaskiri until her trial had been completed and her Circle finalized. Then she would need to separate the young Queen from her Mate and bring him to her mother in Vyruul. *Easy.* Gillian knew she was clever enough to outwit any opponent, but those kinds of tricks only worked so long as your prey did not expect you to strike. Once they were alerted to the threat, they would be much harder to trap.

She had never stopped to consider what would happen *after,* let alone what it would feel like to have to look her prey in the eye each day as she wove her snare more tightly. Helena had been a definite complication. Under other circumstances, Gillian was certain they would have been friends. There had been moments when she forgot what she was supposed to be doing and simply enjoyed spending time with the new Kiri. One visit from her mother had sorted her out quickly enough. The image of what she intended to do to Micha, and not only do but make Gillian participate in, had her running for a basket to empty her stomach. She could not afford friends, not with her twin's life on the line. Instead, she had stopped thinking of Helena as a person and started thinking of her as a means to an end.

It had been much easier after that. Each step of her mother's plan moved forward flawlessly. Although, witnessing the results of the Shadows' attacks had been difficult. She had not anticipated the sheer number of deaths she would be responsible for simply by leading the Shadows to Helena. Her stomach clenched in protest as she thought about the rows upon rows of bodies they had discovered in the days leading up to her final betrayal.

Her mother's army was vast. She hadn't even bothered to send her strongest generals to test the strength of the Kiri's party knowing her victory was already assured without their participation. She had been a cat playing with a mouse: teasing and distracting her with a paw so that she would not see the teeth until they had already snapped closed around her. Gillian could hardly bear to be around the Shadows. Their empty white eyes with the black lines snaking through them and their mindless devotion to their mistress made her shudder with revulsion each time she was near one.

Gillian blinked, coming back to the present. She could not afford to be distracted. Not now, when time was so crucial. Bracing herself, Gillian took one last breath before laying her hand against the solid oak door. There was a soft hum as the wood beneath her hand grew so cold it burned momentarily as the magic in the wood tested her identity. After ensuring she was allowed to proceed, it silently swung open. The lights in the corridor flickered once in response to the release of air from the cell.

There was no sound, no hint as to what she would find once she stepped past the spelled boundaries of the threshold. "Mother's tits, Gillian. You've come this far," she whispered to herself, finally gathering the courage to step forward.

Even though the room was only dimly lit, having no natural light with which to brighten the golden walls, she could see every detail of him clearly. Her eyes scanned Von's prone form, starting from the bottom of the bed. He still radiated strength, despite being bound and in a drugged sleep. He was naked, body splayed spread-eagle; each limb tethered to a post by a length of enchanted rope. His wrists and ankles were an angry red where the cords had rubbed his skin raw in his stupor. The thick stubble covering his sharp jaw was a testament to the amount of time he had been unconscious.

She moved closer to the bed, reaching out a hand to run it along the length of his body. His skin was warm to the touch and he felt like velvet covered steel, soft but unyielding. She trailed her fingers up, lingering to appreciate the way his manhood lay heavy against his thick thigh. It was impressive even though it was as dormant as he was. The only benefit of this particular prisoner, at least in her opinion, was being able to enjoy the feast he made for her eyes.

She let her nails scrape against the muscles of his stomach and up over the tattoo that covered most of his chest and shoulder until it came to rest by his neck. His eyes were moving furiously beneath waxy purple lids. *Still lost to the dreams then*, she concluded with relief. There was no chance he would wake while still under the hold of the *Bella Morte*.

Emboldened by the discovery, she leaned forward, allowing her breasts to graze against his chest and rubbing herself against his silky heat. "It seems as though our play time is not over just yet, lover. Are you ready to have some fun?" she rasped before biting down on the cords of muscle between his neck and shoulder.

Gillian looked up beneath thick lashes to check his face. There was no change and his body remained slack beneath her, not flinching or responding to her attack. Satisfied, she licked up the side of his neck, the musky taste of his sweat arousing her.

She eyed his thick cock and licked her lips, "I wish I could take you for a ride, handsome, but it's no fun when you can't play." With a languid sigh she lifted her head once more, pausing to brush her lips against his. As she pulled back, she bit down and pulled his bottom lip out until she drew blood.

The sight of the deep ruby liquid rolling down his jaw caused her heart to pick up speed. Gillian lapped it quickly, enjoying the coarse feel of his stubble against her tongue.

"Do you think there is power hidden in the blood?" she whispered against his mouth, her eyes closed as she savored the metallic taste of him. "My mother believes that our power is entwined with our very essence, but I have read that our blood contains some of that power as well. Shall we test that theory?"

Gillian lifted up and tilted her head to the side as she studied him. "Perhaps not," she sighed. She couldn't chance her mother finding out.

She stepped back, but not before licking at his mouth a final time. It was time to begin her vigil. She moved away from the bed and sat down in a thickly padded chair. She wasn't sure what she was watching for exactly. She had never witnessed one so far gone to the *Bella Morte*, but she was certain she would be able to discern whether he was waking or fading if any change did occur. Letting out another sigh, she settled back into the chair and braced herself for the wait.

VON WAS SURROUNDED BY MIST. Voices taunted him from its depths. One voice, in particular, caused him to bare his teeth in feral rage. It whispered to him of blood and power; it grated against his senses with an overwhelming sense of wrongness. This was not a voice he wanted in his mind.

There was another voice, however, a gentle one that would call to him from across a great distance. Sometimes he thought he could hear its owner sobbing softly, and he would be overcome with the need to find and protect it. No matter how hard he searched, he could not find the source of the voice. The harder he tried to hold onto it, the quicker it would fade.

The gentle voice would generally come to him after a particularly bad memory. It would find him in the moments just after the vision would fade when he would be gasping for breath, his body coated in sweat as though he had been finishing one of Ronan's workouts. Its sweetness would help calm him down, providing a balm for his ravaged soul and giving him something to focus on other than the pain radiating within him.

The memories were no longer always factual depictions of events in his past. They were twisting, becoming more brutal with each experience. No matter what he had actually done in those moments, within the mist he was his worst self. A man ridden by guilt and anger, no longer capable of mercy or kindness. The worst of the visions were when he was merely a helpless observer. In those, he was able to do nothing but watch the most horrific events unfold one after the other without end. Here in the mist, he had no true sense of time, but each vision felt like it took less time to come than its predecessor. Each one left him more disoriented and battered than the last. At least until the voice that was more than a voice came, wrapping itself around the fragmented pieces of his mind and pulling him back together, back to his true self.

Von knelt there, hands trembling and heart furiously beating. He was not certain how much longer he could withstand these attacks. If he had some way to fight back, an enemy that he could pursue, he might stand a chance. But how can you fight that which you cannot see? These were assaults on his mind and there was little he could do against them. He feared for the time when the voice would no longer reach him, when it would not be there to piece him back together. That's when he would be lost entirely, his sense of self shattering under the strain and leaving him completely broken.

As if summoned, the mist began to swirl and pulse with light.

"No," Von moaned, attempting to brace himself for what it would reveal.

As the mist began to roll back, he saw an aqua-eyed woman staring at him in horror.

"Helena," he gasped with a pain so fierce he felt tears stinging his eyes as it burned through him. Nothing had prepared him for this. Despite all of its cruel tricks, this was the first time the mist had allowed him to see anything of his Mate. He stretched his hand toward her.

All of his longing for her was quickly replaced with fear as an arm wrapped around her waist and pulled her back. Those beautiful eyes rounding as a scarred hand held a knife to that delicate throat.

"Helena," he roared, fear turning to wrath within him. Von tried to go to her, but his body was held fast with invisible ropes. He could not move. His struggles grew increasingly frantic as the knife pressed deeper into her luminous skin. He saw drops of red begin to bead and let out a roar of grief so filled with his fury the hand holding the knife slipped. The blade swept up piercing his Mate's lip.

He felt the resulting sting on his own mouth. Von pressed his hand to his lip and noted the smear of blood with surprise. The pain gave him something to focus on and with a final tug, he pulled himself upright. The arm banded about Helena disappeared. She now stood before him, whole and untouched.

"*Mira*," he groaned, taking a few fumbling steps toward her before collapsing to his knees and wrapping his arms around her. He felt her hands sink into his hair, comforting him.

"My love," he whispered against her, closing his eyes and

breathing in the scent of her. Von waited, anchoring himself in her presence, knowing that when he opened his eyes again she would be gone. He was right.

It was the mist's most diabolical trick yet. It gave him the thing he longed for above all others, only to taunt him with her nearness before proving how quickly it could snatch her away. She would never be his so long as he was trapped here, and the mist would ensure he never again forgot what he was missing.

From the recesses of the mist, Von heard the echoes of the voice, *"I will find you, my love. Wait for me; I am coming."*

He curled into a ball, letting the words wrap around him and surround him with their strength. He found himself mouthing the words as they echoed before fading completely. Once he could hear it no more he let out a harsh breath, begging as he did, "Please, do not leave me here."

CHAPTER SEVEN

*N*ews from Effie's Gran arrived by way of the woman appearing on the Holbrooke's doorstep. Eyeing her now, Helena could not imagine this woman being anyone's Gran; she was tall and slender, her skin unmarked by age. She had light brown hair that was pulled back off her face to fall in long graceful waves down her back. Her eyes were a deep midnight blue and were the only hint as to the years to which she had borne witness.

Those midnight eyes were now pinning her in place with their focus. "Kiri," the woman said in her rich voice as she dipped into a low bow.

Before Helena could respond, Effie rounded the corner at a dead run. "Gran!" she cried, sprinting into her arms.

"Hello child," she murmured, holding the waifish girl tightly. Laughter twinkled in her ancient eyes as she stepped back to examine her granddaughter. "The Mother has certainly graced you with her blessings."

Effie blushed at the compliment and batted her grandmother's prodding hands away, "No more so than you, Gran."

Darrin had been observing the exchange with barely contained amusement. Midnight eyes turned to him as he snickered at the comment.

"You disagree, Shield?" she asked in a deceptively soft voice.

The smile fled from his lips, "Not at all, my lady."

She snorted with derision, "Please, call me Miranda. I am not yours, nor have I ever been anyone's, *lady*." The way she spat the last word conveyed a sense of disgust at the thought.

"Miranda," Helena obliged before Darrin could embarrass himself further, stretching out a hand to the other woman, "It is a pleasure to make your acquaintance. Effie has spoken very highly of you."

"And you as well, Kiri."

The rest of the Circle were scattered behind her. Both Timmins and Joquil eyed Miranda warily, distrust evident in their rigid stances. Kragen wore his trademark smirk as he walked toward the woman and lifted her off the floor in one of his bear hugs.

"Oh my," she gasped, her cheeks flooding with color when he set her down with a saucy wink. "Watch yourself, Sword. I don't care what vows you made, you don't get to my age without breaking a few rules, if you know what I mean." It was Kragen's turn to blush, and Ronan let out loud barking laughs at the sight of his colored cheeks.

Ronan sketched a quick bow to Miranda, smiling as he straightened, "I would hug you as well, lady, but I'm afraid I am spoken for and do not trust myself to behave around a woman as beautiful as you."

"Horse shit," the older woman cackled, pleased despite the crass words.

Unfazed, his smug smile grew and he winked.

"Seriously? Can no one keep their hormones in check these days?" Helena asked dryly.

"I can," Joquil offered from behind her.

Timmins, she noted, remained silent, and she couldn't help but laugh as the image of him lifting the serving woman's skirts came to mind. From the slightly glazed look in his soft blue eyes, she could tell he was lost in the same memory.

Helena shook her head ruefully. These men might be bound to her, but it was clear they took their liberties where and when they wished. She could not find it in herself to begrudge them the chance to find some happiness in companionship, even if it was fleeting.

Her thoughts then turned to Von, imagining how he would react to the woman standing before them. She was sure he would be as charmed as the rest of the men, offering silky compliments and flattering her shamelessly, knowing it would make Helena laugh. All the while, he would be murmuring wicked promises to her through their bond. *"No one could surpass your beauty, Mira. Know that as soon as we are done here, I am taking you upstairs where I can undress you under the soft glow of the moon. Then, I am going to bury myself deep within you."*

Oh yes, she knew *exactly* how her Mate would behave, and she missed his roguish teasing fiercely.

"As much as I enjoy flirting with handsome men, I seem to recall there was a matter of some urgency that led my granddaughter to summon me."

Helena brought herself back to the present, embarrassed at how easily she had been distracted by thoughts of her Mate, but Timmins was already speaking.

"Your granddaughter shared a story with us that she heard from you," he started.

Miranda was nodding, "About the Corruptor and the Vessel."

"Yes, well, I have searched every record I could find regarding the Mother of Shadows prophecy and I cannot find any translation which supports your rendition."

Miranda simply peered at him, as if this were not news to her, "And why would you when it was never written down?"

Timmins bristled, "How can we verify the integrity of your retelling if we do not have a record of it in the Archives?"

Miranda raised a brow, studying Timmins as she looked down her nose. "There is much, Advisor," his title sounding like a taunt as she continued, "that was never written down. It is not the Mother's way to provide all of her Chosen with information they could potentially misuse in their failed attempts to understand it."

Timmins looked ready to explode at the insult hidden within her words. Joquil pressed a steadying hand to his chest and asked, "And how would you know this if there is no record?"

"I did not say there was no record, merely that it was not written down. The Mother chooses her historians with care and tasks them with passing down her wisdom to those deemed capable of possessing it."

"The Masters of Prophecy," Helena murmured.

Miranda nodded again, approval radiating warmly from her midnight eyes as she said, "That is one of the many names the group has been given throughout the years. They are also known as the Keepers."

A grim sort of tension filled the room. The men had just been presented with yet another fact they did not know, on a topic they'd spent most of their lives assuming they were the experts in. Miranda's declarations were so matter-of-fact that it left little room for doubt. She was certain about the matter at hand, almost to the extent that it surprised her when what she said wasn't common knowledge for the rest of them as well. *Almost.* Miranda was certainly savoring having the upper hand.

Helena's lips twisted into a wry smile; in a way it was like meeting a female version of Timmins. While Joquil was the one entitled Master, it had always been Timmins who they turned to in their search for knowledge. He enjoyed problem-solving and sharing obscure, long-forgotten pieces of information with others. His recall for small bits of arcana was unparalleled, at least under usual circumstances; it was part of what made him such an excellent Advisor. It must be driving him absolutely mad to not be the one with all of the answers for once.

"You do not have to simply take my word for it, Kiri. You and your Circle can come speak with the Keepers yourselves. They have been expecting you."

All traces of humor were forgotten as everyone turned wide eyes back toward Miranda. It was true that they had already anticipated the need to travel through the Baelian Forest to meet with Miranda, but it was another thing entirely to feel as though it were predestined. The magnitude of the statement rendered them all speechless.

"May I come too, Gran?" Effie asked with thinly veiled excitement, seemingly unaware of the frisson of apprehension among the rest of them as her enthusiasm broke through the silence.

Miranda stroked Effie's cheek, "Of course child, so long as the Kiri doesn't object."

Effie turned her earnest blue eyes toward Helena, who immediately smiled and nodded her approval. Beaming, Effie wrapped her in a tight hug, "Thank you, Kiri!"

"When are the Keepers expecting us?" Joquil asked coolly.

"As soon as we can get there. Troubling times are ahead, Master, and there is much that needs to be said if your Kiri has any hope of defeating the Corruptor without losing herself to the Fracturing."

The men of her Circle scowled at the implication that she would fail without this meeting. It stung their pride to hear Miranda assume that they would not be enough to protect her from any foe.

"It is your belief the Keepers can help better prepare us?" Timmins questioned.

Miranda nodded once, her eyes scanning the group, "We have been waiting centuries for the opportunity to do so. Just as you have a destiny, so too, do we."

We. There was a pregnant pause as they processed her use of the word. It was the first time she had referred to herself as one of the Keepers, although given all that she had alluded to it was not much of a revelation.

"Why not simply tell us now and be done with it?" Darrin snapped.

"That is not the way of things, Shield. There is a time and a place for such conversations. All will be revealed as the Mother wills," she paused then, closing her eyes and inhaling deeply. When her eyes reopened, a brilliant blue light sparkled in the midnight depths, "There is still time, for now."

"We have already been preparing for this journey for the last several days. We should be ready to leave come morning. Does that suit you, Keeper?" Helena inquired formally.

Miranda smiled as she inclined her head in a small bow, "Yes, Mother of Spirit. Tomorrow will be soon enough. Tonight, I would like to spend time with my granddaughter."

"Of course. Please rest and enjoy yourselves. We shall be off at first light."

The men recognized the dismissal and dispersed. There was still much to be done before they started on another journey. Despite the old woman's warnings about what lay ahead of them, Helena felt only a rush of excitement at the possibility that she was moving closer to finding her Mate. Von was being used as a pawn in another's game, but Helena would find him and repay that foolishness tenfold. No one took her Mate from her and survived the insult.

Outside the wind howled as it whipped through the trees. Shutters slammed against the windows as lightning flared brightly in the sky. Helena's aqua eyes were wild and shimmering with translucence while her smile showed more fang than tooth. She may not yet know precisely where he was, but she was certain that she was about to start the next leg of the journey that would lead her back to him.

MICHA AND NIAL were both waiting for her outside her door. She lifted an eyebrow in surprise to see both men prowling in the corridor beside her room. Pausing mid-step she asked dryly, "Is there something I can help you with?"

Their heads snapped toward her at the words and both men spoke at once: "I am coming with you when you leave for Bael," insisted Nial, while Micha begged, "Do not forget your promise to me, Helena."

Both brows lifted until they nearly touched her hairline, "If you feel that strongly about it, gentlemen, I will not stop you. I am sure we will have need of the additional manpower. Just know that if you slow us down or interfere with our plans, I will not hesitate to leave you alongside the road. The condition I will leave you in, however, will depend entirely on how much you annoy me in the process. Do I make myself clear?"

She watched relief brighten Nial's stormy eyes, while determination continued to shine through Micha's soft green ones. Each man felt he had something to prove, and while she could guess as to what that might be, she was curious to watch it play out.

"We leave with the dawn. Pack only what you need. I do not know how long we will be gone, and I cannot promise this is where we will return."

They nodded their understanding and each hastened off in a separate direction. She shook her head at their dramatic interception. The real reason she had agreed to their coming along was that she had her own feelings of intuition that they had a part to play in the days to come. She just wondered if their schemes would align with her own.

CHAPTER EIGHT

*H*elena finished tightening the strap of her belt with a
frustrated huff. She hadn't slept well and was feeling
decidedly grumpy as a result. Her eyes were scratchy and the muscles
in her back and neck felt knotted. It was not an ideal way to start a
journey, but her dreams had kept her tossing and turning into the first
hours of the morning. Even now the sky was more black than pink, the
sun just starting to peek up from its hiding place beyond the sea.

Helena could not recall her dreams in any real detail. She could
only grasp at the wispy memories, a certain color or feeling all she
could hold onto until even that much had slipped away. The one thing
that hadn't faded entirely was the soul-deep terror she had felt when
her eyes would snap open and her heart would pound between bouts of
dreaming. Her dreams had been some kind of warning; she was sure of
it. It was infuriating that the Mother would find it important enough to
send her the warning, and then not see fit to let her hold onto it. Did
everything need to be cloaked in such mystery? Just once, it would be
really nice to have something neatly packaged and handed to her with
explicit instructions on what to do with it. That would certainly be a
welcome change of pace, given all that had transpired since Darrin had

come to the cottage so many months ago. Apparently, the Mother disagreed.

She was still muttering darkly under her breath when Darrin approached her. "Are you ready to go, Helena?"

"Mother's tits!" she snarled as the leather strap snapped against her skin, his voice startling her despite its softness.

Darrin lifted both hands defensively and stepped back. Kragen placed his hand on the younger man's shoulder, "Perhaps we should get the Kiri some strong black tea before we start. It might do much to brighten her mood."

Unamused, Helena bared her teeth at the men. Feeling more feline than human at the moment, she felt a low growl start in her throat and wasn't at all surprised to see Starshine quietly stalking toward the trio.

Kragen laughed at the display of temper, entirely unimpressed since he knew she had no intention of acting on it. Helena scowled. It was rare for her to be in such a mood, but her growing sense of unease due to the dreams she could not recall, and the lack of sleep said dreams had caused, were taking a toll.

Serena made her way over to join the growing group. She wrapped a comforting arm around her friend and said in a low voice, "Here now, Kiri. Perhaps you would like to ride Starshine this morning? That always seems to help refresh you."

"So she can fall out of the sky when she falls asleep? Look at her; she's barely awake as it is!" Darrin retorted with some heat.

Serena spun toward Darrin, levelling him with a cool stare. She blinked her violet eyes once, twice, and then dismissed him entirely by turning her back to him. Helena's lips quirked up despite themselves and Serena's own lips lifted at the sight.

The thought of riding Starshine was tempting, but she knew how her Circle felt about her being too far out of their sight. She wouldn't allow anyone except Von to ride the Talyrian with her, so her compromise was to ride Karma, Von's Daejaran wolf, beside the others instead. She had her own wolf, Shepa, but since Von's disappearance, both Helena and Karma had found solace in spending time with their human's other favorite companion.

Starshine nudged her mistress with her massive head, the turquoise eyes studying her carefully. Helena buried her fingers in the thick white mane and had just rested her forehead against Starshine's snout when a barely audible gasp had her lifting her head back up to track the owner. Miranda stood near the manor; the hand pressed against her lips did little to cover the growing smile on the Keeper's face. Helena's brows furrowed as her tired brain tried to decipher Miranda's reaction to the Talyrian.

Miranda moved quickly toward the small group. Starshine's reaction was instantaneous. She growled, a deep rumbling sound, and shot a jet of flame at the woman's feet. Miranda jumped back, her mouth agape, but she recovered quickly, "I see you have found your rider."

Starshine's massive head dipped in the semblance of a nod.

Helena looked between the two, her look of shock mirrored on her friends' faces. "Have you two already met?" she finally asked.

Miranda nodded, "Oh yes, the Keepers have always been familiar with the Talyrian pride."

Timmins, unfortunately, chose that moment to join them. It seemed he was destined to be outshone by the Keeper. He had overheard Miranda's last comment and was already scowling when she asked, "What do you know of the Talyrians?"

Helena shrugged, not in the mood for a history lesson. She was far too exhausted for that. "I know that they are very possessive and quite fierce. They can cause the earth to quake, shoot fire, fly, and have no trouble expressing their opinion despite their inability to talk." Despite feeling irritable, Helena was smiling as she spoke. Starshine's gaze was tracking her closely as she turned to face Miranda.

"Your Starshine is more special than you know. A Talyrian will only choose a rider that can match them in power. To try and form a bond with one of lesser power would destroy the rider." Miranda's voice was mild as she shared her information.

Helena could feel her heart begin to race erratically. She sent a startled glance to Timmins, whose own eyes were focused with a single-minded intensity on the Keeper.

"Starshine is the Queen of the Talyrians. Just as the Chosen have a matriarchal society, so too do the Talyrians. She is the most powerful Talyrian in the pride. It says much that she came to you, Kiri. Especially when her ancestors retreated many centuries ago because there were no Chosen who could match them in power."

Helena's entire body stiffened. "I'm sorry," she blinked a few times trying to clear her mind, "what exactly are you saying?"

"With the Mother's power becoming so diluted in the Chosen, the Talyrians could no longer risk linking themselves to their riders. The link between a Talyrian and its rider requires the rider to be able to withstand the additional flood of power. If the rider is not strong enough they would become overwhelmed by the power flowing through their bodies and their minds would shatter."

"Like the Fracturing?" Helena asked in a soft voice.

Miranda's head tilted as she paused, considering. "In a way, I suppose it is similar. The Fracturing is a loss of self that causes a Kiri's power to overtake her body. She is still alive, but she is no longer herself with unique thoughts or desires, merely a receptacle for her power. What happens to a Talyrian rider is more of a slow death. When they are not strong enough to contain and channel the additional power, it eventually burns up everything within them, leaving nothing in its wake that can continue to animate the body and so they die."

Helena was floored. She turned toward Starshine and stared in horrified awe.

Miranda continued, "As a Mother of Spirit you can access all five branches of the Mother's magic: Earth, Air, Fire, Water, and Spirit. Talyrians also possess all five branches, although their ability to wield it is obviously in a different capacity." She paused in consideration for a moment before asking a bit incredulously, "Have you never heard the story of the first Talyrian?"

Timmins scoffed, looking deeply aggrieved, "Obviously not, Oh Wise One, but perhaps you would indulge us, humble simpletons, a little while longer."

Miranda's midnight eyes flashed with annoyance, but she ignored him. Looking back to Helena she said, "I will save that story for another time. For now, it should be enough to know that a Talyrian is a creature of Spirit. Whereas a Kiri has the potential to control or influence with their gift, a Talyrian can link to their rider and share their abilities. My granddaughter told me that when you are angry, you grow claws similar to Starshine's?"

Helena merely nodded while Darrin added in a shaking voice, "And when she's in the midst of one of her tantrums she's also prone to starting storms, but that is hardly a Talyrian ability. It is not like she begins to breathe fire or sprouts wings and start flapping around."

"At least not literal fire," Kragen muttered.

"She has been known to call it from the sky though," Serena interjected, just as softly.

Helena rolled her eyes but remained quiet.

Miranda was deeply amused, "Her power remains her own. How she influences the elements and people around her can manifest in many ways, but this is something unique to her and Starshine. There are some Chosen that can take on the forms of others, but never their actual powers. When Helena channels Starshine through their link, she's taking on actual qualities of her Talyrian. Perhaps she will one day grow wings and learn to fly, but I have never seen nor heard of such a thing happening before."

"I have heard of some Kiris that were able to control animals, is that something—"

Miranda cut Timmins off, "Do you really think the Queen of the Talyrians is going to allow anyone to control her? What woman, let alone queen, would ever be okay with someone else telling them what to do? What she *agrees* to do is a result of her own will and her trust in her rider's decisions. Make no mistake; she is very much in control of her own actions."

Timmins' face was bright red; his lips flattened with annoyance. Miranda's own lips twitched with mirth. She took far too much enjoyment putting him in his place.

Helena was done merely being a silent participant in this conversation. "You said that I can take on the characteristics of

Starshine. Do you mean that I will be able to turn into a Talyrian? Like a shifter?"

Miranda shrugged, "It is possible you could shift into a Talyrian if that were your gift, but you would not *be* a Talyrian. I find it highly unlikely that this link would allow you to become a hybrid version of Starshine and yourself, Kiri. However, those claws of yours are certainly for more than pretty decoration. You and Starshine are both very powerful; who is to say what you will learn to do now that you are linked. I almost feel sorry for the one who causes you to find out."

Helena shivered at that. Starshine pressed against her, those turquoise eyes assessing her. Helena stroked the velvety fur until she felt the deep rumbling reverberate through her hand. *I always knew you were special, beautiful girl, but I never anticipated you were a Queen.* Starshine huffed, little wisps of smoke flaring from the great cat's snout. Helena chuckled, *You're right, I should have known better. Anyone as majestic and as used to getting her way as you must certainly be a Queen.*

Timmins cleared his throat; he was pale now, but desperately trying to retain his position of authority as a member of her Circle. She offered him a gentle smile, empathizing with his consternation.

"It seems we still have much to learn," he said in a stilted attempt at compromise.

Miranda lifted a sculpted brow, "The Mother's Chosen should always be open to learning. It is their mistaken belief in their own excellence that gets them into trouble."

Timmins looked ready to launch himself at the Keeper. Serena and Kragen were trying, unsuccessfully, to muffle their laughter.

"Time to head out you lazy layabouts," Ronan shouted from a short distance away.

Thankful for the distraction, Timmins hurried off without another word. Helena shrugged apologetically as Miranda shook her head, "You think for one tasked with being a pillar of knowledge, he would be more open to learning."

Serena lost it completely and was snorting with her mirth. Helena was little better off. "I... I think he is simply not used to being the one without answers," she finally offered.

Miranda huffed, "His pride is wounded, the foolish male. I will try to treat him more delicately so as not to offend one of your Circle."

"Please don't put me in the middle of it, I beg of you," Helena insisted, still chuckling despite herself. She wasn't sure what "more delicately" looked like, but she had a feeling it would continue to rub her Advisor the wrong way.

"Hmm," Miranda replied, her gaze narrowed as she watched Timmins' retreating back.

Feeling significantly better than she had when starting her morning, Helena gave Starshine one last rub between the ears before starting toward Karma. At least there would be no shortage of entertainment on this leg of their journey. It would be a welcome distraction from what awaited them at the end.

IT TURNS out that entertaining was the absolute last word Helena would use to describe this particular journey. Despite being a smaller close-knit group of friends, the overall mood and energy of the group could only be described as cautious apprehension. There was a palpable underlying tension and little, if any, playful banter between them. In its place, there was only a strained silence that was broken intermittently by half-hearted attempts at conversation.

It wasn't just Von's missing presence that had them on edge either. Traveling again only served as a reminder of what they had unexpectedly stumbled upon the last time. They had been woefully unprepared to come face to face with the remnants of the Shadows' savage attacks, and it was impossible to forget the sight of those bodies lined up alongside the road. Especially the tiny ones. The knowledge of what could be waiting for them kept them ever vigilant. It was exhausting.

The worst part of being constantly alert, at least in Helena's opinion, was that nothing ever seemed to actually happen to warrant that level of focus. They were jumping at every crack of a branch, but so far there had been nothing more threatening to face than their own idling tempers. Perhaps that was threatening enough.

The days were long and the bitter winds of Daejara were swiftly replaced with a thick wall of humid air as they moved into Bael. Bael was a tropical region, the trees thick with ropey vines and the air heavy with the buzz of colorful insects. Where Daejara was a pristine and untouched beauty, Bael glittered like a jewel and seemed to be in a constant state of shimmering motion. There were explosions of color and life everywhere she looked. If it wasn't for the heat that had her shirt sticking to her skin as soon as she stepped out of her tent, Helena thought she might quite enjoy it here.

Miranda and Timmins had started bickering as soon as they stopped for the night to set up camp. She had refused to tell him how much farther it was until they were to meet up with the rest of the Keepers. To be fair, it was not merely that she had refused, rather she had shrugged with a slight smile and stated cryptically, "We will know once we've arrived."

As amusing as she found their disagreements, she wasn't much up for refereeing another one at the moment, so she had peeled away from the group and called Starshine to her for a quick exploration of the jungle around them. When Helena had heard they would be traveling through the Baelian Forest, she had anticipated a traditional forest. One filled with dappled light filtering down through thick branches and dark green leaves, with crisp air scented by the clean smell of pine. Instead, she had been caught completely unawares by the bright bursts of flowers that ranged back as far as her eyes could see. The only thing that seemed to live up to her expectations was a sky primarily concealed by the unseen tops of the trees that towered above her. Even so, she didn't have a name for the massive trees with their waxy green leaves that were as large as she was.

Helena's steps had slowed. She was distracted by visions of the vibrant blooms growing alongside the rest of her favorites in the Palace gardens. It was a peaceful image that captivated her with remembered smells and feelings. Her fingers itched to find the seeds that would make it a reality.

Starshine snorted beside her, the small wisps of smoke seeming to hang in the heavy air. Her wings were pulled in close to prevent them from brushing against the foliage. It was clear the Talyrian was on edge. Helena had assumed that it was because there was a sense of confinement underneath the trees when you were used to soaring in the sky. Starshine shook out her mane and let out a soft huff that emphasized her desire to be elsewhere.

Sighing, Helena was about to give in. As she turned to fully face the Talyrian and tell her it was time to head back, she caught a flash of movement from the corner of her eye. The shadows between the trees had rippled. Startled, she froze, going completely motionless for a series of thumping heartbeats. Curiosity ate at her, causing her to slowly turn her head back toward the trees. There was nothing there. Letting out a breath she wasn't aware she was holding, her shoulders started to relax.

Before she could move, she saw the shadows flicker, flaring infinitesimally brighter before fading back into their normal shade of black. Now certain there was something there, Helena called her magic to her, using it to enhance her senses. Sounds that had been too low for human hearing were suddenly clanging loudly in her ears and the rich scent of damp earth flooded her nose. Each color was so bright it was almost painful in its intensity, but she was able to dilute the effect by focusing intently on the ground.

Nestled between two trees was a patch of darkness that seemed to pulse and grow, feeding itself with the surrounding shadows as it began to take shape. Its form was barely discernable and its edges were blurred, dangling vines momentarily visible around it until they were consumed again by the inky darkness. She felt her mouth grow dry as a distinctly feline shape emerged. It was still cloaked in shadow, but its outline was unmistakable.

There was another ripple and suddenly the darkness came lunging at them. Helena cried out, too stunned to react. Starshine roared and sprang forward to meet the massive shape that was now hurtling toward them. Helena tried to form her magic into a ball of fire, but could not. Frantic, Helena tried again, she could feel the pool inside her slosh, but there was no answering surge. Her eyes widened as she watched Starshine swipe her massive paw at the now-visible cat.

The beast was large, although nowhere near the size of the Talyrian. It was a soft gray with lavender stripes running through its fur. It snarled, saliva dripping from its gleaming fangs that were easily the width of her wrist. Its fur bristled as it crouched in preparation for another attack. Starshine bellowed, jets of fire shooting from her mouth aimed in the direction of the striped beast. It dodged the attack, barely, and let out an angry roar.

Helena was shaking. She could not stand there and do nothing. She pulled at her magic, trying to shift it from her senses into one of the other branches. A small ball of light began to build in her hand and thunder softly growled in the sky.

Her heart raced. She let out a grunt as she tried to make the lightning expand in her hand, but it flickered out.

"No!" she shouted desperately. Starshine's large turquoise eye turned toward her at her cry. Sensing its opportunity, the cat prepared to lunge again, now having a clear shot at Starshine's exposed neck.

Fury built and something snapped within her. Helena could feel her magic rise up and overtake her. The claws pushed out of her fingers and her toes, and her muscles were bunching as she launched herself at the beast. She struck it on the side, knocking it down before those dripping fangs could reach her Talyrian.

Starshine bellowed, pacing behind her. The Talyrian wanted to strike, to defend her mistress, but could not attack without hitting her, so she paced and snarled, her wings flapping uselessly at her sides.

Helena's claws raked at the now-exposed belly of the beast. She could feel the warm blood coating her fingers, but she did not stop. She had turned completely feral. Helena was still snarling and digging into the now dead corpse when arms like steel wrapped around her waist.

"Be easy, Kiri. You have done well."

She was thrashing and snapping in the arms, the voice unrecognizable in her current state.

Her claws pierced through the skin of the one holding her and an angry male voice hissed, "Mother's tits, Helena! Sheath those thrice-damned things! I'm not here to hurt you." The arms about her tightened as bit-off fragments of cursing continued.

Starshine was snarling, crouching low as she approached Helena. Her iridescent gaze met the turquoise one and something began to settle inside her. She took a few shuddering breaths and slumped in Ronan's arms.

She was surprised he was the one holding her, instead of Darrin or Kragen, but then again he was a fearless warrior in his own right. He probably hadn't stopped to think and had simply done what he felt necessary once he saw her.

The claws receded and she was in her normal state once more. She gasped for breath, her heart still racing with adrenaline after the attack. She pushed weakly at the arms holding her; they released her slowly ensuring that she could stand on her own before dropping her completely.

Helena lifted her eyes to his. Ronan's scar was pulled more harshly than usual as his lips were tipped in a frown. His ice-blue eyes shone with worry. She could feel them on her as he searched her face for the answer to a question he had not asked.

She took a deep breath, inhaling the metallic tang of blood. Her brows knit together and she wiped at her nose. Ruby red liquid smeared on her fingers. It was hers. The beast's blood was a silvery purple that matched its matted fur. Helena held out her trembling hand to Ronan, wordless.

He tore at his shirt, a piece tearing away so that he could wipe at her face. "Here, Kiri, allow me. Are you hurt anywhere else?" he asked in the soft voice one reserves for use when speaking with the gravely injured or a frightened child.

She did an internal check of her body and met his eyes as she shook her head in the negative.

Ronan nodded and then pulled her to him for a bone-crushing hug. "I was terrified for you, little one. What would Von do to me if something happened to you while he was away and unable to protect

81

you himself?" the question rhetorical.

Warm tears filled her eyes. "I'm sorry," she rasped, not certain what she was apologizing for other than causing him concern.

Ronan stepped back, clearing his throat. "You have no concern for your own safety. You should have run; the Talyrian could have handled the caebris on its own."

Her brows furrowed at the unfamiliar term he had used to name the beast. She turned her head to look down at it, but he grabbed her chin and firmly shook his head no. She swallowed, her stomach rolling.

No longer satisfied with the distance, Starshine nudged her with her head. Helena automatically began to stroke the velvety fur, "Thank you, beauty, for acting when I could not."

Ronan stilled at that, "What do you mean you couldn't?"

"I-I tried to use my magic and it wouldn't come," she stuttered, shrinking slightly under his harsh scrutiny.

Ronan's frown deepened. She didn't like saying it aloud any more than he liked hearing her say it. Miranda had warned them this was an eventuality the longer she and Von were parted. The sluggishness of her magic, combined with the blood dripping from her nose when she had sustained no attack, were clear signs that the bond was straining.

"Say nothing to the others of this," she ordered, forcing herself to assume the role of Kiri once more.

He moved to protest, and she shot him a narrowed-eyed glare. He muttered to himself before nodding once and saying, "Fine, Kiri, but you will not be without an escort again."

Starshine protested the insult by shooting a small spout of flame at his feet.

Ronan let out a startled shout and jumped to the side, "I meant no insult, lady," he said hurriedly as he addressed the Talyrian, "I just want to assure that your mistress is well protected."

Starshine lifted her paw as though to swat at him. Sensing all he had done was insult her further, Ronan looked at Helena for intervention. Amused, despite the corpse leaking blood on the ground behind her, Helena simply shrugged.

Ronan gave her a glare of his own. "Why weren't you carrying a weapon?" he snapped instead.

It was her turn to look sheepish, "I assumed between my magic and Starshine I would be fine. We hadn't seen anything to indicate..." she trailed off.

"Why do we bother training, Helena, if you fail to use those skills when you need them?"

"I wouldn't say I failed, Ronan. I did kill the caebris after all."

His arms were crossed against his chest, as he considered her words. "So you did, but at what cost?" he asked, referring to her still-dripping nose.

Helena scowled and Ronan shook his head, ready to let the fight go, as the words had stemmed from his concern for her rather than any real disapproval.

"Help me find him, Ronan," she pleaded softly, "before it gets worse."

Ronan's nod was stiff, worry evident in every line of his body. "Let's get you cleaned up and back to the others."

Helena sighed, she was not looking forward to that conversation at all.

CHAPTER NINE

*R*onan's answer to her run-in with the caebris had been more training. The morning after the attack he had woken her by lifting her from her pallet and throwing her into the icy stream. She had stood spluttering, shivering, and shooting daggers at him with aqua eyes swiftly shifting into iridescence. In response, he tossed his sword at her feet and uttered two completely serious words, "Beat me." There was an unspoken message that followed, whispering to her in his rasping growl, *and I will stop.*

He pushed her past every physical limit she thought she had, daily. He woke her up before the dawn and had her running drills with at least one of the others but sometimes two. If one of the Circle was unavailable to be her partner for the day, he would unleash himself on her, holding none of his ferocity back.

Helena was ready to murder him. There was only so much of his taunting she could take. She didn't care that his stubborn brutality had paid off and that she had already far surpassed any accomplishments she had previously bragged about. After a few weeks under his determined tutelage, she could now best most of them in both hand to hand and armed combat more often than not. Except Ronan; that smug bastard continued to beat her, howling with laughter each time he landed a blow or knocked her on her ass.

She remembered the day she had first watched him training with Von, and how he had been the one laying on his back in the dirt cursing at Von to help him stand. Her desire to be the one to put him there, even just once, was what drove her to keep standing long after she wanted to curl into a ball and whimper.

Helena had not asked him for mercy, not once. She knew what drove him to push her so hard was his fear of what could happen to her if her magic ever failed her completely. She could see the concern burning in the back of his icy blue eyes when his calloused hand would reach down to pull her back to her feet. Not that she would allow him to help her up.

Her stubbornness was more than a match for his. If she was being honest with herself, it was because she was just as shaken as he was. The possibility of being in a situation without magic to defend herself, or the others, disturbed her deeply. It had only been a handful of months at most, and already calling her magic to her had become as instinctual as breathing. That was not to say she always had control of it, or even that she was always successful. There were still far more mishaps than she would willingly admit to, but the urge to reach for it was ever present. It was an essential part of her now.

And so they trained, both single-minded in their focus to make her as fierce a warrior as any Daejaran he had trained. The fact that she could already beat both Darrin and Kragen had left her thinking that there was something seriously lacking in the Rasmiri training plan if two of their best could be so easily outmatched, but she would never say so aloud.

"And again," Ronan snapped, his fiery red hair pulled into a tight knot on the top of his head. Sweaty strands were sticking to his cheeks and neck, looking like trails of blood in the glittering morning light.

Helena wiped at the sweat on her brow, her gaze severe as she moved into position. Her magic was rippling inside her, urging her to pay attention to it like a cat purring at her feet. It was hard to deny that part of herself, but the unspoken rule between them was that there would be no magic during their sessions. The whole purpose of her training was to ensure she would not falter if there came a time that her magic was unresponsive, so she ignored the urge to let it wrap itself around her and instead focused on finding an opportunity to strike.

She circled him slowly, eyeing him as a predator assessing its next meal. She quickly weighed and discarded each potential move, already anticipating how he would counter it before her strike would land. He tossed his ax from hand to hand, shifting his weight between each foot; his coiled energy not allowing him to stand still.

Helena forced herself to be aware of the sounds in the early morning air: the low hum of the insects beginning to wake with the warmth of the sun and the soft caw of the birds that sought their breakfast. The jungle was alive around her, but her focus noted it only as a static image. She was aware of it, but only as a means of determining how it could help or hinder her. The rest of her mind was zeroed in on the opponent in front of her.

Her opportunity presented itself when Ronan had started to twist his body to keep her in front of him. Her move was immediate; there was little, if any, forethought before she swept her leg out and knocked his feet out from under him. He had been expecting her to strike with her weapon, not with her legs, and fell with a muffled grunt. He was already using his momentum to spring back up, but she landed on top of him before he could get his feet beneath him.

She knew that his sheer bulk could work against her so speed would be her asset. She twisted her body around his so that she moved from his chest to his back, wrapping her arms around his neck to cut off the flow of air as she did. She increased the intensity of her hold as he struggled to dislodge her.

Her legs were iron bands around his torso, one of his arms also caught in the hold. He continued to squirm, but eventually tapped at her leg as the hold on his neck became too much for him. She released him immediately, the surge of victory sweet. Before she could say anything, he pulled her to him and lifted her in an elated hug.

"Uh, Ronan, I don't think you usually hug your trainees when they beat you," she pointed out chuckling.

MEG ANNE

"Shut up, Hellion," he murmured gruffly, using the childhood nickname he had picked up from Darrin. The Circle had decided it was a very fitting name for their Kiri and had taken to using it whenever they were exasperated with her. Needless to say, they were now using it quite often. Ronan held her tightly, squeezing her in his arms, "Well done, Helena, truly. There are few seasoned warriors that can get past me. That you were able to do so after just a few weeks is incredible."

She bristled with pleasure at his words; the compliment doing much to ease the frustration his weeks of taunting had caused.

"You know what this means, don't you?" he asked as he stepped back from her, still holding onto her arms.

"Again?" Helena asked, trying not to wince at the thought.

Ronan laughed and shook his head, "That's not what I was going to say, although we should definitely test if you can repeat your success. No, Kiri, I was going to say that now that you have proven you can beat not only your team but also your Commander, you have earned the right to wear your Jaka."

Helena went completely still at his words, her eyes going wide at the declaration. She had thought in passing once about asking for a Jaka, the idea of inking her flesh with words of strength and protection a comforting one, but to hear that she had officially earned the right to bear that symbol had tears quickly filling her eyes.

She tried to blink them back, but Ronan spotted them. His smile was warm as he wiped one of her tears away. "He would be so proud of you. You realize that, don't you?"

Ronan's voice was gentle and warm. She sniffed back tears as she nodded, the words causing a ball of emotion to lodge at the base of her throat.

His fingers wove into the tangle of her hair and pulled her back into his chest as tears blurred her vision. "He would fight me for the honor of being the one to mark you, declaring it his right as your Mate, although as the one who trained you tradition dictates that it should come from me."

Helena laughed at that. Von would absolutely balk at the idea of anyone else touching her so intimately, let alone permanently marking

88

her. He would most definitely pull rank and declare that as *his* Commander, the ritual of the Jaka was his to perform, not Ronan's. Despite the fact that no such rule existed and he would be completely making it up.

She pulled out of the comforting embrace and wiped at the wetness on her cheeks with a chagrined sigh, "I'm not usually so weepy."

Ronan offered her a crooked grin, "That's what every woman says when she's caught crying."

Helena rolled her eyes, "I can knock you on your ass again if you're going to insist on turning into a massive asshole."

He laughed at the brazen declaration. "You can try, sweetheart," he taunted.

Helena pretended to consider it, before pronouncing in her most carefully neutral voice, "I think that I've wounded your male ego enough for one day."

His knowing grin made her smile despite herself. He nudged her with his shoulder, "I meant what I said. You did well."

She beamed, the sweat, dirt, and achy muscles long forgotten as they leisurely made their way back toward the camp. "So when do I get my tattoo? Do I get to pick where it goes?" she asked, recalling that both Ronan and Von had their Jakas over their hearts and down their right arms, although she had not noticed the same markings on Serena.

"It is your choice. Most go for the traditional placement," he rested his hand on his chest to indicate his own markings, "but many of the women prefer their back or arms." Ronan shrugged as if the placement did not matter, "We place it over the chest because it is closest to our heart. Thus the words rest above the most vulnerable part of ourselves. But it is merely symbolic. The location does not make the words any more powerful."

Helena considered it, trying to imagine her skin marked with the dark ink. She could not imagine herself with the symbols swirling along her collarbone and over her shoulder, no matter how hard she tried. She liked what Ronan had said about having the words rest above her heart though, which had her asking eagerly, "Can I put it on my ribs? Just under my chest? That way it will still be close to my heart."

Ronan's smile widened, "As you wish, Kiri, although I should warn you that is one of the most painful places to be marked."

Helena shrugged, not overly concerned with his assessment. Pain, she had realized, was subjective. There were jagged edges in her soul where none had ever existed before losing Von. She was already living with the agony of that loss scraping and tearing at her very core every day. She highly doubted the handful of hours someone poked at her flesh would even register. Nothing could possibly compare to the all-consuming ache of losing the most vital part of yourself.

VON WAS LOST in the mist, his nerves frayed and over-exposed. As soon as the mist would begin to fade, he'd break into a sweat and start shaking, terrified about facing the fresh hell it would torture him with. He had watched the most horrific and painful parts of his life replay, sometimes in slow motion, on a continuous loop. His brother's accident. His father's shame when he declared himself a mercenary. Ronan almost dying, his face slashed in half and blood covering his unconscious body. Other soldiers whose names he did not speak but would never allow himself to forget. Men who had died due to his arrogance and the sheer stupidity of decisions he had made because of it. Battle after bloody battle, and all of the bodies of the innocents that accompanied them.

Then there were the other visions. The ones that hadn't happened but still could. Those hallucinations almost exclusively involved Helena, her aqua eyes beseeching him to save her and then condemning him when he could not. Over and over again he had watched her get beaten, raped, or torn apart by one type of savage monster after another. Every time these visions assaulted him, he damn near pulled his arms out of their sockets trying to get free of the invisible chains that held him in place. It was driving him insane watching the nameless and faceless beings torment her. With every failure, he felt his grip on sanity slip a bit more.

He swallowed, his throat still raw from the last bout of screaming.

His lips were cracked and bleeding from biting down on them in his struggles, his body sore and bruised from pulling so hard against his restraints. There were also wounds he could not account for, deep red welts along his wrists and ankles. Their presence did not seem to make any sense as he had never seen any bindings. But then, what of being trapped in this misty place made actual sense? Who could even say what was real or not here?

There was a chattering of voices in the distance that seemed to be growing closer. It was not one of the voices he recognized, or associated, with the visions. Von laid curled into himself, his aching body protesting each movement as he forced himself to try and move into a sitting position. Everything within him objected to the weakness his position conveyed, and yet there was nothing he could do to protect himself against the relentless assaults. Even so, he refused to meet the next bout of torture while lying down like a child. Until they actually broke him, he would continue forcing himself to stand up and face it head-on.

He could not guess how long it had been since the last vision, but he knew since he was mostly coherent that the next round was nearly upon him. The voices which seemed to be beside him now confirmed it. Despite their nearness and volume, he could not make sense of the words, only the underlying urgency.

Something was happening. Von struggled to focus, trying to force his brain to comprehend the sounds around him. He pulled himself toward them, staggering to his feet. He was rewarded with the word "vessel" but alone the word meant nothing to him.

There were two distinct voices now, one of which was clearly angry. He could feel the emotion more than hear it. In fact, that voice was not raised at all. It was more of a harsh whisper he strained to hear. Von could sense the anger of the speaker through the tendrils of ice it wound around him. It was a cold so fierce it burned white hot. The effect caused the hair on the back of his neck and arms to lift in warning. This kind of anger was something best avoided.

The other voice was a soft, protesting keen. *This must be some reprimand*, he decided. Someone must have failed and the keening voice was trying to get out of a punishment. At least, that was the sense he got, given the way the other voice seemed to cut off and speak over the other. *Was it him? Had he failed and this person was taking the blame for it?* He certainly felt like a failure.

Von couldn't understand what the mist was trying to accomplish this time. He felt no personal connection to these voices, only confusion. Although, he was still warily anticipating the emotional blow that was sure to follow. It always did.

Up ahead a dazzling light flared through a crack in the midst. Von squinted, shielding his eyes from the unexpected brightness. *What in the Mother's name is happening?* The beacon of light was new to him, as well. There would be illumination during one of the visions, and there was always an eternal glow in the mist, but not the harsh yellow light which was currently blinding him.

He stumbled toward it, his body in agony at the movement. The light grew brighter the closer he moved toward it, and something was whispering frantically in the back of his mind for him to remain in the safety of the mist. Von laughed harshly at the thought, *the safety of the mist.* What kind of warrior was he, if he was content to remain in the arms of his captors, even the invisible ones?

The light was becoming painful in its intensity; its harsh glow beginning to make his eyes burn. He squeezed them closed to gain some relief but did not stop moving. This was no gentle sunshine; he felt no warmth the closer and brighter it became. His curiosity was eating at him. Von was certain this was some trick of the mist and he was eager to uncover its deception. If nothing else, the end of the vision would allow the soft, lilting voice to find him once more and soothe the ache the vision would surely leave behind. With a final push, he stepped into the blinding center of the beacon and forced his eyes wide open with a ragged gasp.

Rowena paced at the foot of the prisoner's bed. Her anger was making the room turn cold, as ice began to coat the surface of the walls. Gillian shivered and tried to cover her reaction by rising to her feet. It had been four weeks since she had last promised her mother that Von would wake. Four weeks with absolutely nothing to show for it.

She had sat in the room with him so long she had begun to feel like she was the real prisoner. Resentment ate away at her insides; *why should she be trapped so? They had the bait, why did it matter if he was conscious or not? At least this way he was not a threat to them.* The thoughts, though they bolstered her courage, would never be voiced. She knew better than to question her mother.

"Wake him," she hissed.

"Mother, I—" Gillian started to protest.

The use of the word caused Rowena's lips to twist with distaste before her face settled back into its expressionless visage. "Now," she ordered. For all that the word was whispered, it cracked like a whip.

Gillian shrugged helplessly, conscious not to repeat her slip as she added, "The drug has him in its hold, Mistress. There's nothing I can give him to counteract it while he is unconscious."

"You had better hope, girl, that he wakes. My patience with you is waning. I gave you until the turn of the moon, and you have failed to meet your deadline. Does your brother's life mean so little to you?"

Gillian's heart constricted in her chest. *No, not Micha. Not after everything she had already gone through to protect him.* "Please, Mistress. Give me another day. I will—"

"You have one hour, or I will crate you up and send you off to the Vessel myself. Let her have her way with you for all the grief you have caused her. I am sure she has many plans for what she would like to do to you, *Daughter*, if given the chance. It matters not to me. I will still have my prisoner, even if you are too incompetent to follow the simplest of requests." Each word landed like a blow. The fact that this was the first time that Rowena had called her daughter since appearing to her in the mirror cut her more deeply than the rest.

Gillian's back stiffened. She lifted her chin and met her mother's emotionless gaze, feigning a confidence she did not feel. Despite the words "she wouldn't" which repeated in her mind, her mother certainly *would* cart her up and ship her out. She would just enact her own punishment first. Rowena was not one to give someone else the pleasure of hurting someone for her. She was sadistic in that regard and needed to see the effects her brand of brutality could cause. That meant that despite her threat, before she made a gift of Gillian for Helena, Rowena would make certain that Gillian suffered, likely by slaughtering Micha.

Before she could respond there was a sound like crackling leaves that had her twirling to stare at the bed. Von's gray eyes shone unseeing up at the canopy above his bed before blinking rapidly. She was too stunned to move. Only moments before he had been catatonic, the same state he had been in since his arrival in Vyruul. Von turned his head, his eyes landing on her and narrowing. In that moment she was not sure who she was more afraid of, her mother or the madman whose eyes glowed with the promise of a slow and painful death.

She had thought, given how long he had been under, that he would be more disoriented when he awoke. It was clear, however, that Von was keenly aware of his situation, if perhaps not all of the details. Gillian was frozen in place, so startled by the unanticipated change of events that she could not react. This was her greatest fear come to life, save Micha being slain at the hands of their mother. At least he was safely away for the moment. That she even had the ability to feel relief at that realization only underscored how unmoored she had become by Von's very conscious presence.

"You," he growled, his voice no less terrifying despite its harsh rasp. Gray eyes swiftly became a molten, shining gold. With a powerful tug that should have been impossible given the amount of time he'd been incapacitated, Von pulled at the bindings holding him to the bed. The entire bed lurched with the movement. Gillian distantly noted the blood that dripped down his wrists, the force of the impact against his restraints having caused his skin to split. Suddenly, everything went black and she felt herself falling.

CHAPTER TEN

*H*elena was sitting with the other women listening to them share stories about their various conquests. She couldn't help but appreciate the idle chatter after the morning's grueling workout. She allowed her gaze to wander over each of the women, lingering momentarily on Serena's face. The blonde was staring off in the direction of the men. Helena let her eyes follow Serena's path, expecting to find Ronan, and only mildly startled to find Nial instead.

The two of them had been dancing around each other for weeks now. They were overly polite and courteous, both often studying the other before quickly looking away to try and avoid being caught doing so. Helena's eyebrow rose, *when are those two going to admit that they are interested in each other?*

Her next thought followed in quick succession. *Poor Ronan.* She could not imagine her proud friend taking the news graciously. His warrior instincts would demand retribution, or at the very least, the right to fight for his woman. He wouldn't simply allow her to waltz off with a new lover. His pride would never recover from the insult, not to mention his heart. There was little doubt that he loved her with every part of himself; to lose her would be a devastating blow.

Helena sighed. She was borrowing trouble worrying about

something that may never come to pass and she already had more than enough to focus on without adding to the list preemptively. Helena allowed her aqua eyes to fall back onto her friend's face. Serena was frowning now, clearly trying to puzzle something out. As if feeling Helena's eyes on her, Serena's gaze met hers and she turned a bright pink. Blushing was becoming a habit for her where Nial was concerned. She squirreled that thought away for now, determined to tease her friend about it properly another time.

The women had grown silent around her, and it was obvious someone had asked her a question she had missed. Helena blinked, clearing her mind of the errant thoughts in order to focus properly on the conversation. Miranda was regarding her curiously, one of her sculpted eyebrows lifted as if waiting for a response. Effie was smiling brightly, sitting on a log beside her Gran with her legs tucked up beneath her simple red dress.

"Apologies, Keeper, my mind seems to have wandered. What were you saying?"

Miranda's smile was warm as she repeated her question, "No need to apologize, Kiri. I was just wondering if you had any luck with your training. I know that you've been working with the fierce one." Her head gestured toward Ronan who had his arms crossed and was glowering at Timmins, "But what of your powers? Are you still struggling to control them?"

Helena tried not to scowl. She had finally made progress after weeks of effort with Ronan, and instead of being able to enjoy the accomplishment for a few hours, she had to answer for the fact that her magic was more like a prepubescent teenager than a prophesied ruler.

She opened her mouth to respond when a voice answered for her. "Our Kiri has never been one to lord her talents in front of others. She hates showoffs," Darrin's quietly amused voice responded as he took a seat next to her.

Helena smirked at him, remembering all of the times growing up when she had told him she wouldn't be his friend anymore if he always insisted on showing off. Mostly she had been annoyed he had been able to do so many more things that she had, and it was her way of trying to level the playing field. Not that it ever worked for very long.

Miranda's midnight eyes were shrewd as she pointed out, "I never said anything about showing off, I was asking about control."

"Some days are better than others," Helena responded dryly, refusing to elaborate.

If Miranda was startled by the shortness of her tone, her face did not betray it.

Micha was the one to respond, which surprised everyone. He had barely spoken more than a handful of times since they had left the Holbrooke estate. Taking her words before they had left to heart, he had blended unobtrusively into the background and had chosen to remain silent and watchful during their trek.

"That is true for all of the Chosen, Kiri," he mumbled, stepping closer to the group.

She smiled thankfully at him, appreciating the show of support.

Miranda harrumphed, annoyed that she had not gotten a straightforward answer, but seemed resolved to let it go. Helena couldn't help but wonder why she was so concerned about it in the first place. *It was really none of her business, was it?* The thought troubled Helena. As if to underscore her unease at the line of questioning, there was a low buzzing just under the surface of her skin. She rubbed her arms without conscious thought.

"Are you all having a party without me?" Kragen asked in his booming voice.

Helena rolled her eyes, "I would hardly call a bunch of women sitting around in the dirt a party, but to each their own, Sword."

There were murmurs of protest at her words, Serena feigning wounded pride as she shouted, "Hey!"

"That simply means you aren't doing it correctly, Kiri. I find that a group of women in the dirt can be quite an enjoyable time," Kragen smirked.

"You would," she retorted, trying to hide the smile his words had triggered.

"I second that," Ronan laughed, wrapping his arm around Serena, who gave him a tight smile.

"And I," Darrin chimed in.

"Because you would know," Helena sniped sarcastically turning to Darrin. "Tell me, Shield, when was the last time you had a group of women playing with you in the dirt?"

Darrin turned pink but answered gamely, "I seem to remember a time, Hellion, when you –"

"And that's enough of that story!" she said quickly, knowing exactly what he was about to share and wanting nothing to do with it. Helena frowned and began rubbing her arms in earnest, the harsh buzz beneath her skin growing painful.

"Cold, Kiri?" Nial asked softly from behind her. She tried not to flinch at his voice, but she had not heard his approach. Helena shook her head but did not respond.

Timmins and Joquil were the last to join the circle, joining in on the cacophony of happy and relaxed voices that surrounded her. She was smiling softly, enjoying the comradery, even as she shifted in her seat uncomfortably. Her behavior was starting to draw some concerned looks from the others, but no one mentioned it.

"The last time we sat around like this Timmins was telling us one of his stories," Joquil reflected.

"When isn't Timmins boring us with one of his stories?" Kragen asked and then quickly ducked as a rock came hurtling toward his head.

"Har har har, you jackass," Timmins said dryly.

Helena laughed despite herself.

"I believe it's Miranda's turn to tell us a story," Ronan called out loudly as he pulled Serena into his lap. Nial frowned before wiping his face of all expression.

"Oh yes!" clapped Effie, "Please Gran, you promised to tell the story of the first mate. It's one of my favorites!"

"I thought it was the Talyrians?" Kragen asked Darrin in a carrying whisper.

Miranda looked around the group sprawled about the clearing. The stars were just starting to appear in the sky as the sun began its descent. "I suppose it is the time of day made for storytelling," she said finally.

There was rustling as everyone settled in, making themselves comfortable. For her part, Helena was struggling to simply stay present with the people around her. Her skin felt as though she was being prickled with thousands of electrified needles. Fairly certain she was experiencing another side effect of the separation from Von, Helena didn't want the others to realize what was happening. She bit down hard on the inside of her cheek, trying to use the pain as a distraction. It worked. She focused on it, grinding her teeth slowly back and forth to increase the pressure. The buzzing only receded slightly, but it was enough to allow her to hear Miranda's lilting words.

"When the Mother first walked among the world she had created; she did so alone. As a being comprised of energy and intent, she was nothing like the two and four-legged, or even the finned creatures she had made. Thus, while she was surrounded by the beauty of her creation, she was never truly part of it. She spent many centuries with the beings she had molded from her power, infusing bits of herself into them so that they could continue to evolve as the years passed. This is how the Talyrians, Draconians, and even the Macabruls came into being."

Kragen nudged Darrin, "I told you it was about the Talyrians!" His over-enthusiastic exclamation caused the rest of them to snicker.

Miranda's midnight eyes glowed with warmth as she continued, "Eventually the first humans were made, and the Mother felt more drawn to these beings than any of the others. She was still too powerful and *other* for their simple minds to comprehend, but she studied them anyway. She was convinced they were the answer to her loneliness, if only she could find a way to bond with them. Despite infusing them with greater parts of her essence than ever before, it quickly became clear to her that the only way the humans would be capable of interacting with her would be for her to make herself more like them. These humans became the first Chosen. They were beings with raw and undiluted power, capable of magic we have not seen for millennia. Even still, the Mother's power was too vast for them."

Helena struggled to pay attention, but the buzzing returned in full force. Her ears were ringing and each word Miranda spoke sounded as if it was coming from far away. She bit down until the metallic taste of her blood was coating her tongue and tears were filling her eyes. In the distance, Starshine roared.

Miranda's storytelling halted, and the others shifted nervously in their seats. Kragen and Ronan both stood, hands unsheathing their weapons. Starshine's roar had been a call to battle: one they were answering. No one seemed to be looking at Helena, although in their own way, each person around her was seeking to protect her. If only they knew that their so-called enemy was not one they would actually be able to fight.

Helena's eyes lost focus, so she squeezed them shut. Within her, there was a sharp snap and she felt the bond that ranged between her and Von, the one that had been nothing but an endless chasm of silence for so long, pull taut. There was another roar, but this one was solely in her mind and it was a voice she had secretly feared she'd never hear again. *Von.*

When her eyes snapped back open, they were not a shining blue but swirling iridescent mist. Her teeth were bared in a feral snarl, her nails growing and curling into deadly black claws. She heard shouting around her and let out a low warning growl. All of her attention was turned inwards. Where there had once been nothing, she could feel a growing rage.

"*Von?*" she asked frantically. There was no answer.

Helena tried not to panic. She didn't want to know why she could only feel his emotions. All that mattered was making sure the bond did not go silent again. She honed in, flooding the tether between them full of her magic, pulling every last drop from the pool within her and sending it toward the howling wrath. If he was surrounded by enemies, she would make damn sure they could not hurt him again.

There was a loud crack of lightning, roaring thunder, and the sharp scent of burning wood. More screams called to her and she hissed. It was a final warning.

She felt as though she was using their bond like a rope, climbing and pulling herself toward him. Helena knew the moment she found him. There was a shiver of awareness that ran along her skin, although she was only passingly aware of her physical body. Helena was wholly focused on the thin barrier that was separating his mind from hers.

She sent her love for him to press against the barrier. It was a request for entry, the equivalent of a lover's gentle caress. She would not force her way into his mind, to do so would be the worst sort of invasion. If he was still in there, she would give him a chance to grant his permission before breaking the barrier.

The barrier rippled in answer before fading completely. She was in. Helena had a sense of being surrounded by mist before a room came into sharp focus. She could still feel her actual body, crouched on the jungle floor, from a world away. At the same time, she could also feel restraints biting into her, no... Von's wrists.

Their individual consciousness' were blending, and she could feel his jumbled thoughts like a rush of water washing over her. There were no complete sentences, only assorted words and phrases: *the voice, stay in the light, Helena...*

Upon hearing her name, she called to him, *"I'm here!"*

There was a surge of confusion that was quickly replaced by fury. Von's head turned. Helena was seeing through his eyes. Gillian was standing above them, her already milky skin deathly pale and her mossy green eyes showing white.

"You!" Helena shouted although it came out in Von's harsh rasp. They pulled against the restraints, the entire bed jerking beneath them as the wood gave way under the force of their joint strength.

With a roar, they were free and lunging toward Gillian. Her green eyes went white with snaking black lines moving beneath the surface. That was when Helena became aware of the other woman in the room.

ROWENA WATCHED Von break free and acted swiftly. She sent her power into Gillian's body. The girl was too senseless to move to defend herself. Rowena shuddered as she pulled the essence into herself, feeding off of the girl's power and bolstering her own strength. Her lips curled in an almost sexual smile. The extra flood of power was always heady.

She threw out an arm as Von launched himself at Gillian and Gillian's body lurched like a marionette before collapsing to the floor. She had not drawn enough to turn the girl into one of her Shadows. That would require a complete drain of power, and she still had plans for the girl before she could allow that to happen.

Von stopped short, now crouching on the bed. His hands fisted around the restraints at his ankles and pulled. The supple leather broke cleanly in two. He faced her, eyes a glowing molten gold.

Rowena smiled wickedly, "So glad you are back amongst the living, Mate. I was growing weary waiting for you to wake. Now the games can really begin."

She lashed out quickly sending her twisted Spirit magic toward him. Von's eyes narrowed and he snarled before speaking in a voice that had the smile fall from her face. "You do not know who you play with, woman, or you would not be so eager." His low rasp had transformed into a melodious and richly layered voice that she had heard only once before.

Rowena's bolt of magic bounced off Von with no more effect than a feather. His head had dropped down to assess the smooth skin of his chest before his lips curled with amusement and those molten eyes lifted to stare up at her through his lashes.

"My turn," the voice-of-many purred as Fire erupted from Von's hands.

With no choice but to retreat, Rowena snapped the purple stone from its resting place in her ring and vanished.

"HELENA!"

"Kiri, come back to us!"

The voices were tugging at her, but she resisted their pull a bit longer. For all that she was in Von's body, it was clear he was not conscious of her presence. She could feel him there, but he was diminished. Whatever had him in its grasp had not let go entirely. Helena sent her awareness through his body, seeking out the source of the corruption. She found traces of it throughout him, like gray smudges marring the shining brilliance of his soul.

Her magic was beginning to wane, the extent of power required to submerge herself within him more than she had ever used before. With what little she could still use, she wiped at the smudges until they were gone. His body shuddered and took a ragged gasp when the last of them disappeared. His eyes were heavy; the urge to sleep and let his body finish repairing naturally was overriding her ability to keep it awake.

She could not hold onto him for much longer. Recalling a trick that Von had used once before, she whispered to him, knowing the words would be waiting for him once he woke. *"We are coming, my love. It will not be long before you are in my arms again. I love you."*

With those words, she felt herself snap back into her own body, the chamber he had been in momentarily superimposed over the jungle clearing. Her eyes swam in and out of focus before she fell over in an unconscious heap.

CHAPTER ELEVEN

When Helena came to, she was dizzy and disoriented, her body feeling more than a little battered. The air was thick with the acrid smell of smoke, causing her to wheeze painfully. Blurred faces were hovering over her, but even blinking she could not call them into focus.

"Helena," a frantic Darrin called. She felt him take her hand in his and even that small shift had her groaning.

She turned her face toward the direction of his voice, but the movement caused stars to explode behind her eyelids. She tried to open her eyes but quickly closed them again. Something was wrong with her eyes. Helena tried re-opening them, but instead of seeing faces or bodies, she could only make out swirling colors. Where Darrin should have been there was a flicker of deep forest green. *Earth*, she realized. She was seeing his gift. *How is that possible?*

Helena allowed her eyes to roam and was able to catalog where each of her friends were, without being able to discern any of their physical features. Her Circle seemed to glow more brightly than the others since their gifts were threaded liberally with a soft shimmering lavender she recognized as her own. *I must be dreaming*, she decided, although the overwhelming pain shooting through her body contradicted that possibility.

She felt a cool hand brush her matted hair off of her face. Helena whimpered, the touch was gentle and yet it still grated. Helena opened her mouth to try and speak but was shushed by the owner of the hand. She assumed it was Miranda who was currently trying to pump her full of healing vitality. Rather than dull the ache, the power seemed to make everything come into sharper focus. It was as if her mind had wrapped her in some sort of protective fog to alleviate the pain, but Miranda's magic was stripping it away and forcing her to endure the full extent of her injuries.

"You need to let it go now, Kiri. You're still trying to use your power and it is fighting you. Release it. There you go sweet child," the kind voice murmured, punctuating each order with another soothing sweep of her hand.

Helena didn't feel like she was using any magic, she felt entirely depleted in all honesty, but she went through the mental process anyway. She visualized pulling the tendrils of her magic back into her and then letting them flow back into her inner pool. Usually rippling and shining, it felt muddied and almost completely empty.

Fear had her gasping, but strong hands held her down.

"Be still, Helena. Please," the strong voice was begging with no small amount of desperation. *Kragen*. She had scared him. *What have I done?* All Helena could recall were those moments she had been joined with Von. None of the corresponding moments her physical body experienced were available to her.

"Wha—" she croaked in a terrible rasp.

"We're not entirely sure, Kiri," Timmins murmured from close by, anticipating her question. She detected a subtle quiver of concern in his voice.

"What he means to say is that your power fucking exploded," Serena interjected, not one to mince words. Despite their crassness, her words were spoken in a very subdued tone. If Serena was subdued, then it must be *bad*.

Helena blinked a few more times before her vision finally began to clear, her friends' faces taking shape around her. Ronan stood back with Effie cowering in his arms. She was obviously terrified. Micha was white-faced and solemn, standing a little to the side of them. Nial was crouched beside Serena, not touching her, but obviously trying to bolster her with his silent support. The Circle were all touching her in some way, their hands pressed against various parts of her body. Helena let her gaze wander further, eyes trying to catalog and make sense of what she was seeing.

There was smoke everywhere. Trees to the side of the clearing were burning and the sky was a deep, angry black. In the swirling mass of clouds above them lightning flared brightly before an answering crack of thunder rolled in the distance. Helena blanched, *did I do this?*

From the clouds, small gray flecks were floating to the ground. It was clear that it wasn't rain. *What is that?* She squinted, trying to make sense of the objects. Her eyes widened and she croaked, "Ash."

The sky was raining ash down upon them. Peering closer she could see a dusting of the gray soot coating them all.

"For her reign shall be one of ash," Miranda intoned. Beside her Timmins and Joquil stiffened, exchanging furtive glances before turning back toward her. "Welcome back, Helena," Miranda continued as if she had not been quoting words of prophecy mere seconds before.

A question must have been apparent in her eyes because Darrin was quick to supply an answer, his voice filled with giddy disbelief, "Your eyes went all misty, like they do when you access your power, but this was different. You weren't in control; it was like it overtook you. You were growling and muttering things under your breath. A storm began to rage around us, the lightning hitting a few of the trees and cracking them in half. Then you smiled vacantly, not really seeing any of us, before saying 'My turn.' That was when fire began to fall from the sky. It didn't seem like there was any way we could avoid the flames, but not one of us was harmed. Finally, everything died down and you collapsed. When you woke your eyes were still swirling with that rainbow mist, but they are blue again now."

Helena was dumbstruck by his recounting and beyond horrified to see the consequences. She had thought her magic was only being used where Von's body was, but apparently she had pulled so much that it was unleashed around her body as well. The thought of that much power and destruction was more than she could process. Helena swallowed, her throat raw. "I saw," she paused to drag in a ragged breath, "Von." It was all she was able to say before her voice failed her.

Nial let out an audible gasp, while Ronan and Serena asked in unison, "Where?"

"How is that possible?" Effie whispered to no one in particular.

"Was Gillian with him?" Micha demanded, bracing himself as if for a blow.

Helena closed her eyes and dipped her chin in the semblance of a nod.

The man dropped his head and his shoulders slumped. He had been hoping that despite the story of his sister's betrayal she had been innocent. Hearing she had been with Von was as good as declaring a notice of execution.

"Can you still feel him?" Miranda asked with calm authority from her place at Helena's head.

Helena allowed herself a moment to seek out the thread that connected them. She plucked at it tentatively, weak with relief when she felt the solid presence at the other end. There was no answering thrum down the bond to indicate that he was conscious yet, but he was alive, and she could feel him again. It was more than she'd even thought possible after the last few months.

"Y-yes," she rasped.

Nial's eyes closed at the news before he slouched against the smoking remains of a tree behind him. He jumped forward with a startled yelp and rubbed his back. "Hot," he said by way of explanation, his cheeks pinkening with embarrassment. Kragen snickered and even Timmins let out a few amused chuckles before covering them up with a polite bout of coughing. The moment of levity allowed the group to relax, notwithstanding the fact that Helena was still lying in the dirt looking very much the worse for wear. Her complexion had taken on a waxy sheen and there were large purple smudges below each of her eyes. Her cheeks were hollow, her lips cracked and bleeding, while her overall appearance was emaciated and frail. Helena's magic had used her body to fuel its rage leaving her as little more than a shell in its wake.

Despite her ravaged body, Helena's mind was alert and sharp. It was a frustrating contrast. Knowing that Von was alive was pushing at her to get up and keep going, but she could barely lift her hand without it shaking badly.

"You need to rest," Miranda insisted firmly as if sensing her internal battle of wills.

"Keepers," Helena countered.

"We aren't far now. I am sure they will come to us given the state of things here. Besides, you are clearly not fit for travel at present."

Helena scowled, or she tried to, as any movement at all left her wincing.

Serena stood, "Here, let me make up a tent for you."

"I'll help," Effie offered, following close behind.

They had only intended to stop here for a quick break and meal. Their plan was to continue on a bit further before resting for the evening, so no formal camp had been set up. Apparently, plans had changed and they would now remain here for the foreseeable future. As much as she wanted to rush off, Helena couldn't deny that sleep sounded wonderful. It was all she could do to keep her eyes open. They started to drift closed but an errant thought had them flying back open.

"Starshine?" she demanded.

"Your Talyrian set off once the storm started in earnest. We think that she sensed the threat and went to keep watch. We have not seen her since," Joquil supplied in his usual matter-of-fact manner.

Helena frowned at the news, hoping she was alright. That was Helena's last coherent thought before the world went dark.

VON COULDN'T PLACE his finger on what was different, only that something was. The mist wasn't gone completely, but it was greatly diminished. He was reclining in a field he didn't recognize, beneath a clear blue sky. There were no discernable landmarks nearby and he had not heard any voices since waking.

All the pain and fear were gone, in fact, it was actually peaceful. Von stretched and rose to his feet, deciding to explore. For the first time since finding himself in this place, he was curious as to what he might find. The walk was a pleasant one, the breeze keeping him cool despite the presence of the sun. He had no clear destination in mind, but he did feel a strong pull to continue following a stream he had come across.

After some time, although he could not say how long, Von saw a garden materialize on the horizon. This he recognized. Picking up his pace, Von hurried toward it. It was the Kiri's garden from the Palace in Elysia. A smile tugged at the corner of his lips as he remembered the day Helena had unknowingly summoned him here.

He had been in the middle of a conversation with Ronan. They had been discussing their men's rotation schedule which they had decided was necessary given the Chosen's hostile response to their presence at the Palace. Ronan had been listing off the pairs when Von had felt a sharp tug in his chest. He'd looked down, certain that someone had a hold of him but saw nothing. Then there'd been a tickling at the edge of his consciousness. A feeling that he was needed somewhere. Then, like now, he had followed that intuition until he found Helena sitting on a bench in the garden. Her eyes had been closed and she had been smiling, her rosy cheeks giving him a pretty good idea of what she'd been thinking about.

Von blinked. As if the memory summoned her, Helena was sitting at a fountain he had not noticed. Her fingers were trailing along the surface of the water and her eyes were downcast as they watched the ripples.

Von swallowed thickly, *Mother she's beautiful*. Her dark hair was pulled up off her neck, but strands had gotten loose and were falling about her face in soft curls. Her body, which he had always appreciated for its curves, was wrapped in a lilac dress that revealed more than it concealed.

Here's a vision I don't mind being lost in, Von thought with a leer.

He saw her freeze, her eyes lifting from the water before her body turned to face him. The aqua orbs widened when they saw him standing there. To his shock, they filled with the sheen of tears before she launched herself at him. He stumbled back slightly, his arms wrapping around her to hold her tightly against him.

"*Mira?*" he asked, "What's wrong my love?"

"You're gone," she whimpered, her voice sounding small and lost.

Von chuckled at that, "I'm right here, Mate."

"You're not real," she mumbled dejectedly, sniffling into his chest.

Von ran his hand along her back, enjoying the way she felt in his arms. Feeling inspired, he let his hands roam lower and squeezed appreciatively. His hips pressed into her and he lowered his mouth to whisper into her ear, "That feels pretty real to me, Mate."

A shiver raced down her body and she pulled back to meet his gaze. "I must be missing you even more than usual if my dreams have taken this kind of turn," she murmured. Her eyes had gone soft and thoughtful, but they were no longer wet with tears.

"Your dreams? Sweetheart, I'm pretty sure you're visiting mine." Von laughed, letting his eyes run down her body and appreciating the swell of her breasts revealed by the low cut dress.

He watched her brows furrow thoughtfully, her nose scrunching up as she considered what he said. He pressed a kiss to her nose, tilting her chin so that her eyes met his again, "Why does it matter whose dream it is, so long as we are together?"

Her eyes sparkled mischievously at the thought before she broke out into a large grin, "I suppose you're right."

"Do you mind saying that again?" he asked, pretending to clean out his ear. "I'm not certain I heard you correctly."

Helena laughed and slapped his chest playfully, "You were lucky I admitted it at all."

"I suppose that's true. Can we take advantage of our good fortune now?" he asked, lips hovering above hers.

"If you don't, I may have to tell everyone about how you've lost your skill at seduction," she said a bit breathlessly.

Von snorted, "As if anyone would ever believe that. You should aim for a more realistic threat next time."

Helena shrugged before closing the space between them and kissing him. Von groaned low in his throat and pulled her closer. She tasted amazing. His hands moved up her body until they were framing her face and his fingers were woven into her hair. Cradling her head between his hands, he adjusted its angle so that he could kiss her more deeply. He felt her pulse fluttering wildly against his hands as he did.

She bit his lip and then licked it sweetly before running her tongue along his; her hands roaming across his chest and pulling at his shirt until it came loose. Von pulled back somewhat, chuckling at her whimpered protest as he lifted the piece of cloth up and off.

"Why the hurry, love? Not that I'm complaining mind you," he asked with a grin, breathing hard as he stepped back to her.

"I'm not sure how long we have, and I don't want to wake up and not have felt you inside me again," she panted, running her hands along the now exposed skin.

Her words left him reeling. This must be his dream indeed if his sweet but somewhat shy mate was speaking so. Not a man to take one of the Mother's rare gifts for granted, he grabbed her about the waist and lifted her until her legs were wrapped around him. "By all means, Mate, do not let it be said that I denied you."

She was giggling and flushed until he pressed his hips into her center and continued with the gentle rocking motions. Her eyes widened and then closed, her head lolling back as she pressed down into him.

"Like that do you?"

"I've missed this," she murmured, "the way that your body fits mine so perfectly. How with just one touch from you I feel like I'm on fire."

Von felt his head empty; the thought of teasing her and prolonging their time together disappearing completely as he sank to his knees on the grass. He maneuvered their bodies until he was on his back and she was straddled above him. Helena settled against him, causing him to harden even more.

"Take what you need, lady," he whispered hoarsely.

Her eyes were shining as she moved to free him from his leathers. "I need you," she professed.

"I am yours."

"Mine," she growled in affirmation, her eyes beginning to swirl before she closed them and captured his lips. He was thrusting helplessly into her hand as she began to work it up and down. Von moaned when she stopped until he felt her shift and start to slide her hot center along his length.

"Helena," he groaned.

She slid down him in one long thrust. Von's hands were clenched on her hips, holding her down while he enjoyed the sensation of being buried completely inside her. *Finally.* It was like coming home. Her breath hitched as she began moving above him, his own breath coming out in shallow pants as he matched her thrust for thrust, driving into her.

She increased the pace until her inner muscles began to spasm around him. Helena threw her head back yelling his name. Von came right behind her, pulling her down so he could kiss her as he emptied himself inside her.

They laid there, wrapped around each other under the sun's warm rays, slowly coming back to themselves. She went to lift herself off him but Von protested, tightening his hold on her, "Not yet."

Helena laughed and peppered kisses over his face. She lifted herself up slightly until she was resting her weight on his chest and looking down at him. Her fingers traced over his eyebrow and nose before moving down to his lips. He caught them in his teeth, biting down gently.

"I miss you," she whispered brokenly.

He released her fingers with a gentle kiss before replying, "Not nearly as much as I miss you, Mate." His gray eyes met hers solemnly and in their shared silence, she could feel all that he had endured since they had parted, knowing he was experiencing the same. They were wholly connected, hearts and minds completely in sync despite the time they had spent apart.

"I'm sorry—" she started, her voice thick with emotion, but he placed a finger against her lips and shook his head.

"You never need to apologize to me. Not for that. It was I who had wronged you, my love. More than that, I had many opportunities to come clean about what had happened—"

Now it was she who cut him off, "No, Von, please don't. It was Gillian's fault. She's the one who bewitched you. Without her trickery, you never would have done anything to apologize for in the first place."

Von gave her a lopsided smile, moving to place a curl behind her ear, "You have a kind heart, Helena, but I am not blameless here. Her magic ensnared me, yes, but it was not as if I was without memory of the incident. It was my pride that kept me from telling you what I had done. When you spoke of your trial and what you had witnessed, that was a warning for both of us. I should have told you then, but it was easier to let myself believe you'd never find out..." he trailed off.

There was a longer silence, their eyes saying what they could not. Helena kissed him, a sign of her forgiveness and love. With that kiss, another broken part of him settled back into place.

She pulled back, swirling aqua eyes meeting his as she declared fiercely, "I am coming for you. I *will* find you."

"I know you will, my love. I will be ready," he promised as he kissed her again, and pulled her back into his arms.

Helena settled against his chest, listening to the familiar thump of his heart. She smiled and pressed her lips against his skin, right over his heart. Their hearts were still beating in time, as they had been since speaking the words that bonded them to one another. It was a small detail but it brought great comfort. No matter the physical distance between them, they would always be one. She closed her eyes, still smiling softly. Eventually, they both began breathing deeply, lost once again to their individual dreams.

HELENA WOKE UP SMILING. Despite the chaos that had ensued earlier that day she was more at peace than she had been in months. She no longer felt any pain from her power's earlier outburst, which was a welcome and pleasant surprise. She shifted slightly, disrupting the soft furs that were wrapped around her. While there was no pain, her body did ache, but in a familiar and enjoyable way.

"Von," she whispered in hushed awe, pressing her fingers to her lips which felt swollen and slightly bruised. It may have been a dream, but in her heart, she knew it had been real.

"Mate," came the faint but fierce reply.

Helena's closed her eyes as her shoulders began to shake, a lone tear snaking its way down her cheek. She'd done it. When she had connected with him and removed those stains, she must have gotten rid of whatever had prevented them from reaching each other through the bond. It was still a strain, neither of them at full strength, but it was a start. At the very least they should be able to communicate and that was enough, for now.

In the quiet darkness of her tent, Helena began whispering words of thanks over and over, "Mother if you are listening, thank you."

CHAPTER TWELVE

*M*iranda had been right. The morning after her little tantrum, as Ronan had started referring to it, the Keepers sent word that they were on their way. That was it. Keepers were notoriously cryptic, so no one was surprised that they had not provided an estimated date for their arrival. Helena snorted derisively and rolled her eyes when Timmins relayed the message, but secretly, she was relieved not to be traveling for a while. Her body had yet to fully recover from the power-storm even days later.

Helena wasn't the only one still feeling lingering effects from the storm. While the sight of the damage she had caused left her wincing with remorse each time she witnessed it, her friends looked at her in much the same way. She couldn't blame them; her body had been slow to recover. Each one of her companions had taken it upon themselves to care for her and as such, she'd had an almost constant parade of visitors. This morning, Effie had arrived with an apple for her to snack on, and then Miranda strode in no more than two minutes later with a soft blanket for Helena to wrap herself in. Less than five minutes after that, Kragen appeared and made a snarky comment about how terrible Helena looked and forced everyone out so that she could rest. On and on it went, each of her friends trying, in the ways they best knew how, to ensure she got well. It was sweet of them, really, but Helena was starting to wish they would just leave her alone.

If it weren't for the worry that burned brightly in each of their eyes when they looked at her, Helena would have ordered them away by now. Instead, with each demand, she merely bit her tongue and relented. She was fortunate to be surrounded by those that loved her. There were many others that could not say the same.

As they had every few moments since she woke up, her thoughts spun back to Von. Helena sent an idle caress along their bond; it was a gesture so filled with tenderness it was as though she had run her fingers through his hair while he slept. There was no answer, nor had she expected one, but she could feel his steady presence at the other end. The feel of him within her was enough to keep her satisfied. From what she had experienced when joined with him, his mind and body had been in a condition similar to the one she was currently in: utterly battered. Unfortunately for her Mate, he did not have the benefit of well-meaning friends to care for him. Rather, Von was at the mercy of the enemies that surrounded him.

The thought of Gillian and that blonde woman had Helena's lip lifting in an unconscious snarl. She knew without having to be told that the woman with emotionless blue eyes was the one Effie referred to as the Corruptor. She had felt the perversion of magic when the woman struck out at Gillian.

The memory caused Helena to shudder with revulsion. What she had felt while in Von's body was nothing like the warmth she associated with her own power. Her magic felt familiar, almost like she was greeting an old friend or beloved pet when she called it to her. In comparison, the wrongness of the other woman's magic had grated against her senses like razor sharp nails sliding along glass.

All that she had learned from Joquil about the rare Spirit magic indicated that the wielder must employ restraint at all times. Helena had her own handful of mortifying reminders of what could happen when overwhelmed by emotion to help reinforce that particular lesson. Spirit magic took many forms, as did every branch of the Mother's power. However, it was the only branch that had the potential to control someone completely. In its basest form, it was the ability to influence another with your will and when used, it should be a mere coaxing, not a full-on assault.

As the ultimate representation of the Mother's own power, Spirit magic was revered. It was why those that had the ability to weld it became Kiri, or Damaskiri if they did not pass their trial. In either case, they were the Mother's representatives amongst the Chosen. To twist such a sacred gift... it was utter blasphemy and beyond reprehensible.

Helena's eyes were beginning to burn with iridescence when she heard a tentative scratching at the entrance to her tent. Serena peered around the flap and raised her eyebrow in silent question when she saw Helena's furious expression. Helena forced herself to shake off the rage that had started to swell within her and focus on the woman before her. "Yes?" she asked, her voice sounding mostly calm.

"They have arrived, Kiri," Serena replied formally.

The use of her title was a code. Helena had come to realize that her Circle and those closest to her would use it as a sign of caution when surrounded by potential enemies. That Serena did so now while referring to the Keepers gave her a moment of pause, *Weren't these people coming to help them?*

Helena nodded, to indicate that the warning had been received, and pushed herself out of her chair. The blanket Miranda had brought her earlier fell to the floor. Helena eyed it for a moment before deciding it wasn't worth the effort. As it was, it was a struggle just to keep her legs from buckling as she took slow, measured steps toward the tent's opening.

Serena reached out to offer her support, but Helena shook her head. She already knew that she looked awful, but no one else needed to see that her weakness was more than skin deep. Her power flowed into her at the thought, a gentle reminder to never refer to herself as weak. The flood of magic helped calm her quaking limbs, and when she left the tent, she did so gracefully. More importantly, she did it on her own.

The light that filtered through the trees was a weak and watery green. The effect of it was startling. Each of her friends looked more than a little sick. Helena would have laughed at the thought, except that their expressions were all schooled into hard lines. That alone was enough to stay her reaction, but it was the sight of Effie's sweet face completely devoid of her usual smile, that had Helena faltering slightly. Even Miranda, who was a Keeper herself, was facing the three hooded figures solemnly.

Helena could not make out any facial features under the blood-red hoods. They were each tall and slender, standing shoulder to shoulder, as they faced her friends. The Circle was more scattered, effectively providing a thick barrier between Helena and the Keepers. Ronan and Kragen were standing the closest, each of their thickly muscled arms crossed over their chests. Ronan was scowling, but Kragen was expressionless. Behind them, and slightly to the left, Darrin stood with his hands at his sides, his twitching fingers the only sign of his unease. Effie was at his side, her own small hand moving to curl around his and stop the outward sign of distress. Helena was thankful for her small gesture of support, as she continued to take in the scene in front of her.

Joquil was to the far right of the clearing, his body leaning casually against a tree. Micha was at his side mirroring the posture. Timmins was beside Miranda, standing at the far left of the group, his brows lowered in displeasure. Nial was in the back, Serena having moved to stand next to him after leaving Helena's tent.

It was an odd sight, certainly less welcoming than she had expected, given Miranda's association with the group. Schooling her features to conceal the thoughts that were whirling through her mind, Helena made her way to the front. Kragen and Ronan shifted to make a space for her between them. The not-so-subtle drop of their hands to rest beside the hilts of their axes had her lips lifting in a bemused smile.

Before Helena could settle upon the appropriate greeting the Keepers swept into low bows, the ruby-red fabric of their cloaks brushing the dirt floor.

"*Kiri*," they rumbled in unison, their voices echoing spectrally in her mind. Helena stiffened at the sound. This was the first time she had heard a voice in her head that wasn't Von's and she wasn't sure how to feel about it. The shifting of her friends underscored their own disquiet.

Helena weighed the option of bowing in return but Miranda caught her attention, the older woman having stepped forward to stand beside her. She cut her chin to the side, a discrete but emphatic no. It looked like she would not be returning their bow after all.

"Keepers," Helena said with more bravado than she was feeling, "thank you for joining us."

The figure in the center moved forward. Long skeletal fingers appeared from the bottom of its sleeves to lift the hood back to reveal its face. There was a startled gasp behind her, but it was the only sound in the entirety of the clearing. Even the animals had decided to make themselves scarce for this particular meeting.

Helena couldn't blame them. The Keepers were terrifying. There was no other word for the beings that stood before her. The other two followed the lead of the first and removed their hoods. She swallowed thickly, silently wishing they would put them back on.

Their faces were gaunt, hairless, and a white so pale, she could make out the pulsing of purple veins beneath the thin skin. Their eyes were pits of black and their mouths were stitched shut, thick black cords woven in a crisscrossing pattern along the length of them. The only distinguishing marks between them were the swirling tattoos that covered almost every visible inch of skin. The markings were a deep navy blue, but as Helena stared at them, they seemed to shift and move in a serpentine fashion.

Without conscious thought, Helena decided the only way to get through this encounter was to brazen it out. "It would seem that Miranda got the looks in the family."

Behind her Kragen and Ronan snickered with appreciation, while she saw Timmins close his eyes in dismay. Miranda's own lips curled in an approving smile.

"Kiri, may I introduce you to the Triumvirate," she said by way of introduction. "These are the oldest of the Keepers, those who have sworn their loyalty to the realm and have shaken off all vestiges of their past lives in order to lead and offer guidance without any of the bias of mortality."

"One could argue that it is mortality that allows for the most valuable of guidance," Helena murmured.

"*Our Kiri is wise,*" the voices hissed in her mind. It was hard to discern any type of emotion, but Helena could have sworn she sensed amusement.

"You will have to forgive my ignorance," Helena replied, "I had not realized the head of the Keepers would be gracing us with their presence."

"Nor had I, Kiri, or I would have better prepared you," Miranda said drolly. There was a hint of censure in her voice, as though she was not pleased by the appearance of the Triumvirate.

The figure in the center tilted his head to the side as though examining her. "*Perhaps it is us who should ask your forgiveness. We were merely curious to see whom the Vessel would be, after carrying the prophecy for so many years. We could not miss an opportunity to meet the woman who is responsible for the fate of the Chosen.*"

"No pressure," Ronan muttered.

Helena raised an eyebrow in response, "I hope that I have not disappointed you after such a long wait."

"*You are more than we allowed ourselves to hope for,*" the voices echoed.

Helena shivered at their response, not feeling overly comforted despite the words.

"Seeing as we are all aware of the prophecy, how is it you think to help us?" Timmins asked. It was the most outright disrespectful she had ever heard her Advisor and Helena turned toward him in surprise.

The Keepers' faces turned toward him in unison. "*You know of the Mother of Shadows, of what will befall the Chosen if the Vessel becomes corrupted, but you know nothing of the Corruptor. Nor what it will take to defeat her. We merely offer information... and a choice.*"

"A choice?" Helena repeated, her eyes snapping to the central figure.

There was a slight dip of its head, "*There is always a choice, Kiri.*"

"Convenient," she bit out, her stomach twisting inside of her.

"Our words will be for you alone, Kiri, if you wish to hear them."

Helena swallowed back her fear and stepped toward them, "Very well." As she spoke, all three lifted their hands toward her.

"Helena!" Darrin cried out in warning.

"Kiri!" the others' voices echoed, the whistle of blades being drawn sounding behind her.

The black pits where their eyes used to be began to glow scarlet. Helena could not look away, drawn to what she saw within the fiery depths. As one, the Triumvirate touched her. Helena heard someone scream and had the distant thought that it might be her. There wasn't enough time for her to consider the notion further because she was already falling.

CHAPTER THIRTEEN

*V*on was stretched out on the bed, bonds firmly back in place. His eyes were closed, feigning sleep. He didn't want to let on that the effects of the drug had already worn off. It was a game he'd been playing since that little red-haired bitch dosed him again. Every day since he'd broken free she had been force feeding him healing brews liberally dosed with a sedative that knocked him back into unconsciousness almost immediately.

Once he finally came to he would pretend to be asleep, while Gillian and the blonde one plotted and schemed in hushed whispers over his bed. The women were careful never to reveal any specifics, but Von knew that eventually, they would divulge something useful. Until then, he would bide his time gathering strength and seemingly inconsequential information. One never knew what could be important later on, and he had every intention of paying their hospitality back in kind.

The warrior in him began to assess his enemy's strategy. *What reason would they have to keep me docile but not completely out of commission?* The answer came to Von almost instantly; the demented bitches wanted to make Von one of their puppets. For him to have the most value, he needed to be in peak condition, but they couldn't risk him fighting back. Thus the drugs. They wanted Von at full-strength and firmly under the blonde's control, but the only way that would ever happen is if he was unconscious when she made her move. *They are biding their time as well,* Von mused.

Von let his thoughts continue to wander, knowing the answer he sought was lingering at the fringes of his mind. As a Commander of his own men, he was well-versed with this kind of strategizing: weighing and evaluating an enemy's strengths and weaknesses, looking to strike when it would have the biggest impact... this was his bread and butter. He was absolutely confident he'd be able to discern their plot, and then do everything in his power to undermine it.

It can't just be my health they are waiting on, he decided. While it was true that the *Bella Morte* had delayed their plans considerably, keeping his mind trapped in the misty place while sapping his body of strength, there had to be at least one other piece out of place. When the answer came this time, it was like a gentle caress: *Helena.* They were waiting for Helena.

Von hoped his lips hadn't twitched with the smile he suppressed at the thought of her. His Mate's visit left quite an impression on his jailors. They had spoken of little else in the days since. Unfortunately, the entire reason he was still strapped to this bed was because of the state he was in after her visit. Once her spirit left him, his body had collapsed into an exhausted sleep, leaving him vulnerable to his captors. The women had made their move, acting quickly since they knew there was no way they could control him if he was fully conscious and gaining his strength back.

Luckily for him, they hadn't realized that Helena had been able to reestablish their bond, if they were even aware the bond existed in the first place. His connection to her provided an added level of consciousness and protection. So while he was lost to the darkness of the sedative, there was an untouchable part of his mind working to peel back the fog encasing it. This allowed him a few hours of hard-won clarity each day. Clarity he fully intended to use to whatever advantage he could manage.

It had taken him awhile, at first, to brush off the webs clouding his mind, but each day it was easier. The combination of Gillian's healing brews, plus Helena's reservoir of power was doing much to speed the process. He should have been able to do it on his own regardless, his power more than enough to combat the effects of such a drug, but the *Bella Morte* had done considerable harm. His own power was perpetually drained due to the constant work required to repair the damage. In his current state, there simply was not enough left over to fight off anything else. This meant that as badly as he wanted to communicate with Helena, he hadn't been able to do more than seek her glowing warmth at the other end of their bond.

Von tried to push back the wave of frustration that threatened to overwhelm him. Patience was not one of his virtues. He was a man of action. One that liked to weigh his odds, decide on a course, and then act swiftly. The fact that he was literally chained to a bed while his woman was about to battle her way through their enemy's forces, without him, did not sit well with his warrior's heart. Although, the part of him that recognized his Mate as a warrior fiercer than even himself allowed Von to quiet the need to act. He might be stuck here, but he was not entirely useless. He still had a part to play.

A sense of peace washed over him. Helena was coming for him, even now she was preparing to do so. Von settled back into the bed, trying not to rattle the magically reinforced chains as he did. He would continue to collect information and once he was able; he would pass it on to Helena to help her prepare her strike. He would use this time wisely.

Thinking back to Gillian and the other woman, Von was slightly taken aback to learn their plan revolved around attempting to control him and then use him against Helena. What a bunch of fucking idiots. It was growing increasingly clear to him that they had no idea who was coming for them. How these women could continue to underestimate their opponent, especially after the little fire show she had demonstrated for them last time, was surprising. Perhaps they simply didn't realize how much power truly simmered beneath such a sweet-looking face. Von allowed himself a mental shrug, let them continue to underestimate her. It would only make his Mate's job that much easier.

He must have made a sound because he heard a rustling that grew louder with proximity.

"Awake so soon, dearest?" Gillian asked in a saccharine voice.

Von knew it was pointless to try and deny it. Opening his eyes, he stared up at her with blatant malice. His gray eyes had darkened to the point that they were almost black.

"Oooh," she cooed, batting her green eyes, "someone is feeling fierce today. The tonics must be working."

It was all he could do not to bare his teeth at her. Instead, dark brows lowered over glowering eyes.

"Come now, precious," Gillian chided, her cheerful bedside manner making him want to stab her in the eye, "I'm helping you feel better. No need to be so rude."

Von had no need for words as he stared up at the female leaning over him. The promise of a slow and painful death was glittering in his eyes for all to see. He might even enjoy her death more if he got to watch it happen, rather than keep the promise himself. Von's amusement grew as he began to imagine all the ways his Mate would repay Gillian for this. He was already grinning by the time he began to picture Helena cocking back her arm to slam her fist into the other girl's throat. The redhead tried to blink back the apprehension that clouded her eyes once he began chuckling.

Gillian cleared her throat uncomfortably. It was the first time she had been alone with him in this room since he had woken up. There had always been at least one or two other guards with her, if not the blonde woman as well. Apparently, he really was waking up more quickly than usual. He'd have to be more careful not to alert them, or he might lose the moments of awareness he'd been fighting so hard for.

Von refused to back down, staring up at the woman unblinkingly. Let her be uncomfortable, the stupid cow. She was a pathetic excuse of a woman, allowing herself to be manipulated and used by another. She was probably too stupid to realize that she wasn't going to be alive at the end of this. There was no way the other one would let her live once she had accomplished her goal. Assuming, of course, that Helena didn't handle the problem first.

Von was smirking as he mentally hurled insults at her, berating her for being stupid, weak, and ugly, among a litany of other shortcomings. The more childish and petty the insult, the wider his smile grew.

"Yes, well," Gillian's pale skin flushed as she pulled out the bottle of healing tonic.

He eyed the soft blue liquid balefully, not ready to fall back into oblivion just yet. "She is coming for you," he taunted, his voice a harsh rasp.

Gillian stiffened, the hand holding the bottle spasming at his words.

"When she finds you she will *destroy* you," he vowed, his voice dipping deeper with each word. "There is no version of this where you do not pay with your life, Gillian. It is foolish of you to cower here thinking you are safe behind these walls. No walls could ever protect you from her wrath. Aren't you supposed to be smarter than that? You were always so quick to point out how much cleverer you were than everyone else in the Palace, but I guess those were just more empty words. No one with any actual capacity for intelligence would remain a sitting duck while death itself came for them."

"Death comes for us all eventually," she responded primly, her voice brittle and strained.

"Yes, and if we are lucky, it will be gentle. Yours will not be."

Gillian swallowed, visibly shaken. "I liked you better unconscious," she finally snapped.

He gave her a grin that was too feral to appear anything but threatening, "I will like you better when my Mate has finished draining the life from your body."

Gillian lashed out with Air, using it to cut off the supply of oxygen in his lungs. He tried to counter, willing Air to keep the organs inflated, but he was just too depleted. He felt his lungs seize and his mouth opened on a gasp. Gillian poured the minty liquid down his throat, causing him to sputter. He tried to spit it back out at her, but his body had reflexively taken great gulps of air once she cut off her attack. She had won this round, getting him to take the sedative, but she had not come out unscathed. Von could see the way his words twisted around her, ensnaring her with their promises. She was petrified.

Good, he thought smugly, eyes already drifting shut, *she should be*. That was his last coherent thought before darkness came for him.

CHAPTER FOURTEEN

The feeling of falling was disorientating since she wasn't actually moving at all. There was a part of Helena that could still sense her body standing in the clearing with her friends, and another that felt as though she was tumbling down a deep hole. Her conscious mind was being pulled into another reality while her body stayed in the physical world.

Helena took a moment to get her bearings once the whirling motion settled and she could reestablish the feeling of being still. A small gasp left her mouth as she identified her surroundings. The Triumvirate had pulled her into the chamber from her trial. She glanced down quickly and noticed she was no longer dressed in her traveling clothes, but was now wearing her simple tan trial gown instead. Confused, she spun in a slow circle, searching for anything that would give her an idea of why she was here.

There was no sign of the Triumvirate, so she was alone, at least for the moment. Without their guidance, she was uncertain what, exactly, she was supposed to do. The last time she was in this chamber, the room swirled with mist and her trial had begun. Helena hesitated for a moment, wondering if something similar would occur again. It did not. She had the feeling that the trio was testing her, and would not be remotely surprised to learn that they were playing an elaborate game. Growing annoyed, she let out a huff of breath and decided to investigate the chamber.

Once she lifted her foot to step forward, the chamber came to life around her. Gone were the smooth stone walls and in their place was a sprawling hillside that stretched out as far as she could see. Helena blinked and shaded her eyes; the bright sunlight blinding in its intensity after the relative darkness of the room. The scene was familiar but she was having difficulty placing it, as if it was a place she had been once long ago. There were no landmarks that she recognized, although there did seem to be some type of building far in the distance.

Left with no other option but to walk toward it, she did so tentatively. The scene rippled and changed, growing progressively more dark and stormy with each forward step she took. Helena couldn't stop her little jump when the sky began to crackle with lightning and growl with thunder. The ominous backdrop was further intensified by the presence of roiling purple clouds in a starless navy sky.

She squinted up at the sky as she felt the first few drops fall from above. As the wetness met her skin, she was surprised to find it warm rather than icy. Touching her fingers to her face, she felt the thick liquid smear across her cheek. The fingers she pulled away were stained a deep red. It was not rain that fell from the sky but blood. Helena felt her stomach lurch in response to the realization but managed to keep walking, certain that whatever it was she was supposed to see would only be revealed if she continued with her search.

As she began to crest the hill, the blood-rain began to fall in earnest. Her hair was hanging limply where it was not already stuck to her face and neck. The plain garment she wore had turned crimson and was clinging to her damp skin. Helena wiped at her face once more, trying to keep the blood from dripping into her eyes and noticed that her fingers had curled into black claws. A deep sense of foreboding had her moving more cautiously, knowing that her claws only appeared when she felt threatened. That was when she saw the first of the bodies.

She was forcing herself to walk quickly now, trying hard not to linger and search the faces of the dead. It was an impossible feat. Each step showed her another person she recognized. Helena swallowed hard, trying to breathe through her mouth as the stench of decay caused her stomach to roll. Death was everywhere.

Helena was stumbling now, trying to scale a growing mound of bodies. A sea of familiar faces stared up at her, their eyes accusing in their vacancy. This was her fault they seemed to shout at her. She took another step and felt something roll and crack beneath her feet. Falling, she threw her arms out, trying to catch her balance. Her hand made contact with something soft and warm.

"No," she moaned, already knowing what she would see when she moved her hand.

It was the final scene of her trial. The bodies of her friends twisted and broken beneath her feet. The sky thick with smoke and still raining both blood and fire. It was a slaughter.

Helena's breath caught in her throat, her eyes starting to sting due to the smoke. It was becoming too much for her.

"Why are you showing me this?" she shouted angrily, feeling her power build in response to her distress.

The Triumvirate's spectral voices greeted her then, speaking separately and all at once:

"Chosen One."

"Vessel."

"Mother of Spirit."

"You have a choice before you."

"Loyalty or love?"

"Mercy or vengeance?"

"Life or death?"

"The path you choose will decide our fate."

"The fate of all the Chosen."

The voices were indistinguishable, each picking up where the other ended, sometimes harmonizing in one richly layered voice.

"What will you choose?"

"You cannot choose both."

"Your choice will be our salvation."

"Or our demise."

She could feel the brush of air against her ear as if the next words were being whispered straight into them by invisible lips.

"Know this: you require balance."

"A tether to this world."

"One to hold your soul in place."

"The tether is fragile."

"Stretched too far and ready to snap."

Helena was shaking as they spoke, the words reverberating so that she could feel them with her entire body. They were deadly soft but crystal clear.

"Without the tether, you will fracture."

"Eternally lost to the darkness."

"No way to return."

"The choice will be made for you."

"You will damn us all."

"See the cost of your choice."

Helena shuddered as the bodies that had been still beneath her began to writhe and moan in misery. "You show me only one path!" she cried, as desperate for clarity as for the end of the vision. She was not sure how much longer she could stomach the sight of her friends' decaying bodies. "What is the other future?"

"Unknown," the trio hissed, the word echoing around her.

"What is the point then? You show me this but speak to me in riddles. You're no help at all!" she roared. Her magic was swelling within her, responding to her strained nerves and emotions, yet trapped in her body as it had no focus for its release. She could see the sparks begin to form and leap on her skin, her body a conduit for the magic that was rising to dangerous levels.

The scene around her began to fade. As it did, Helena's eyes looked up and noticed a small figure staring at her from one of the windows in the tower above her. She was too far away to make out the features but could not mistake the pale blonde hair that seemed to shine like starlight in the darkness. She felt her resolve strengthen. She may not have answers, but perhaps she had a focus after all.

THE FEELING of returning to her body was overwhelming. Her skin felt tight and itchy as if stretched too thin over a frame it no longer fit. She could only assume it was because of the growing tide of magic welling within her. The sparks that she witnessed in the vision were present here, her friends shouting out and trying to reach her once it was clear she was back among them.

Her entire body began to shake with the force of her restrained magic. It needed an outlet, but she knew that if she let it go, she could easily destroy everyone around her. Helena bit down on her lip, immediately tasting blood as she tried, unsuccessfully, to concentrate enough to ground her power. It was not enough; she simply didn't have the control required to manage that much power. That was when she felt her knees buckle, her body starting to tumble to the ground.

With a roar, Ronan reached her, pulling her shaking body into his and taking the brunt of the fall. Her power snaked across his skin everywhere that it made contact with his. He grit his teeth against the assault of magic.

There was hardly time to see what was happening in the chaos around her. Miranda was hurling obscenities at the now-empty place the Triumvirate had been standing. Effie was snarling and muttering under her breath, tugging against the arm Darrin had banded about her waist. He was barely holding her back from launching herself at her grandmother. Kragen, Serena, Nial, and Micha all had weapons drawn and were forming a tight circle around Ronan and Helena. Timmins and Joquil were chanting something from just outside the formation, their hands beginning to glow with the combined force of whatever power they were calling forth.

It was Ronan's terse words that brought her back to herself, "Ground it damn you."

Helena was panting with the effort to push her magic back into her reservoir. It was fighting her, like a cornered animal that wanted to defend itself. She was pleading with it, begging it to calm down, but it would not listen. Her power had a mind of its own.

Ronan could sense what was going to happen before she did. Helena looked at him with pleading iridescent eyes.

"Do it," he snapped harshly before shouting to the others, "Get down!"

Around her the others all dropped, not questioning the order.

Helena threw her head back and screamed, her power tearing up out of her body and launching itself into the sky in one solid beam of purple light. The beam began to arc and spiral until it finally burst and fell back in millions of sparkling pieces to the earth. It was both beautiful and terrifying. Unsure of what would happen once those fragments of power made contact, Helena held her breath. Her body was still trembling from the torrent of power, but she could feel what still lingered flowing back into the pool.

The first of the glowing motes touched the top of a charred tree. Helena sucked in a breath when the branches were illuminated with that same purple light. Almost immediately the tree began to swell and grow, small green leaves unfurling and then turning to luscious blooms. All around her, everywhere her magic made contact, it was the same. It would seem that her desire not to harm had her magic sending pure vitality into the land she had damaged so badly only days earlier.

She watched in mute amazement as the land came back to life around her. The places her magic did not touch were quickly concealed by vibrant green leaves that were growing to abnormally large sizes. She had thought the flowers in Bael were big before, but they were nothing compared to the melon-sized blooms that were popping up now.

Ronan slowly lifted his body off of hers, moving more quickly once it was clear that there was no danger. His look of surprise was so comical that Helena snickered and then began to laugh in earnest. He turned to her as if questioning her sanity, which only made her laugh harder. Realizing that she was laughing at him, he scowled at her and snapped, "Overcompensating much?"

Helena had tears streaming down her face from laughing so hard. Her stomach was sore from the force of it. It wasn't that there was anything funny about what had happened, but the sheer absurdity of a warrior staring up at a flower like it was about to sprout fangs and attack had her snorting with hilarity.

Ronan let her fall to the dirt, feigning disgust while barely concealing his own relieved smile as he watched his Kiri rolling around on the ground. One by one, her friends slowly walked to stand around her, their faces shining with varying degrees of wonder and concern. As they took in the land around them, and her unharmed body, they relaxed until they too joined in.

CHAPTER FIFTEEN

*N*ight had fallen on their camp. Gone were the joyous sounds of laughter and in its place was a strained silence. It was time for answers.

Miranda cleared her throat while the men in Helena's Circle all glowered at her. It was evident they all believed that the Triumvirate's visit had been some sort of trap. Even her granddaughter seemed uncertain as she looked over at her with wide blue eyes. Darrin remained at Effie's side, the violence of her earlier reaction had caught him off-guard. He kept looking at her like he wasn't entirely sure what to do with her. His puzzled expression had Helena biting back a smile. A man who seemed confused about a woman was always quality entertainment.

As for herself, Helena wasn't sure what to believe about the Keepers or their parlor tricks. She had not sensed any malicious intent from them, although there was much to be desired about the way they delivered their messages, not to mention their overall countenance. The thought of those stitched lips and glowing eyes had her suppressing a shudder.

Kragen caught the movement and wrapped a protective arm around her shoulder. She smiled up at him, appreciating the gesture of support.

"Did you know?" Timmins finally demanded, barely able to restrain his fury. His face was flushed and his blue eyes were narrowed as he waited for Miranda to answer.

The woman opened her mouth, ready to flay the skin from his bones with her words, when she caught the expressions on their faces. She sighed, seeming to age before them. Her shoulders drooped, and she clasped her hands in her lap. Miranda's eyes met hers, "I had, and still have, no reason to believe that they had any intention other than assistance." Both her eyes and her voice were imploring Helena to believe her. She did.

Helena nodded once, "Nor do I."

There was rustling as the men turned annoyed glances in her direction. Apparently, they didn't want her to be the one talking right now. *Well, they could just go right ahead and stuff it.* Her temper flared. She was the Kiri, Mother bless it, and she would do whatever she damn well pleased. If they didn't like it, nothing was stopping them from leaving. Except for the vows they had made.

The memory of the night they had made those promises to her, and she to them, had her swallowing her own harsh words. These were her protectors; it was their duty to worry and care for her. Sensing her shifting mood, the men tried to look appropriately chastened. Only Nial and Serena seemed to be looking at her with any amount of lingering amusement.

Rolling her eyes, Helena continued, "I do not deny that their methods were questionable, but it is the only way they were able to communicate."

"Don't make excuses for their behavior, Kiri," Joquil admonished. It was rare that he would speak against her. Even more rare for him to have such deep lines of worry bracketing his lips.

"I'm not making any excuses, merely stating facts," she replied calmly. "There is much we do not know about the Keepers, that is true. However, they did show me, once again, what is at stake if I make the wrong choice. They also left me with a warning."

"What did they say?" Miranda asked cautiously.

Timmins scowled at her and the older woman responded by

sticking out her tongue. Helena shook her head and smiled. The way those two bickered was like watching two children resort to hair pulling because they were uncertain of how to show their affection.

"I think they were warning me of the Fracturing, letting me know that if I do not find Von soon, I will not have a choice to make at all."

Their words floated through her mind, no less disturbing the second time.

'Without the tether, you will fracture.'

'Eternally lost to the darkness.'

'No way to return.'

'The choice will be made for you.'

'You will damn us all.'

"What will the choice cost?" Effie asked in a small, subdued voice.

Helena looked at her with haunted eyes, not needing to use any words to convey her answer. The girl's shudder was indication enough that she understood. Vividly.

"So the course is clear. We make for Vyruul and find Von," Ronan declared.

"You say that as if it will be easy," Miranda scoffed, "the journey from Bael to Vyruul is a long one, or have you already forgotten?"

"Perhaps if we hadn't been wasting time in this Mother-forsaken jungle we could have been well on our way by now," Timmins snapped.

Miranda leveled her gaze at him, a sharp edge in her voice as she responded, "If I recall correctly, you are one of the ones that helped make the choice to come here. Furthermore," she continued, raising her voice to speak over his sputtering protests, "we all decided to stay when our Kiri's health demanded rest."

Helena tried not to squirm at the mention of her title; she wanted no part of their feud.

"We all wanted to see if we could learn anything further about the prophecy," Joquil said neutrally, studying his hands with interest.

"And none of us would risk Helena's health," Serena added while the others nodded their agreement.

"It would not be a far journey by Talyrian," Helena said lightly as if her words would not have the impact of a verbal explosion.

"Absolutely not!" Kragen and Ronan yelled in unison while Darrin shouted, "I forbid it!"

She raised an eyebrow, daring them all to try and stop her.

"And what is your plan once you get there?" Micha asked softly.

As one they turned to look at him. Helena noted the color staining his cheeks and almost felt sorry for him.

"What do you mean?" Serena asked.

"Well you do not simply arrive and politely request Gillian hand over your Mate and expect that to work, do you? She will be expecting you, planning for your arrival. You need some plan if you expect to get what you seek."

Now Helena's cheeks burned. It was not that she had forgotten what would be waiting for her once she got there, but the pure logic of his comment left her feeling foolish.

"What would you suggest?" she challenged, trying to regain some semblance of authority.

Micha looked startled, surprised that she would ask him such a question. From the looks Darrin and Ronan shot her, they were as well. Helena shrugged, "You know your sister and the lay of the land better than anyone here; what would you suggest we do?"

His eyes shuttered as he thought through a list of potential scenarios. When he met her gaze again, he seemed slightly defeated, "It is clear I do not know my sister as well as I thought I did. I never imagined her capable of something such as this. However, she is very clever. I would expect a trap. She will have prepared for every possibility and have planned accordingly. You will need to do something unexpected."

"A distraction," Kragen mused.

"Yes, exactly," Micha nodded, "Gillian's biggest weakness is that she does not anticipate anyone to be as clever as her. She will think your first move is your only move. She will not expect a diversion."

Helena could sense the wheels beginning to turn in her warriors' minds. She was glad for that. It would take their collective energy to come up with something good enough to trick the sneaky bitch.

"Use me," she said suddenly.

"What?" Timmins snapped as Darrin snarled, "Excuse me?" Kragen and Ronan just looked at her with lowered brows, displeasure at her statement obvious. Joquil and the others remained calmly quiet, waiting for her to elaborate.

"Use me as your distraction. They will not expect me to come on my own. I will offer myself up in exchange for Von. While I keep her busy, you can sneak in and go to work on their forces."

"That seems too simple," Darrin frowned, "and I do not like the idea of you meekly offering yourself up like a calf to slaughter. You shouldn't go into the enemy's camp on your own."

"Who said anything about meekly?" Helena responded with a terrifying smile.

"Hellion…" Darrin trailed off, his green eyes scanning hers as he asked, "what are you planning, wicked girl?" Years of understanding passed between them and even he could not stop the smile that grew as he began to anticipate her reply.

Her answering smile was smug as she asked, "What kind of damage do you think a Talyrian could do?"

"Kiri! You will be a flying target," Joquil protested.

"You must not think much of my shielding abilities if you think that is the case."

She saw the considering looks on the others faces. Turning back to Micha she asked, "Do you think it could work?"

He tilted his head, playing out the scenario in his mind before nodding slowly. His green eyes were sad as he said, "I do. She does not know what a Talyrian can do, so she would not know how to plan for it. You will cause enough chaos that she will be quick to surrender and hear you out, leaving the field open for your men to move in."

Ronan and Kragen were nodding, "It's certainly a start." The group gathered closer as they began to brainstorm in earnest. Miranda remained seated and was looking at her thoughtfully. Finally, her eyes met Helena's and she murmured in a voice so low Helena was certain the others couldn't hear, "and her reign will be of ash."

"That's the second time you've said that," Helena commented in a low voice, moving to stand next to the older woman.

"I do not believe it will be the last," she retorted.

Helena shivered as the woman's words wrapped around her, the scenes from the Keepers' vision fresh in her mind. "Let's hope that is not the case," Helena whispered, her face ashen.

"From your lips to the Mother's ears," Miranda replied, just as softly.

CHAPTER SIXTEEN

*D*ays were passing quickly as the group made their way to Vyruul. Despite the number of miles that had been reduced between them, the distance Helena felt between her and her Mate didn't seem to lessen. She was still keenly aware of his absence beside, as well as within, her. Although she couldn't decide what she missed more: the feel of his body pressed against hers or that deep growling voice calling her *Mate* within the recesses of her mind.

Their bond was intact, something she checked compulsively multiple times a day. Whenever she plucked at the mental tether that bound them, she was always able to feel his flickering presence along its length; however, they had not had any meaningful contact since she had found him in her dreams. Helena was sure that it was because of his captors, although she could only guess as to what they were doing to him that interfered with his ability to access his magic. Everything she pictured only caused her fury to grow.

Helena's rage had become a living thing always simmering just below the surface. These days a thought was enough to make it boil over and send her spiraling into the darkest recesses of her mind. Whether it was because they finally had a plan, or that they were mere days away from finding him, she couldn't say. In either case, her need for vengeance had become all-consuming.

She had withdrawn from her Circle, choosing to visualize all the ways that she would repay Gillian's treachery instead of making idle conversation. For a girl that had grown up in a quiet cottage, it would seem that Helena had quite the sadistic imagination. She was fairly certain this was not a discovery her mother would be proud of, although there was no question Von would approve. The thought had her lips curling in a feral smile.

Ronan picked that moment to turn to her. Whatever he saw on her face gave him pause, but after a moment he maneuvered his wolf toward her. "Kiri," he said by way of greeting.

She lifted a brow at the formality. "Bastard," she returned, the word thick with warmth and gentle teasing despite the iciness of her eyes. It was Von's preferred greeting for his oldest friend, and Helena had used it intentionally, knowing Ronan would pick up on the sentimentality of its usage rather than any perceived insult.

As predicted, a smile stretched across his scarred face. "It would seem you are feeling more yourself, lady."

"As opposed to what, exactly?" she asked mildly.

"Your body has regained the weight it lost during our time in the jungle and there are no longer shadows beneath your eyes."

"Oh," she said, shifting in her saddle so that her cloak draped around her more loosely. She was only a little surprised to find that he had been paying attention that closely, but it still rankled that he felt the need to comment on her weight at all. His answering grin was all teeth. The smugness of the expression had Helena rolling her eyes, "I suppose you'd like a cookie for your expert observation skills?"

"Not if you made them," he countered.

Helena sputtered, "I will have you know I make delicious cookies, thank you very much. You would be damned lucky if I ever offered to share them with the likes of you."

"I don't think Von would let you share your *cookies* with anyone but him," Ronan retorted dryly.

The subtle emphasis on the word had Helena studying him more closely. The satisfied look in his eyes took away all of the indignation she was feeling. "You're provoking me on purpose," she accused.

"It worked," he said simply.

"Why?" she pressed.

"Because there has been a weight to your thoughts that doesn't belong there. I have noticed it often the last few days, and its presence disturbs me. You are sunshine, Helena. There is no place for darkness in those eyes." His words had the effect of a pail of water being dumped atop her head. They were a frank assessment, but no less effective for it.

Helena sat there, her mouth opening and closing like a gaping fish while she processed what he had said. That he had actually cared enough to intervene. Not even Darrin had nerve enough to call her out on her temper.

"Thank you," she said softly, humbled by this man and his words. It had stunned her that he knew her well enough to know what she needed, even better than she did. And not only that but also by the way he always seemed to look after her, even when it had never been his responsibility to do so. There were those in her Circle, bound to her by life vows, who paid less attention to her subtle shifts in mood. It spoke deeply of his commitment to Von, and to her.

They shared a look that said more than either of them could verbalize. The moment hung between them, stretching until Ronan finally ended it by clearing his throat gruffly, "If you had wanted to postpone getting your Jaka because you were too scared of a little needle, you could have said so. I don't think you needed to stage a tantrum to get out of it. That was a little much, even for you."

Understanding was shining in her aqua eyes as she sneered playfully, "Please, I bet you cried when you got yours, you big baby."

Ronan laughed, a deep guffaw that had the others turning in their seats to stare back at them curiously. "Ah, Hellion, that's more like it."

She grimaced at his use of her nickname but smiled all the same. "Does this mean that I still get my Jaka?"

Ronan nodded, "Whenever you are ready, Helena, it would be my honor."

147

"Tonight?" she asked, suddenly eager to bear the mark of protection.

He lifted a brow but nodded his agreement, "Sure. Usually, it takes a couple of days to get the ceremony organized—"

"No," she cut him off, "no ceremony. Just us." There was no hidden meaning in the words; she simply did not want to be bared for so long in front of the others.

"Serena is more than capable of doing it, if you'd rather," Ronan offered, his ears suddenly red.

Helena laughed, amused that her friend was having a bout of modesty at her expense. "No, you are my Commander, are you not? It should be you."

He was pleased to hear her words, although it took a while for the color to fade from his face. "As you wish," he said finally. They rode beside each other in companionable silence until finally breaking for camp that evening. As she dismounted Karma, Helena was pleased to realize that she had not thought of torture or blood once that afternoon.

HELENA FOLDED the simple gown she had selected, tossing it in her knapsack once she was done. Serena and Effie had helped her modify the garment so that she could undo the ties over her shoulder and peel the fabric down instead of having to remove it entirely. Serena also helped her fashion a cloth that tied around her chest so that she could retain some modesty while Ronan tattooed her. She had appreciated their help, and the sound of their soft voices as they had gossiped and laughed together that afternoon. It had given her mind something to focus on.

She was alone now, however, and the silence was overwhelming. Needing to distract herself until it was time to meet up with Ronan, Helena decided to bathe in the secluded glen not far from the campsite. While she had asked Ronan to forego the official ceremony, Helena liked the idea of cleansing herself in preparation for her Jaka. It was a sacred mark of the Mother, and receiving it while coated in sweat and dirt was highly unappealing.

Checking to make sure she was not forgetting anything, Helena allowed her eyes to scan her tent before she finally nodded and stepped out. A cool breeze greeted her and had her shivering slightly. The weather had started to turn in the last few days, the humidity of the jungle yielding to the cooler temperatures of the north. Helena had never been to Vyruul, but what she had heard about the mountainous region had her anticipating jagged peaks reaching toward the sky from a sea of ice. And if the last few days were any indication, the temperature would only continue to drop as they moved deeper into Vyruul. They were a day or two away from the border, and none of them were quite sure what to expect once they arrived.

Shaking off the thoughts of what may or may not be waiting for her in Vyruul, Helena let out the low whistle that called Starshine to her side. After a few moments of silence, the sound of beating wings filled the sky. She looked up, smiling when she saw the Talyrian flying toward her.

Starshine landed with a soft huff, smoke flaring out from her nose, her turquoise eyes luminous.

"Hi girl," Helena said softly, lifting her hand to brush the velvety snout in greeting. A deep rumble started in the Talyrian's chest, causing the ground to tremble slightly.

Helena snickered as she began to scratch behind the large cat's ear, "Feel good?"

Starshine closed her eyes in response and began to purr louder.

After a few moments of indulging Starshine, Helena gave her a final pat and asked, "Keep me company for a while?"

Starshine huffed her assent and nudged Helena with her massive head, pushing her in the direction of the pool. She stumbled slightly and laughed over her shoulder, "In a hurry all of a sudden?"

The Talyrian didn't justify the question with a response, which only amused her further. "So what have you been up to, lady?" she asked aloud, not expecting a response but enjoying the playful banter regardless. A turquoise eye rolled toward her and then away as a small jet of flame lit up the darkening sky.

"Killing things?" she guessed, only half joking.

Starshine snorted.

"Hunt, kill, same difference," Helena amended, laughing at the absurdity of carrying on a one-sided conversation.

Starshine shook her head, seeming to disagree with Helena's assessment. The silvery mane shone brightly as she did.

"Did you have a Mr. Starshine to keep you company? A he-cat to help you pounce on unsuspecting bunnies? Or to pounce on you?" she teased while mimicking a cat pounce.

Starshine stopped her slow prowl and just looked at Helena without blinking. The Talyrian queen was clearly not impressed with Helena's pouncing skills.

"I'm sorry, were you the one pouncing on him?" Helena asked deadpan, blinking up with wide innocent eyes at Starshine. The Talyrian stared steadily back, unmoving. "Were you off pouncing with multiple Mr. Starshines?" she pressed, enjoying herself entirely too much as she barely held back her laughter.

The Talyrian seemed to sigh, resigned to her mistress's baiting, and let out another deep huff before she started walking again. A large plume of smoke curled up in the air and was floating behind her as she moved through the trees.

Helena waited a moment and then started after her, "What, too personal?"

Starshine let out a low growl, which only caused Helena to break out into happy peals of laughter. "It's not like you don't make your opinions clear about *my* mate. I only thought it fair to inquire about your own..." Helena trailed off searching for the right word, "companion." She had finally caught back up to Starshine who paused only long enough to lift her giant paw and swat at Helena.

The duo had just reached the small clearing beside the shallow pool when the sound of splashing greeted them.

Starshine's teeth bared in a warning growl, while Helena reached for the hunting knife she had strapped to her thigh. They took a cautious step forward, all amusement fleeing in the wake of a potential threat.

The sound of a girl's high-pitched giggle had her freezing in place. Two more steps confirmed what her ears had already recognized. It was Effie, splashing in the water. Helena felt her shoulders relax and was just about to call out a greeting when another person came into view. *Darrin.*

"Well isn't that a surprise," she murmured to her feline friend, not sure what to think about the couple currently splashing around in the water.

Starshine moved her head in the semblance of a nod.

"I guess you aren't the only one that goes off to pounce with a tom," Helena mused.

Starshine growled softly, but there was no temper in the sound.

A pang in her chest kept Helena from announcing her presence. She didn't want to interrupt them and rob them of the moment they were having. Effie's face was flushed with color, as she laughed and tried to run away from Darrin who was pursuing her. Her blonde hair was hanging down her back in a golden stream, her blue gown clinging to her curves in a way that Darrin was helpless to ignore. She watched the way his eyes trailed down Effie's body before reluctantly dragging back up to her face, his own eyes bright with predatory interest.

With a lunge, Darrin wrapped his arms around Effie's waist and pulled her down into the water. She popped up, sputtering and pushing her wet hair out of her eyes. As she rose, she was face to face with Darrin, barely any space between them. Their laughter slowly died as they stared at each other as if finally seeing each other for the first time. The smile fell from her face, and Helena could see Effie's chest frantically rising and falling with her shallow breaths. Darrin stared down at her, his green eyes intense as he lifted a hand to brush stray drops of water from her cheek.

Helena felt her breath hitch, suddenly uncomfortable with bearing witness to such an intimate moment. "Come on, girl," she said under her breath, nudging Starshine as she started walking away from the couple in the water, "let's go down a bit further."

Her movements felt leaden as she walked, and Helena told herself firmly it was just the long journey and not jealousy that weighed each step down. Too bad she wasn't buying it. It wasn't a longing for Darrin that made her heart heavy, but the simple fact that she wasn't the one experiencing that stolen moment of sweetness with her Mate, that she had experienced so few stolen moments with him before he was taken from her. She could feel the ripple of magic that rose in response to her anger at the reminder. The sudden tidal wave of emotion caused her face to flush as her thoughts turned again to the red-headed girl who was responsible for her current lack of moments. *Gillian*, Helena snarled softly.

Sensing her rapidly diminishing mood, Starshine headbutted Helena to pull her attention away from her thoughts. Unfortunately, the move had the unintended side effect of sending Helena flying into the water, arms flailing wildly. At least, she thought it was unintended. When she popped back up out of the icy water, Starshine sat at the banks, licking her paw while her tail twitched behind her. If she didn't know better, she would have sworn the Talyrian was laughing at her.

CHAPTER SEVENTEEN

*H*elena braided her hair as she made her way back toward the camp. Starshine prowled behind her until the others came into view and then let out a soft sound that could have been a farewell, before she moved into the shadows.

Her dress was still damp from having fallen into the water, despite Helena having called some Fire to help dry it off. She moved toward Ronan who was seated beside the campfire, staring off in the direction of Serena and Nial. Seeing the two heads bowed closely together while they whispered animatedly had Helena sighing heavily.

She said nothing as she moved beside the red-haired warrior. His hair was unbound and hanging in thick red waves down his back. Helena had the completely improper thought of running her fingers through it to see if it was as soft as it looked. She stroked her own hair instead, pouting slightly when she realized Ronan's hair was probably softer than hers. The inane thought made her chuckle.

Ronan turned slightly in his seat and lifted his eyes to her. He gave her a smile that didn't quite reach his eyes and turned back toward Serena. "I've lost her," he said in a rough voice.

"But she hasn't—" Helena started, almost horrified at the thought.

Ronan glared at her, offended on Serena's behalf, "No, she hasn't said or done anything so final. But it only takes a look to see what is between them."

Helena studied the blonde, whose cheeks were flushed and violet eyes were shining under the warm glow of the fire. Although, it was more likely that the dark-haired man with stormy eyes was responsible for her friend's happy blush.

Turning to Ronan, she watched as his eyes devoured the woman who had been his lover and partner for most of their adult lives. You don't have that kind of relationship with someone and not learn every nuanced expression on their face. He obviously saw something when he looked at her that made it clear she was falling for the other man. Then again, Helena had known immediately that there had been something between them.

"Will you not fight for her?" Helena asked quietly, no judgment or censure in the question, only curiosity.

He smiled up at her wryly, "If I thought there was a chance, do you think I'd be sitting over here watching that?" There was a bitter edge to his words that cut deep.

"I suppose not," she replied, smiling as she imagined him throwing Serena over his shoulder to carry her off and remind to whom she belonged.

"One cannot fight what's between them. I've seen the mating bond falling into place before. I recognize the symptoms," Ronan's voice was low and thick with the emotions he struggled to hide.

"Mating bond?" she repeated stunned, turning to study the couple more carefully. "You think they are mates?"

Ronan laughed without humor, "What else would snatch her from me so easily? I've loved her since we were kids, and she has loved me. There's never been another for either of us, until she met him. Now she barely remembers that I exist." Helena heard the way he struggled not to choke on the words; the admission was costing him dearly.

She placed a hand on his shoulder, squeezing slightly as she offered silent comfort. They stood there quietly, and Helena saw the moment that resignation wrapped itself around him like a mantle. He lowered his head and took a shuddering breath, staring into the flame for one, two, heartbeats before slowly coming to his feet. When he turned to her, his glittering blue eyes were lost.

"Is there no hope then?" she asked, her own heart breaking for her friend.

A side of Ronan's lip curled up as he considered the question, "As long as the Mother watches over us, there is always hope. But I will not make her choose, Helena, not to assuage my pride. Not when the Mother pulls her to another."

Helena wrapped her arms around him, giving him a quick and fierce hug. When she pulled away, they both pretended not to notice the tears still shining on the other's cheeks. "Come, you have a job to do," she said firmly, making the words an order that would help him refocus.

Ronan nodded, a true smile growing as he looked down at her, "My needles are yours, Kiri."

"You don't have to look quite so gleeful at the thought of making me bleed," she muttered, his chuckle following her into the tent.

HELENA STRETCHED out on the faded green blanket that Ronan had laid out for her.

"Get comfortable, we'll be here awhile," he ordered, turning to set up his supplies while she got into position. She maneuvered herself so that she was laying on her side, her head cradled in the vee of her arm.

Turning toward her, Ronan's eyes scanned her with professional assessment, "Over the ribs and heart?"

After a steadying breath, she affirmed, "Yes."

He nodded and moved to sit beside her. As he shifted away from the makeshift table he'd set up she noticed that the liquid in the small glass dish was white not black. Seeing the questioning look in her eyes, he answered, "I thought something subtler would suit you better. Besides, I already told you, you are sunshine. Your mark should shine as you do."

"And will it?" she asked surprised.

"I added some powder to the ink that should give it a metallic hue once it heals."

Pleasure filled her at his words. Noting her reaction, he grinned smugly, "You are my Kiri, not just another warrior in the ranks. You deserve a mark as unique as you are."

She smiled up at him, eager to see what it would look like, "So what are you waiting for?"

He shook his head and rolled his eyes, moving into position with his hands hovering just over her skin. She could feel the heat rolling off of him and closed her eyes to concentrate on her breathing.

"Ready?" he asked softly.

She gave a terse nod and grit her teeth.

The first prick of the needle caused her to flinch. The second and third came in rapid succession until each was lost in the other, becoming a string of scratching fire that worked its way along her skin. She felt sweat break out all over her body in response to the pain, but she laid as still as possible, thinking only of breathing in and out.

"You are faring better than Von did," Ronan said after a while.

Her eyes flew open at that, "I am?"

Ronan nodded, biting down on his lip as he focused intently on the placement of the needles. He sat back and wiped at her skin before dipping his needle back into the ink and moving back over her. She tried to ignore the sight of the smeared blood on the cloth he absentmindedly placed back on the table.

"He was cursing the entire time. If I recall correctly, he was so creative with his insults that our Commander was blushing and finally threatened to beat him bloody if he didn't shut his mouth."

Helena smiled at the thought, imagining the abuse Von hurled at those around him. Ronan adjusted her positioning slightly so that she was more on her back than her side, starting to work his way toward the center of her chest. She took in a sharp breath; the pain was more intense there.

"I offered to hold his hand," Ronan said quickly, to distract her.

She blinked at that, too startled to laugh, "And did he take you up on your offer?"

"What do you think?" he asked, raising a brow.

"Which body part did he threaten to remove if you tried?" she responded.

Ronan just stared at her, letting her arrive at her own conclusion.

"And did Serena have anything to say about that?" she asked, before wincing at her use of Serena's name. She looked up at him apologetically.

He shrugged and his smile, when he looked down at her to respond, held only a hint of sadness, "She informed Von that if he went anywhere near my cock, she would rip his off and shove it down his throat."

Helena tried not to laugh, but a snicker escaped anyway.

"I guess it's a good thing you did not end up holding his hand then."

"No, not his hand, just him."

"Excuse me?" she asked incredulously.

Ronan nodded, "Oh yes, I had to hold him down. He was squirming so badly it was nigh impossible for our Commander to continue."

Helena was having trouble imagining her Mate in that depiction. She gave Ronan a questioning look, doubting him momentarily.

"Ask him about it yourself, once we get him back. He won't be able to lie to you."

She shook her head in amazement, "I suppose I'll have to."

They grew quiet for a while as he continued his steady pace.

"Will you tell me what they mean? The symbols," she clarified when he did not begin speaking right away.

"Each one on its own means something different, but when they are woven together, they become a blessing, enchanting you with the Mother's protection. This one," he said indicating the symbol he was currently outlining over the center of her ribs, "is the symbol of the Mother herself. It is always placed closest to the heart, since we owe our existence in this world to Her. She is at the center of everything, and so too is her mark." He finished a complex swirl and sat back to gesture to the looping symbol that linked with it before flowing into others along her ribs, "This one is strength and that one balance. And these here are for accuracy, agility and speed."

Helena nodded her understanding.

"We're almost done," he said quietly, noticing her expression as he moved to fill in the Mother's symbol.

"I'm fine," she panted as the needle stabbed at her. Ronan raised a brow, calling her on the lie. Rolling her eyes, she bit down on her lip and nodded for him to continue, feeling light-headed as the sound of her heartbeat pounded in her ears.

"Individually, the symbols do not *do* anything, but when they are combined like this, they become a sort of enhancement, infusing your power with their abilities."

"I don't feel any different," she murmured, trying to focus on his words and not the pain.

"That's because I'm not finished yet," he retorted.

"Perhaps you should hurry up," she said with mock sweetness.

"Would you like me to do this right or quickly?" he taunted.

"Why not both?" she asked seriously, her hopeful look dropping at his expression. "Just don't mark me with anything offensive," Helena said finally, a bit resigned.

At his silence, she lifted her head to study his face again, "You didn't mark me with anything offensive did you?"

He scowled down at her, "No, Hellion, nothing disrespectful. But it is customary to incorporate something personal into the Jaka, as well as something that reflects its bearer."

"Isn't that what you did with the ink?"

He shrugged, "In part, I suppose."

She hesitated before asking, "What symbols did you add to represent us then?"

"For you, I added the symbol of life, since you are the Mother's Vessel," he murmured as he gestured toward something that looked like flowering vines wrapping around the symbol of the Mother.

"And yours?" she asked, trying to lift her head to see what he was doing.

He scowled at her and pushed her back down, "Settle down, or I'll call one of the men in here to hold you down."

She made a rude gesture to show him what she thought of that suggestion.

Ronan shook his head as he laughed, still not answering the question.

"Hey! I'm waiting," she reminded him.

"Patience," he murmured, refusing to answer.

Just when she was about to push him, he sat back and nodded, "Just one last thing and we'll be done."

He set his tools down and cleaned her throbbing skin with a cool cloth, wiping away the excess ink and blood. Once she was clean, he rested his hand above the Mother's mark and bowed his head. She watched his eyes flutter closed and he said something hushed she could not understand.

Once he was done speaking she felt a tingling rush work its way through her body. The colors in the tent had grown muted as it became dark outside. However, they were now blazing brightly. Helena blinked, trying to get her eyes to adjust. She turned toward Ronan, who was looking at her with something akin to wonder, his mouth hanging open in a way that frightened her.

"What?" she asked, startled to hear her voice come out in the richly layered way she associated with her magic.

He blinked a few times, "Your eyes," he said hoarsely.

She reached for a mirror he had set to the side and pulled it to her face. Staring back at her were twin pools of swirling iridescence. That was nothing new. Unexpected, but not new. It would seem the Jaka had called her magic forth.

Curious to see what her tattoo would look like with her enhanced vision, she moved the mirror down to see her Jaka for the first time. Her skin was red with irritation, which only made the shimmering mark stand out in sharper contrast. Helena's breath left her in a whoosh. It was beautiful.

The twirling lines seemed to sparkle like a cloud of diamond dust along her skin, catching and pulling the light to the symbols now inked into its surface. She studied the Mother's mark first, which looked like two hands cradling something between them. Her own mark, twisted around it like a vine with flowers in various stages of bloom. Helena followed the vines, moving the mirror as she did, noting the symbols he had already indicated and picking out a few others. She opened her mouth to ask him about them when realization dawned. He had included a symbol for each of her Circle.

"Ronan," she whispered awestruck, as she peered more closely.

There was Darrin and Kragen, the runic shapes representing a shield and sword hidden along a snaking piece of vine from her own symbol. A little beside them, also hidden in the vines were the symbols of knowledge and power, Timmins and Joquil respectively. Von's mark left her speechless. Her fingers fluttered above it, aching to touch it. At first glance, it was nothing special, but upon deeper inspection, it was a spiral of stars that worked itself around the vine and ending just below her heart. It was the symbol for completion blended with the symbol for the soul.

"It's perfect," she breathed, trying to push down the emotion that threatened to spill over. She'd had enough of tears, and this was not a moment for them.

Before she set the mirror down, she caught one final symbol, barely visible to her at the base of her ribcage. It was the very tip of the tattoo, a trio of arcing lines that connected into a tight knot.

"Loyalty," Ronan supplied in a subdued tone.

Her throat too tight for words, Helena reached out and grasped his hand firmly in hers. She squeezed it tightly before letting go and turning to him.

"Thank you."

Ronan bowed his head. As he did, she felt a small ripple in her mind. It was not the feeling she associated with her connection to Von, but it was familiar all the same. Focusing on that sensation, Helena quickly realized what it was. Her glowing eyes studied the man standing before her. She was experiencing Ronan's feelings.

As she turned deeper into herself, she found that there were five new threads in total, one for Ronan and one each for the rest of her

Circle. The tether connecting her and Von was unchanged although it now seemed to pulse with increased awareness. The other strands were vibrant and steady within her, and it was not difficult to identify which strand represented who.

She reached for the one that felt like Ronan and waited. There was no reaction from the man standing before her, although she was able to focus more clearly on what he was feeling. His sense of pride at her happiness with the tattoo warmed her.

Smiling, she focused on the others. Helena felt flickers of awareness, but not an actual connection. Whatever Ronan had done when he'd incorporated himself and her Circle into the tattoo had deepened her empathetic connection to each of them, but it was not the two-way bond that stretched between her and her Mate.

Helena wondered how long it would take for the others to realize what had happened.

CHAPTER EIGHTEEN

*G*illian paced back and forth between two of the pillars in the throne room. Her mother had summoned her and she had no clue what to expect. Things with Von were progressing, albeit more slowly than her mother would have liked. The dose of the healing brew that she had been giving him each day was no longer necessary, although she continued to use it as an excuse to keep him sedated.

Stupid male with his stupid eyes, she thought darkly. He was the one who was chained, not her. What did she have to fear from him, really? The memory of their last interaction rose in answer. *Right.* She shuddered and began biting at the soft flesh beside her thumbnail. There was something about that cold silver gaze that made her edgy. She much preferred when he couldn't look at her. Perhaps Rowena would be willing to consider blindfolding him so that she could avoid it even in his waking hours. Gillian did not go out of her way to ask for favors from her mother, but this one might be worth it. If for no other reason than to escape the sinister promise lurking in those eyes.

The soft click of a door shutting halted her steps and had her spinning to face the throne where Rowena now sat. Being seated did nothing to diminish the icy power that radiated out of her.

Gillian clasped her trembling hands together and was glad for the folds of her dress that concealed them. "M-mistress," she said by way of greeting, hating herself for the nerves that made her stutter. Once she had finished her approach and stood before Rowena, she genuflected and nervously lifted her eyes up to assess her mother's mood.

Rowena stared down at her without moving, her face an expressionless mask. Only the slight tightening of her mouth alluded to her temper. "The bitch queen moves with her band of rogues to surprise us. Even now they approach our border. How can that little fool really believe that anything she does would go unseen in my lands?"

"Her underestimation works in our favor," Gillian pointed out, blanching when her mother narrowed her eyes. The question had been rhetorical and she had not be given permission to speak. Lowering her gaze, Gillian bowed her head apologetically.

After a long moment of silence, her mother continued, "We will be ready for her with a little surprise of our own. It's time to ready the prisoner."

Gillian lifted her eyes, unsure what her mother meant.

Seeing the question on her daughter's face, Rowena rolled her eyes with exasperation, "Must I do everything myself? Bring him to me so that I may begin drawing from him."

Understanding dawned, and Gillian clenched her hands into tighter fists, her nails cutting into the soft skin of her palms. "Of course, Mother. It will be done."

"See that you do not waste time."

Gillian nodded to show that she had heard her and swiftly made her way out of the room. She had mixed feelings about her mother's twisted use of power. There was something about it that grated against her and left her unsettled for days after witnessing it. While she was no great fan of Von's, other than using his body for her amusement, a part of her could not stomach the thought of him as one of her mother's puppets. To see such strength cowed... it was a shame.

Shaking her head to clear it of the unwanted sympathy, she steeled herself for what lay ahead and made her way to Von's room so that her mother could begin the process that would turn him into a Shadow.

"KIRI," Timmins said in a respectfully subdued tone from the entrance to her tent.

Helena looked up from the map Micha had sketched for her and idly asked, "Why is it we never seem to stay anywhere that has actual walls. These lands have inns don't they?"

The side of Timmins' mouth curled up in an amused smile. That question had become a familiar refrain as the climate continued to drop the closer they came to the heart of the Vyruul mountainside.

"You know it is not safe to announce our presence here."

Helena's answering smile acknowledged his words of caution, while the shiver that ran down her spine reinforced them. The truth was, something knew they were here already. Helena had never felt anything like the bone-deep certainty that she was being watched; she had been tense and on high alert for days.

Sighing, she turned to face him fully, "What did you need, Timmins?"

Her Advisor looked at her carefully before speaking again, "We are less than a day's ride from the keep, according to Micha."

Helena nodded, her indication that he should continue.

"We will need to select our base camp and begin preparations for the attack."

She raised her eyebrow at that, "What do you mean begin? Preparations started days ago."

"I just meant..." Timmins trailed off and looked at her with concern etched in his expression. His usual confident demeanor was nowhere to be found as he noticeably deflated before her. Helena could feel his worry tugging at her from the depths of their Jaka-enhanced connection, but she didn't need it to know something was weighing on him. She could see him struggling to find the words he needed, so she did not press him and remained quiet as she waited for him to continue.

"Helena, I - I do not have a good feeling about what awaits us. You said yourself there was another woman in the room when you joined with Von. Gillian is not the only one we will face and I highly doubt she was the mastermind behind kidnapping Von. We need time to better plan and prepare for the true enemy—"

The change in Helena was instantaneous as she cut him off, "One enemy or thousands; the plan does not change. They took what is *mine*," the word came out in a snarl that echoed in the voice of her magic, "and now they must pay." Her hair flew up around her, rippling in a non-existent breeze while her eyes twinkled with iridescence. It was not Helena talking; it was the Vessel.

Timmins stared at her with wide-eyes.

"Do you doubt my ability, Advisor?" she asked in a deadly soft croon.

"No, Kiri," he replied, his voice even and his answer immediate.

She waited a beat before speaking again, letting him feel the weight of her power fill the room. "You do bring up a good point, though. One I had already been thinking on, in fact. We cannot prepare for something that is unknown."

"Kiri?" he asked, his tone wary as if anticipating what she was about to say.

The smile that curved her lips was filled with bloodthirsty promise, "I think it's time we do some spying of our own."

HELENA ROLLED her eyes as her men fussed around her. They had moved her away from the campsite and into a large snow-covered clearing, so that if she lost control again, her magic would not destroy anything of value. If she did not agree, at least in part, with their assessment that this experiment could yield potentially dangerous results, she would have already begun the mental descent that would take her to the threshold of Von's mind.

Since being marked by Ronan, she had felt more centered and in control of her power than she had since Von disappeared. She had also been feeling increased flickers of awareness along their mating bond as they closed in on where he was being kept. The result was that Helena was stronger than she had ever been, and she was ready to test her power.

"Are you sure about this, Helena?" Darrin whispered, crouching beside her.

She pressed her palm to his stubbled cheek and offered him a reassuring smile, aqua eyes staring into green as she said, "I need to do this, Darrin. He needs to know that we are close so he will be ready when we come for him. Not to mention the fact that we would greatly benefit from any information he has gathered. I know that I can reach him," she finished fiercely, her voice was strengthened by her conviction.

"You may need to do it, but I don't need to like it," he muttered darkly.

Helena couldn't contain the chuckle that escaped at his petulance, "Were you hoping to talk me out of it?"

The stubborn set of his jaw was answer enough.

"And how, exactly, did you think you were going to stop me?"

Darrin shrugged and looked away as he said, "I would have found a way."

"Mmm," she murmured, the disbelief in her tone evident. Helena called her power to her, feeling it readily respond. "Look at me," she demanded in the multitude of voices.

Surprised at the change, his eyes snapped back to hers.

"I am the Mother's Vessel. I do not need protection. It is those who seek to oppose me that require protection from *me*."

"I am your Shield," he protested in an angry whisper, "It is my duty to protect and defend. You are too important to our people to be so careless with your life."

"It is because of our people that I cannot afford to hide behind you. I am their leader, Shield. Let me lead." There was no room for argument and he knew it. Helena could almost see the frustration rolling off him in waves as he stood and argued anyway.

"And I am your Shield!" he shouted, "let me fucking protect you! Mother's tits, Helena."

Infusing her voice with her power she stood slowly, "Do not forget to whom you speak, Shield. You made a vow to be in service to me and my will. Obey it."

"I made a vow to protect you from those who would seek to destroy you. I *am* staying true to my vow, you stubborn ass!" he fumed.

The sky cracked in half as a bolt of lightning and the answering growl of thunder lit up the sky. In the distance, Starshine roared, sensing her mistress's temper and seeing it as a call to battle, one that she was clearly eager to answer.

"Kiri," a soft voice called.

Helena whirled around, hands balled into fists. Effie stood just off to the side, her trembling hands held up in the position of surrender, "He means no harm, Kiri. He is just worried about you. We all are." The rest of her Circle flanked Effie, unwilling to step in the middle of this particular argument. From the set of their jaws and crossed arms, Helena could tell that they were not necessarily on her side.

Seeing the wary way Effie and the others waited for her reaction was sobering. Helena took a shuddering breath, trying to reign in the temper that still rose too quickly to the surface. "I know." She turned to face Darrin again and said more softly, "I know."

"It is not just the Chosen who need you," he said softly, "I need you, too."

Her eyes softened, and she looked from Darrin to Effie, "But Von needs me more. Don't you understand yet? Without him, I will cease to be me. This has to end, Darrin, for all of our sakes," her voice carried despite the gentle way she said the words. She watched as the fight left him, his shoulders drooping as he released a deep breath.

"Then I will stand guard while you do what needs to be done." With those words, Darrin turned on his heel and stomped off.

Helena's eyes still shimmered with iridescence as she turned back toward the others. The added level of awareness her Jaka granted pulsed as she met the steady gaze of each. If she were to close her eyes, she would be able to identify who was standing where simply through that connection. Each man had their own unique sensation, some combination of their power and personality, that was unmistakable. And now, when amplified by the intensity of their emotion, it was a force she couldn't ignore if she tried.

The feel of them was overwhelming, especially since her own emotions were riding high. It should be too much for any one person to bear, all of these conflicting feelings swirling through her: Darrin's receding anger, Kragen's steady strength, Timmins' gentle concern, and even Joquil's quiet displeasure. But she didn't have a choice. As the Kiri's Circle, these men were bound to her. They had placed their lives in her hands, and she was responsible for their well-being. That included dealing with mercurial moods.

Something shifted within her, settling into place. She was their ruler and the decisions she made would affect them all. While that meant she owed it to them to listen and take their opinions into consideration, it also meant that it was ultimately up to her to trust herself to make the right decision. They needed her to lead, to make the choices that they could not. So she would.

Sensing the shift in Helena, Serena stepped forward. "We will all stand guard," she said softly. The others nodded their agreement before moving away to stand in a loose circle around her.

Nial was the only one who hesitated, walking toward her and placing a hand on her shoulder. "I know that I have made no formal vows to you, Helena, but I still serve. It is my brother you are bound to, which makes you family. If you have need of me, for anything, my help is yours."

"Nial—" she whispered.

"I serve, Kiri," he said firmly, before squeezing her shoulder and backing away.

Those not in her Circle traded looks with each other before kneeling. Effie, Miranda, Micha, Nial, Serena, and Ronan each bowing their heads in a formal show of respect. Her Circle, seeing the others and sensing the importance of the moment, also dropped to their knees. Helena opened her mouth to protest, feeling overwhelmed at the sight of her friends submitting to her in this way.

"We serve," they said, their voices booming across the clearing.

"You guys," she whispered, her fingers pressing into her lips to stave off the emotion that was threatening to overpower her. She needed to focus now, and could not afford to let go of the righteous anger that had been guiding her until now.

Ronan's eyes met hers first, his smirk full of male arrogance as he said, "I never swore loyalty to Von; hopefully he won't be too butthurt when he finds out about this."

Snickers met the comment and Helena felt her lips twitch as she said dryly, "I won't tell him if you don't."

With a wink, Ronan stood, and the others followed. "What do you need us to do?"

Amusement fled as quickly as it had come. "Be ready," she said, her power making her hair dance and eyes glow, "this visit may not go unnoticed."

CHAPTER NINETEEN

*V*on woke with a start. Something was coming and his instincts were screaming for him to prepare. He shifted in the bed, arms and legs still bound with magic-enhanced chains. Von snarled and pulled, feeling the chains go taut instead of give. Growling with frustration, he worked himself into a sitting position and stared in the direction of the door.

He could feel his heart racing, but instead of panicking he felt himself slip into the intense focus that always preceded a battle. Even chained he would put up a fight. Von's eyes took in every detail of the room, searching for something that he could use while also cataloguing potential threats. During his assessment, he felt a gentle tug along his bond with Helena. It was the strongest the bond had felt since being trapped here.

The tug came again, more insistent this time. Von hesitated, torn between staying vigilant and wanting to follow the pull. Was this what had awoken him? The possibility gave him pause. Maybe it was not a threat after all. Focusing on their bond, he tentatively asked, *"Mira?"*

The answering voice was not the sweet, slightly husky voice he associated with his mate. It was raw power that responded, *"Mate."*

Von snapped to attention, his own magic rising to the surface in response to Helena's. This was not to be a moment shared between lovers then, but a Kiri calling upon one in her Circle. There was a part of him that mourned the fact, wishing to feel her body move beneath his again, even if only in their shared dreams. However, the part of himself that belonged to her could not deny the call to battle he heard in her voice.

From his place on the bed, Von grinned. There was no joy in the expression, only a feral hunger as he answered, *"Kiri."*

"We have need of your services, Mate."

He appreciated the double meaning of the words, and could not help the sexual purr that laced his voice as he asked, *"I am always ready to service you, Mira. But perhaps you could specify what it is you require?"*

Von felt her amusement and the punch of arousal his words evoked. He closed his eyes as he felt the gentle pull of fingers through his hair followed by a sharp tug and the sting of a bite along the corded muscles of his neck.

"Focus, Mate."

"Apologies, Lady. What do you need?" Von willed his body to obey as he waited for her to reply.

"Information. We are close, perhaps only a day away. Can you tell us anything about where you are being kept?"

"Very little, unfortunately. I have not left this room, at least as far as I am aware," he replied apologetically.

There was no censure in her voice when she asked, *"What of your captors?"*

"The blonde is the one calling the shots. There's no question about it. She only visited me the one time you were present, but it is clear that she has something on Gillian. As to what that is I couldn't hazard a guess. I also couldn't say which of the Mother's branches she's been gifted with. I have never felt it's like."

"Corrupted," Helena rumbled, still using the harmonious voice that indicated she was channeling her power.

Von considered the word and nodded, *"Yes, that is what I feel. She has twisted her magic; it makes her... unpredictable."*

He could feel her sigh, disappointed that they had so little to go on. Not wanting to let her down, he offered, *"Gillian still visits me daily. She is usually only here long enough to drug me, but perhaps there's a way for me to get past her."*

There was a pause while Helena thought over his offer. Finally, she said, *"Not alone, and certainly not while bound. It is not safe for you to wander through the castle on your own. Especially since we do not know enough about the enemies you could encounter. No, Mate. Stay put. I have another idea, someone else who might be able to tell us about the blonde."* Helena paused again and then added, *"Just because you cannot escape, does not mean you should have to remain chained."* Von felt a surge of molten power rush through him and then all four chains snapped. He pulled his arms down, his muscles protesting and welcoming the movement in equal measure.

"While I truly appreciate the freedom, Mira, could we not have started with that part?" he snarked.

"Apologies, Mate. I did not think to try intentionally using my power in this way," came the chagrined reply.

"I was only teasing, Mira. There's no need to apologize. And were you referring to using your power through our bond again?" he asked while rubbing the tender skin at his wrists.

More magic filled him, soothing and alleviating the pain in both his wrists and ankles as she said, *"Yes, exactly. It feels like I am trying to send something as vast as the ocean through a hole the size of a pin. There's just too much power to funnel in that way, especially if my intention is not to destroy. Instead, it is safer and easier to tap into our bond and have my power reinforce your own. Then it's as simple as thinking of your body as an extension of mine. I just need to picture what I want it to do, and it responds. Honestly, it's still foreign and a bit awkward, like I am trying to put on a pair of trousers that were made to fit someone else. But it's getting easier."*

Von laughed at her analogy, and asked, *"Do you think you could make that connection with someone else? Use your Spirit magic to influence their actions from a distance?"*

There was a pause before she spoke again, *"I'm not sure. It's possible, I suppose, but I think it would be hard without having the kind of bond that you and I share. It would likely not work in the same way."*

"You would have to use force," he clarified, following her train of thought.

"Yes, I think so. Generally, when my magic influences other's, it is tied to the intensity of my emotions. I am sad and so others cry—"

"Or you are thinking of me and suddenly everyone has need of a dark room," Von teased.

"Sometimes they don't even wait for the room," Helena replied dryly, *"but yes. It is my emotion and power that drives them to act, but the actions they take remain their own. To manipulate their will to the point that I am forcing them to behave in a specific way... that is something else entirely. Add distance to that equation, and it only becomes more unlikely. It is our bond that allows me to tap into your power at all, and even still the distance between us interfered in my ability to reach you until now."*

"Not just distance, but two meddling bitches who kept me trapped within the mist. You could not reach me because I was lost; the part of me that is my essential self was locked within the furthest depths of my mind," Von said darkly, as the familiar burn of anger flared within him.

"Yes," she agreed sadly, *"you were lost, but I could still feel you. I just didn't know how to find you or even where to even look. Our bond is a tether; it connects us even beyond something such as space. When you are close enough, it acts as a compass; an instinctual pull that will unerringly lead me to you. If we are too far, it is simply a psychic link. A way to remain in contact and know if you are safe. I think, had you not been taken so far away, even trapped in the mist, I would have been able to reach you. We were too far apart; our bond was stretched to its limit."*

There was something in her voice, something she was not saying, that had him tensing on the bed. The torture, being unable to save her and forced to watch while she was torn apart... his visions had not been just meaningless nightmares. They had been a side effect. A warning. *"The tether was breaking,"* he said with a feeling of horror so great he could hardly process it.

"I-I think so."

The thought of losing their connection, of losing *her,* was too much to even contemplate. He could not imagine a future, a life, without her in it. *"I would have died there, had you not found a way back to me,"* he concluded with certainty, the image of his broken body curled around itself coming back to him. *"Had the tether snapped and I lost you, Helena, I would have ceased to exist. There is no place for me in a world without you."*

"Stop, please," she begged, and Von could feel the tears she was fighting back choking his own throat. *"I cannot bear the thought of it. I have already seen what happens if the tether breaks. If something had happened to you, Von... something worse than you merely being kept from me. If the day came where I could no longer feel even a hint of you within me... I would have torched the earth in my despair. What was left of my soul would have died with you, and everything that makes me who I am would be gone. Except my power, which would remain, unchecked."*

"Your trial," he remembered, haunted by the memory of her covered in blood in her bed as she told him what she had seen.

Helena did not need to confirm his words. Instead she said, *"You keep me grounded and whole. My power is too great for me to contain on my own. As my Mate, you are the balance. If I lose you, Von, there is nothing that will stop me from destroying everything and everyone."*

"Mother of Shadows."

"That would only be the beginning. By the time I finished, nothing would remain," she gently corrected.

"So you will not lose me," he declared. He could feel her struggling to contain her emotions and did the only thing he could to comfort her. *"No need to be so dramatic, Mate. You could simply settle for telling me that you love me, like other wives do."*

Von felt her incredulity and the wave of astonished mirth that came in response to his words. *"And what do you know about other wives, Mate?"* she asked in a dangerous purr before adding more to herself, *"besides, you started it."*

Von was grinning despite her revelations. All he knew, was now that her voice was once again in his mind, he felt more whole than he had since first waking from the nightmare he'd been trapped in. They had shared moments, but nothing close to the true strength of their bond. He had felt its lack more than he had realized.

"I have missed this, Mira."

"As have I, Mate." There was a sadness that tinged her words and he wanted nothing more than to take her into his arms and hold her.

"Soon," he promised fiercely.

"Aye, but first we deal with the bitches who thought to come between us." The promise of violence in her voice excited him more than it should have. He loved that his woman was as much of a warrior as he was, that he did not have to apologize for, or hide, that part of himself from her.

"Aye," he agreed, echoing her words as a cruel smile curved his lips. *"I look forward to bearing witness to your justice, lady."*

"Not as much as I look forward to giving it," she crooned. He could feel her sigh as she said a bit wistfully, *"I must leave you now, I need to conserve my power for what lies ahead."*

He bit back the whimper of protest at her words.

"I cannot do much about you being physically alone... not yet," she continued, *"but know that you are not alone. I am here if you have need of me. Don't forget to make it appear as though you are still bound when she comes for you."* A whisper-soft caress stroked the length of his body and he felt her pull away from him. When he tried to follow, protesting the growing distance, her voice swelled in his mind, *"I am still here, my love."*

He flushed, embarrassed at the need for her that clawed at him. Hearing her in his mind again, and feeling her steady presence, was a balm to his soul. He had been lost to the mist for so long; he had forgotten what being whole felt like. Not that he was whole, not yet.

He wouldn't be until there was not even a breath separating him from his Mate, but it was a start.

Instead of responding, he settled back into the bed and waited, knowing it would not be long before he would be whole again.

CHAPTER TWENTY

*R*owena watched her daughter's retreating back from her place on the throne. Her patience had long since worn thin. It was time to play the aggressor once again and force the imposter to come out of hiding. There were whispers that she was finally drawing near, but Rowena had been on high alert ever since the girl's mate first came to stay in the castle. So while she skulked about in the forest, believing that she would be the one to start this war, what she didn't realize was that Rowena was already ten steps ahead of her. It had been her intention, after all, to initiate this exact scenario. Now that the time for action drew near, however, Rowena found that she was no longer willing to wait for the other woman to make the next move.

Her fingers tapped restlessly on the wooden arm of her throne as she waited for her daughter to return with their prisoner. It was insulting that she should have to wait at all but Rowena forced herself to remain calm. No good would come from her losing her temper now, and these things take time.

Minutes ticked away and Rowena shifted restlessly in her chair wondering what was taking her daughter so long. That girl was getting more useless with each passing day. Soon the threat of her brother's life would not be enough to ensure her willing compliance, but that was a problem she could easily deal with just as soon as she handled the imposter.

The silence around her grew as she waited, but Rowena didn't mind silence. After spending years in the Palace surrounded by sycophants and the incessant chatter of voices she almost appreciated it. Once she was back on the throne, she would have her fill of company again. For now, the remoteness of her family's home suited her just fine. If nothing else, it allowed her to build up the army of Shadows that had become so useful these past few months. The mindless beings with super-human strength were very effective at quelling protests and rebellion. Rowena's lips curled into a smile at the thought.

Rowena felt a ripple along the current of her power, followed by a stinging lash, much like a whip, against the edge of her awareness. The pulse of power caused Rowena to freeze in place. *Was it possible that the little bitch had found a way to sneak in after all? No*, Rowena realized, *her arrival would have much more fanfare than that.*

Precautions had been taken to ensure that their prisoner would not be in any state to access or use his own power. Even so, Rowena placed sensors in his room so she or her guards would be able to act quickly in the event he got free. The power flare she felt was one of the sensors going off. Since it was tied to her own strength, the release of power instantly alerted her wherever she was. She was more than a little intrigued that it would go off now after so much time had passed. Just when she was about to put the next step of her plan into action.

It was also too much of a coincidence for her to ignore. Rowena rose swiftly and crossed the room. Apparently, it was time for her to engage in a more direct manner with their prisoner.

GILLIAN STOOD outside of the door, hesitating only for a moment before pressing her hand to its cool wooden surface and stepping inside. Von's eyes snapped to her, tracking her movements like a predator assessing prey. She swallowed, uncomfortable with the comparison. She did not appreciate feeling hunted when he was the one in chains. Relieved to see that much, at least, had not changed, Gillian braved a few steps closer to the bed.

She eyed him dispassionately, only mildly disappointed that he was no longer naked. As much as she had appreciated the visual feast, her mother had ordered that she dress him after dosing him a few nights ago in "preparation" and she was not about to force the issue. Gillian wasn't sure how giving him skin-tight leather pants and a fitted white tunic did much to prepare him for anything. If she had to guess, it was more her mother's way of removing the distraction of his heavily muscled body, since a naked Von was hard to ignore. Mother knows she had enough trouble ignoring that temptation herself.

Mouth suddenly dry, Gillian licked her lips and cleared her throat.

"Meal time already?" he drawled insolently.

Gillian shook her head, "You have indulged in our hospitality for long enough, Holbrooke. It's time for you to get to work paying your debt." She knew it was the wrong thing to say as soon as the words left her lips.

Silver eyes glittered with malice, "Let me loose and I'll begin repaying you for your hospitality right now."

Gillian forced herself to let out a shaky laugh and roll her eyes in a show of haughty amusement. "Oh, Von, always so quick to threaten violence. I was merely teasing. Let us start again, shall we? No more secluded meals in your room. Now that you are well, you will be joining me upstairs."

She waited for a reaction to her announcement, but he did not so much as flinch.

Taking a steadying breath, she tried again. "You are coming with me," she announced with false bravado.

The smile that stretched across his face showed how easily he saw through her. Lifting a mocking brow, he asked, "Who's going to make me?"

"I am," said a voice just behind her.

CHAPTER TWENTY-ONE

*H*elena could feel the tendrils of her magic melding back into her reservoir of power. She took a deep breath, the weight that had been lodged in her chest for months no longer present after finally being able to speak with Von through their bond again. There had been so much she wanted to say, things she could feel that he wanted to say to her as well, but it had not been the right time. They would have time for such things once she was able to hold him in her arms again.

Feeling a dripping wetness at her nose, she lifted a hand and wiped at it. Seeing the smear of red against the stark paleness of her skin gave her pause. It would seem that even despite her power's increasing strength, and the renewed connection between her and Von, the side effects of the Fracturing had not diminished.

As she refocused on the world around her, Helena's eyes found Ronan's across the clearing. He was frowning darkly, having tracked the movement of her hand across her face, but said nothing. Her eyes met his steadily, and she offered a helpless shrug. There was nothing she could do about it, save rescue her mate, which they were already in the middle of doing. What good was there in calling attention to the urgency with which they needed to act, when everyone was already moving as quickly as possible?

Ronan shook his head, his brows lowered over glittering blue eyes. Helena could tell that he understood her predicament, but it was clear that he was not happy about it all the same.

Perhaps it was because she was still attuned to Ronan after their years together, or maybe it was simply her position at his side, but Serena sensed the shift in his attention and turned to face him. Her blonde brow was lifted in question as her eyes scanned his face. When he did not acknowledge her, she followed his brooding stare to where Helena was sitting. Seeing that her friend was back among them, Serena quickly stood and closed the distance between them.

"Did you learn anything, Kiri?" she asked in a hushed voice once she'd reached her side.

Helena met her friend's gaze, noting the concern mixed with eager anticipation in her violet eyes. With a rueful shake of her head, she was forced to admit, "No."

Disappointment quickly replaced anticipation in her friend's eyes. Serena worked quickly to hide her reaction, but it was too late. Helena pushed away her own sense of frustration, knowing that even though they were no better off than when she started, at least in terms of gathering information, she still had come out of the meeting with a plan. Just because Von was unable to tell her about where he was being held, didn't mean that there wasn't one among them that could.

Serena opened her mouth to ask a question, but Helena beat her to it by shouting, "Micha!"

The young man ran forward, startled to hear his name. "Yes, Kiri?" he asked tentatively, as if uncertain that she had really called for him.

"I have a couple of questions and am hoping that you can help me, Micha," Helena stated in a more subdued tone. "Are you aware of a blonde woman that might be working with your sister?"

Micha's face scrunched up as he replied, "No, Kiri. No friends that I am aware of. The only blonde I have ever seen Gillian spend any meaningful amount of time with was our mother, before she rejoined the Great Mother, of course."

Helena frowned at the news, having been hopeful he would have been able to finally solve that mystery for her. She sighed before mentally shifting gears and asking, "But you are familiar with where your sister is staying?"

"Well yes, Kiri, of course. If my sister is staying in Vyruul, then she is most certainly at my mother's estate. It was where my mother was raised, and where we would go to visit her family when my mother was tired of our antics and wanted us out of the way for a while."

"So you grew up there?" she asked intently.

"Yes, Kiri," he confirmed, "more or less. The Palace was our home while my mother ruled, but I am well-versed in the layout of the estate, if that is what you are asking."

"Tell me, Micha, if a prisoner was being kept there, where would that be in relation to the entrance?"

Micha looked at her with confusion, not because of her question; it was clear she was asking where Von was being kept. He was confused because he had never had any need for a room that would be used in such a capacity.

After a moment of contemplative silence, Micha green eyes brightened and he said, "My mother had a series of rooms that only she could enter. The doors were spelled with a lock that would only open under her touch. If I had to guess, I would assume that Von was being kept in such a room. They were several floors underground, far away from any of the living quarters. I believe she used them as storage. We were not allowed down there, of course, so it is hard for me to say exactly. But you know how it is when you tell a child they are not allowed to do something. It becomes their personal mission." Micha was grinning with the memories the words called to the surface of his mind.

Helena chuckled, no stranger to such childish antics. She and Darrin had been much the same when they were younger. They were always quick to devise a plan that would surely land them on the business end of a belt, or at the very least, one that resulted in a stern lecture. Either from her mother, Anderson, or if they were in serious hot water, both.

She shook her head, pushing away the memories so that she could focus on the matter at hand, although an amused smile lingered in her aqua eyes.

"I must admit, it would have been too good to be true, if we could have simply snuck in and rescued him without garnering their attention. So, I'm not surprised to hear that we will need to find a way to get them to open the door for us. But I think I have a plan that will help with that," Helena could not entirely keep the excitement out of her voice. There was a lot at stake but the thought of pulling one over on Gillian, after all that she had put them through, was heady. It would be especially rewarding to fool her using one of her own tricks.

The men in her Circle, having noticed her conversation with Micha, had already moved to encircle her.

"I am going to walk through the front doors as an invited guest."

Kragen raised an eyebrow, while Timmins and Joquil exchanged confused glances. As always, it was Darrin that spoke first. "And how in the Mother's name do you plan on getting them to do that? Are you actually planning on waltzing up to the front door and knocking?"

"Well, yes." Helena's face was serious, but there was an unmistakable twinkle in her eyes, while she awaited the men's reaction.

They were dumbfounded and had nothing to say in response to that. In fact, the Circle could not seem to find any words to say at all.

"Allow me to point out, if you don't mind," Ronan started carefully, "that seems like the quickest way to find yourself trapped in a room of your own. How exactly do you plan on avoiding capture, or is that part of your plan as well?"

It was hard not to laugh. Helena could tell that the men wanted to shake her and were barely restraining themselves from doing so. Feeling the need to put them out of their misery, Helena let them in on her plan. Her full plan. "Gillian is not the only one with the ability to alter her appearance. You have seen me do so a handful of times, although I've never tried to fully shift into another person."

Realization dawned on their faces as she continued, "There is perhaps only one person who could very easily walk up to the door and be let in without being thrown into some dungeon."

"You are going to transform into me," Micha whispered in amazement.

"Yes," Helena confirmed.

"That is absolutely absurd," Darrin snarled.

Helena shrugged, "Is it? She has no reason to question his appearance there, since he has knowledge of the estate's existence. In fact, it would be more surprising if Micha didn't go looking for his sister upon hearing of her disappearance. It would be the first place to look if he was trying to find his sister."

Kragen was nodding his agreement while Darrin continued to frown in annoyance.

"It is not easy to assume the identity of somebody else. Especially not when you're trying to fool someone who knows them best. It is not merely enough to look like Micha, you will need to be able to adopt his mannerisms and knowledge as well," Joquil pointed out in a carefully neutral voice. The men could not argue with her reasoning, but that did not mean that her plan was entirely without holes.

Helena nodded, "Yes, there is much that I will have to learn in order to pull this off. Even though I should only need to be Micha for a short time if all goes well."

"When it comes to war, darling, you can never assume that anything is going to go well," Ronan said dryly as he crossed his arms over his broad chest.

"That's what you're here for," Helena said with a smile before turning her aqua gaze back to Micha's stunned face.

He looked like he wanted to protest but could not find a good enough reason to argue. His shoulders drooped and he sighed before asking, "What is it that you want to know?"

"I think the real question is, what do I need to know?" Helena countered, "You are the only one who can tell me what Gillian is going to expect from me. You are her twin, after all."

Micha nodded grimly, "Yes, I suppose you're right. If you will grant me a little bit of time, I can better anticipate what information you may need."

Helena nodded her consent as Timmins said, "You should not go far, Micha. If our Kiri is to learn your mannerisms, she will need to be able to observe you."

"I've always wanted to train a monkey," Kragen said, grinning widely before looking at Micha and adding, "dance, monkey, dance."

Micha scowled and snapped, "I'm not your fucking monkey. I'm only here to try and save my sister. It would serve you well to remember that, Sword."

Kragen's smile vanished as quickly as it appeared and his eyes glittered with menace as he replied, "Did you not just make your own vow of allegiance? She is still your Kiri, regardless of your sister's actions. Your loyalty is owed to her, regardless of who you share blood with. You're still alive because you serve a purpose, monkey. But everyone's purpose runs out eventually. Perhaps it would serve you better to remember that."

The two men stared at each other while Ronan and Darren stepped closer to where Kragen was standing with his hands balling into fists at his sides. Knowing that he would not survive a fight against any of them, let alone all of them, Micha simply walked away.

"I did not think the child had it in him," Ronan muttered once he was settled out of hearing.

"Every man finds his balls eventually," Serena stated calmly, not even flinching when five sets of male eyes landed on her.

"That may very well be true," Helena said, wiping tears of laughter from her eyes, "but I do not think they appreciate you pointing it out."

"No more than you would enjoy me commenting on the size of your tits," Ronan confirmed.

"I did not comment on the size, merely pointed out that he found his," Serena said mulishly.

Helena's smile grew as she said, "True enough," before turning to Ronan to say, "And you only mention my tits because Von isn't here to repay you for doing so."

"Allow me," Darrin said, slamming his fist into Ronan's arm with considerable force.

Ronan grunted, rubbing his arm as he said, "Make sure to remind me to pay you back for that."

Helena threw back her head and laughed, so grateful for the friends that were around her. There was too much at risk for them to give in to the emotions that were always riding a killing edge. These moments of mirth were as essential to their continued sanity as breathing.

"As much as I'd love to continue with this conversation," she said finally, "I think we should probably eat. It may be a few days before we have anything resembling a real meal again."

"It's your turn to cook," Darrin pointed out.

Helena frowned playfully, "But I'm the Kiri... doesn't that get me out of chores?"

"It didn't when you were seven, and it sure as shit doesn't now, Hellion," Darrin replied with a warm smile.

She rolled her eyes as she stood, bumping him with her hip as she passed, "Then get out of my way."

Dipping into a mocking bow, Darrin called to her retreating back, "As you will, Kiri."

CHAPTER TWENTY-TWO

"*I* am." The cold voice caused Gillian to jump violently and spin toward the open doorway.

Gillian's mouth opened and closed helplessly, as if she wanted to say something about the unexpected appearance, but one narrow-eyed glare from the woman in the doorway kept her silent. It was obvious that the blonde had decided to change the plan without informing Gillian. Von tucked that information away for later examination while trying to see what he could learn through a quick study of his newest visitor.

He was not moved by her beauty, although there were some that might be. He much preferred laughing aqua eyes and cheeks that always seemed to be tinged with a sweet blush when he was near, to this woman's coldness. There was something about the set of her lips that was too cruel. While the angles of her face and body were too harsh to inspire anything other than a strong desire to put as much distance between oneself and her as possible. This was an adversary that required he tread carefully, not a woman that could be won over with soft words.

The woman in question clearly fancied herself some sort of monarch; a crown of dark metal sat atop her almost colorless hair. The black stones which ringed it seemed to suck in the light rather than reflect it. It was an object that should have inspired respect but fell woefully short. The effect of the crown was such that it appeared a gash across the top of her head standing out in harsh contrast rather than any form of glittering adornment. She was trying too hard to be a symbol of power and strength, and the crown seemed to mock, rather than reinforce, her authority.

Von, sensing that his disinterest would garner a reaction nothing else could, asked in a bland voice, "And you are?"

His disrespect proved effective. He watched the woman flinch and press her lips together, her cheeks flooding with color as she snapped, "The rightful ruler of the Chosen and your new Mistress."

"Mmm," he murmured, "then we appear to have a problem. I've already made a lifetime vow of service to another woman. And maybe no one had the heart to tell you, but you seem to be confused. I happen to have it on good authority that our Kiri is a beautiful and vibrant woman in her prime, not some dried-up corpse."

The blonde's icy eyes were shooting daggers at him. Von also noted the way her metal-tipped fingers dug so hard into her fleshy palms they drew blood. Deciding to press his advantage and taunt her further, he added, "Couldn't find a man with the balls to bed you so you decided to steal hers? Here's the thing, sweetheart, you might have me tied down, but you still can't make me fuck you."

Gillian went pale at his words, cringing when the blonde snapped in a voice so filled with ice-cold fury that the walls began to twinkle with frost, "You arrogant—"

"Asshole? Bastard? Twice-forsaken son of a whore?" Von merrily supplied, grinning widely while staring her down with hard gray eyes. He couldn't help it; he was enjoying himself. There was something about sizing up a new opponent that made him feel alive. He might be her prisoner, but by the time he was done with her, he would make this woman beg for mercy.

Her eyes widened and her nostrils flared. Von had a moment of self-preservation and sent a thought to Helena, *"Darling, now might be an excellent time to join me."*

The blonde lifted her hand, blood dripping down her palm and onto the floor as she said in a voice lacking inflection, "I should have realized you would want to skip the foreplay." Her ice-blue eyes drained of all color before turning completely black and she began rapidly muttering under her breath.

Her words were unintelligible and Von was just getting ready to goad her further when he felt the first slam against his mental barriers. The blow was so unexpected he curled into himself. It was like receiving a blow to the lungs, and it knocked the breath from him momentarily. Bile rose in his throat at the feel of her trying to peel back the layer of his mind that protected his deepest thoughts. His skin turned clammy as he grit his teeth and focused on repelling the invasion.

Von noticed the moment that the blonde realized something was wrong. She frowned deeply, her black eyes lightening to blue as she stepped closer to the bed. She hadn't anticipated his being able to resist her attack. Not that Von felt like he had resisted much of anything.

She must have seen something in his eyes because a wicked smile bloomed across her face. Curling her bleeding hand back into a fist, she allowed her blood to drip onto his leg as she began chanting with renewed effort.

"Helena!" he shouted desperately down the bond, his body arching up off the bed as his vision began to fade. He had no clue what she was doing, but it felt as though he was being flayed alive, his mind and body left bare for her to pluck and prod to her liking.

THE PAN DROPPED from Helena's fingers as electricity hummed painfully over her skin. She could hear Von calling for her along the length of their bond, but the corrupted power she could feel clawing at him kept her from being able to form words. It was as though she was under attack as well.

"Helena!" Effie shouted, trying to move to her side.

"Kiri!" a multitude of male voices exclaimed at the same time.

Helena was unable to do or say anything. She could feel herself being pulled back to Von. It was not a conscious choice, more like her power's instinctive response to the attack. The transition from campsite to the stone room was both instantaneous and disorienting. Helena could feel her physical body collapsing to the ground near the fire but she was also aware of a much larger body reclining on a bed beneath her.

There was no mistaking where she was; her magic had pulled her back into Von's body. A sweet numbness filled their joint body as they pushed up off the bed, no longer retaining the illusion of being chained. "We've got to stop meeting like this," she purred in the voice of her magic, as Von's eyes made the shift from steel to molten gold.

The blonde's eyes widened and her smug smile fell from her face. "You!" she snarled, lurching away from Von's body. Turning toward Gillian, who was watching the scene unfolding before her with horror, she shouted, "Don't just stand there you little fool!"

"Mother!" she whimpered, as Helena threw out an arm and ribbons of Fire wrapped themselves around the frightened redhead.

Helena felt a moment of shock as she processed the word, *how was that even possible?* Batting the thought away to deal with later, she kept her attention on Gillian. The blonde backed out of the room, eyes never leaving them.

Von's lip curled in a sinister smile, enjoying Gillian's mewls of pain as the Fire began to singe skin and cloth alike.

With a frustrated growl, the blonde stepped into the hall, "If your final act is to buy me time, so be it, at least your death will be more useful than you ever were!"

"Help me! Please, Mother!" Gillian sobbed as the blonde fled.

Helena protested the retreat, knowing the true threat was currently escaping and wanting to pursue her. She looked back to the cowering girl, an annoying sliver of sympathy worming its way into her heart, despite everything she had done. No one should have to face such betrayal from a loved one. Especially a mother.

"Give me one reason I should spare you," Helena demanded in the harmony of voices; Von's approval radiating along their joint consciousness at her words.

"I-I," she stuttered, crying out as the bands of Fire drew tighter. Tears filled the eyes that were so like her brothers, suspended from her eyelashes like drops of rain caught on a branch. "Mercy! Please, Helena. I was only protecting Micha."

Helena loosened her hold on the Fire, startled by Gillian's words.

"She does not deserve mercy," Von snarled.

"We cannot kill her, my love. Not yet. We will need her if my plan is to work," Helena cautioned.

"You think that blonde bitch will let her live after this? She does not care what happens to her daughter. She all but left her for us to finish off."

"It doesn't matter, we cannot risk it. She might be our only chance. Gillian lives."

Von's growl of frustration escaped and caused Gillian to flinch.

"Just because she must live, does not mean she needs to be conscious." Drawing back his arm, Von let his fist slam into her jaw. Gillian's head snapped and she crumpled to the floor.

Helena looked on in amusement. She might feel sorry for the girl, but it didn't mean she hadn't deserved it. Not after what she had done. A sense of disorientation grew and Helena had a vision of the campsite superimposed on the small room. A wave of nausea hit her causing Von to stumble.

Von took a tentative step toward the door, knowing this might be his only chance at escape. Helena tried to refocus on him and the room, but could feel herself being pulled back.

"Be careful!" she warned, her voice thin along their bond. Her magic was fading, having been pushed too far already.

Already Von's eyes had returned to the usual gray. She could feel a gentle caress along the bond, and his concern for her.

"Do not worry about me. Just stay safe until I get to you."

With a final fervent *"I love you"* their connection was severed, neither certain who had sent the thought.

PULLING his focus back to the present, Von's eyes scanned the room. Gillian was out cold; she was not going to be an issue. Stepping into the hall, he checked for signs of others. There was nothing. Balls of Fire flickered from glass orbs which floated every few steps along the otherwise dim corridor. There was a muted fabric, that had once been a vibrant red, running the length of the hall. It was clear this was not an area that received much attention.

Letting his instinct guide him, Von shielded and took off at a run. Reaching a corner, he slowed, peering around the dank stone wall before continuing. After several more turns he reached a dead end.

Von slammed his fist into the wall. Earth infused the blow causing the wall to tremble under the force, small bits of dust raining down from hole he'd left behind.

"Leaving so soon?" a cloyingly sweet voice called.

Von spun, his lips pulling back as he bared his teeth like a cornered animal ready to strike. The blonde was standing there surrounded by a small army of Shadows awaiting her command. Von lost count at seventeen and knew, without a doubt, that he was completely and utterly fucked.

Feigning indifference, Von shrugged and allowed his body to relax, "With a hostess like you, you can't blame me."

The blonde tilted her head, studying the change with interest, "Do my Shadows not concern you?"

Von's answering smile was pure arrogance as he replied, "Woman, I've single-handedly destroyed entire cities. What's a handful of mindless corpses?" With a quick move, Von threw out a wave of his power, but it was significantly weaker than it should have been, harmlessly sparking when it came into contact with her shield. Apparently, Helena wasn't the only one who was drained. Von did not allow his expression to alter, despite the failed attack.

Looking entirely too gleeful, she simpered, "Why don't you be a good little boy and get down on your knees? There's no reason to lose a warrior as strong as you to such foolishness."

"There's only one woman I will ever kneel for, and you are not even fit to speak her name."

The amusement fled from the woman's face and she scowled, "You dare speak to me that way?"

Von's arms crossed against his chest as he defiantly lifted his chin, "I just did. Do you need me to repeat myself?"

Rowena threw out an arm and Von heard a sickening crack. Looking down he noticed a finger hanging crookedly at the wrong angle. His own shields were no match for whatever power she was wielding. Von's shoulders began shaking with laughter and his eyes met hers, "Is that all you have bitch queen? It's going to take more than that to bring me down." The laughter died down and he said in a voice filled with venom, "I. Will. Not. Kneel."

"Yes, you will," she ground out, eyes narrowed into slits, as another wave of magic hit his body. There was another crack and Von was falling.

Looking down he noticed the bone in his shin sticking out of his leg. There was another loud crack and the world around him began to dim. As his hands slammed into the stone floor, he felt the sticky warmth of his blood. The last clear thought he had before everything went black was *If I get through this, I will need Nial to make me one of his chairs.*

CHAPTER TWENTY-THREE

*H*elena came back to her body in a rush of sensation. The colors of the forest seemed too bright to be real, while the sound of her friends' voices felt like they were being screamed directly into her ear. With a wince, she covered her ears and ducked her head in between her legs to try and drown out some of the intensity.

Miranda was the first to notice she had returned to them. She placed a warm hand on Helena's shoulder and was holding out an embroidered linen kerchief when Helena was finally able to meet her gaze. Confused, Helena raised an eyebrow.

Miranda gestured toward her face and pressed the cloth into her hand. Understanding dawned; she was bleeding again.

"I thought these side effects would have abated somewhat now that we are closer to one another," she muttered wiping at her nose.

"Physical distance is only part of the problem. The Fracturing is a result of the bond being significantly weakened to the point it is entirely severed. You and your Mate have not had a chance to properly reinforce the bond, although you have been able to keep it stable enough through the strength of your connection," Miranda explained, while motioning for Helena to keep the kerchief when she tried to hand it back.

"It just thought..." Helena trailed off, staring into the blood-spattered cloth.

"Thought what, Kiri?" Miranda prodded gently, her voice filled with warmth and understanding.

"It just seemed like things were starting to get better. We have reestablished our mental connection, for the most part. At the very least I've been able to feel flickers of him, if not connect with him outright. I was even able to find him once through our dreams. And now the Jaka has also seemed to further reinforce the bond." Helena listed off each of the things as she thought of them, seeming a bit lost to learn that they weren't enough to prevent the side effects of the separation.

Miranda took Helena's hand in her own, forcing her to look up before saying, "Those things are definitely helping. They are, perhaps, the reason that the side effects are progressing so slowly. But think of it like filling a dish that has a hole at the bottom. There's only so long the dish will remain full before it starts to drain again. Your connection to your Mate is the same. Until you two are together again, you will keep wasting energy trying to keep the bond whole. It is an impossible task."

Helena frowned, "So the mood swings, the physical tolls and effects, not to mention my power's ability to overwhelm me... those will all continue until we are reunited?"

"Yes, Kiri, if it does not worsen in the meantime," she said a bit apologetically.

"Lovely," Helena murmured as she tried to stand. Stumbling, Helena fell into the older woman. Miranda caught her with a muffled grunt. Flushing she said softly, "Apologies, Keeper."

"None are necessary, Kiri," Miranda replied as Joquil and Kragen rushed over to them.

"Are you alright, Hellion?" Kragen asked in his deep rumble.

Helena nodded wanly, "Yes, fine. It seems like I can only project my consciousness for so long until my body protests and pulls me back."

Joquil studied her with serious amber eyes, "Your soul is determined to reattach to its other half, which is why you feel the pull to reconnect to Von so strongly, but your physical body cannot stay empty for long without beginning to break down."

It was similar to what Miranda had said, but Helena still found the words surprising. "Is that what I'm doing? Sending my soul to his body?"

Joquil nodded, "You would not be able to call your power to you and use it through him otherwise. It is one thing to share a mental link, to speak to one another and be aware of each other's emotions. It is something else entirely to fuse your power."

Helena looked at Miranda for confirmation, but the woman only shrugged. It hadn't been a lack of power that pulled her back then, but her body's need for her soul. That certainly explained why her body felt so weak, despite the deep pool of her magic still rippling within her.

Distracted by the realization, Helena did not hear Micha's approach.

"Kiri?" he asked.

As her eyes focused on his, she felt her rage begin to spiral. Memories of what had happened, and what she had heard, while connected to Von had her curling her hand into the material of his shirt. Overhead, the sky began to darken and let out a warning crack of lightning.

"How, by all that is holy, is your mother still alive?" she asked in a guttural snarl, her teeth bared as she leaned into him until her nose almost touched his.

Micha's green eyes widened with a mix of shock and fear, "W-what do you mean, Kiri? My mother di-died." She could see his Adam's apple bob as he swallowed back his panic.

"No, Micha, she did not. Your mother is very much alive. She is the one behind Von's capture." Aqua eyes bore into his, daring him to protest, but the confusion in his expression could not be faked. Letting him go, she watched as he stumbled before regaining his footing.

Having overheard the encounter, the rest of her Circle had already joined them.

"How can she still be alive, Timmins?" Helena demanded.

Timmins expression was dark as he admitted, "I do not know, Kiri."

Joquil spoke from beside her, "Traditionally, a new Damaskiri does not rise until the current ruler dies. I did not even know it was possible for one to come into her power while the other still lived. She must have employed powerful magic indeed to fool us."

"You don't say," Helena snapped.

"At least we know who we are facing now," Miranda said prosaically. "It will help with strategizing, yes?"

Helena looked back at Micha who had completely retreated into himself before saying slowly, "I would not count on much of anything when it comes to the Corruptor." Speaking quickly Helena filled them in on what had happened when she was with Von.

After she finished, the only sounds in the camp were the crackles and snaps of the fire and the distant roll of thunder. Taking a fortifying breath, Helena said, "The plan does not change, but the timetable must be pushed forward. We cannot leave Von with her any longer. She has already tried to turn him once. Now that she knows she cannot, there's no reason for her to leave him unharmed."

Nial was the first to respond, his voice hesitant, "I want to save my brother as much as you do, Helena... but shouldn't we be fully prepared before rushing into this battle?"

"We've already discussed this," Helena said flatly, meeting each of their eyes in turn. Her friends' expressions were grim but accepting.

A feeling like a spark of fire in her hand had her yelping and shaking her hand in surprise. Seeing nothing wrong with her hand, she sent her focus deep, ignoring the startled shouts of her friends. Before she could do more than establish Von was alive, pain lanced up each of her legs, causing her to drop toward the ground. Hands reached out to grab and steady her, but Helena saw nothing but glittering black rage.

The sky cracked in half with a blinding bolt of lightning, while thunder shook the earth.

"That bitch!" Helena roared, pushing her friends off of her and starting to run toward a larger clearing, shouting, "Starshine!"

It took only a moment before Starshine's brilliant white fur gleamed against the darkness of Helena's storm as the Talyrian shot twin flames from her snout. She landed quickly, causing the ground to tremble in response. Helena was already moving to mount her but was brought up short.

"Helena! You can't mean to go right now. She'll be expecting you," Darrin shouted, before releasing her arm.

Spinning around, she pushed him back and said with deadly fury, "Try and stop me again."

Startled, he froze in place. Helena looked at the rest of them, daring them to so much as move. "Rally the troops, I will find you once I have him. This ends now."

"Kiri!" Ronan shouted. Helena's narrowed eyes did not faze the warrior who only said, "Bring him back to us."

With a nod, Helena climbed onto Starshine's back. She pressed her heels into the Talyrian and without so much as a backward glance, they took off toward the sky and the man that meant more to her than breathing.

CHAPTER TWENTY-FOUR

*H*elena stood at the edge of the forest, staring out at the twinkling white land that was sprawled out before her. The massive black structure was half-hidden in the snow-covered mountains and seemed to have been carved out of the rock that surrounded it. Its many twisting spires were reaching up through the mist and into the inky sky.

It had taken the rest of the day and most of the night to reach the castle. Above her, the sky was just beginning to fade from black to a deep navy. The sun had yet to make an appearance over the horizon but stars had already begun to slowly wink out. A few of the stalwart sentinels remained, ready to stand witness to the battle to come.

"It's not very welcoming is it?" Helena asked.

Beside her, Starshine let out a huff of agreement, her breath turning to curling wisps of steam in the frigid air.

Despite the large number of windows, not a single light was ablaze in any of them. "If I didn't know better, I wouldn't even believe there were people in there," Helena mused aloud, more from an effort to avoid thinking about what lay ahead, rather than any need to voice the thought.

The cold was overwhelming and her cloak did little to stave off the chill. Helena called some Fire to her, using it to warm both the garment and herself.

"I suppose this is where you leave me," Helena said once she was warm, turning to fully face the Talyrian queen.

Starshine's ears flattened, a clear indication of her disapproval.

"I'm sorry, beautiful, but I can't pretend to be Micha with you following me around. It's going to be hard enough to pull this off as it is."

Starshine huffed again, her annoyance unmistakable. The large feline sat back on her haunches and pulled her wings tightly into her body, refusing to leave. Helena sighed and rolled her eyes but did not force the issue. It would have been a waste of words. Instead, she chose to use the time wisely and begin her transformation into Micha. Unsure of any official way to do so, she simply let her instinct act as a guide.

Helena closed her eyes and called forth an image of Micha as she had last seen him: mussed russet hair framing a pale and slightly freckled face, mossy green eyes and long lashes that went blonde at the tips, and rumpled but well-made clothes that hung off of a tall and lean frame. Once the image was clear in her mind, she willed her body to duplicate it, taking the time to carefully focus on the specific features and characteristics that made up the man.

At first, nothing seemed to happen, but then she could start to feel her bones and muscles lengthen and stretch. Looking down, she noticed that her curves had disappeared, although there was a new bulge that had her blushing and quickly averting her gaze. It may technically be her body, but there was something that didn't feel right about showing too much interest in that particular detail. Lifting a hand, Helena noted that her fingers were no longer slender with oval-shaped nails in desperate need of filing. Rather, she had the thick blunted fingers of a man.

"Weird," Helena murmured, startled to hear the deeper timbre of her voice. With a small chuckle and a shake of her head, Helena made to move back to Starshine. Before she could take her first step toward the Talyrian, Starshine let out a long, threatening growl that forced her to take a few stumbling steps back instead.

"Starshine it's me. It's me, girl," she said holding up her hands.

The great cat went silent, tilting its head until those luminous turquoise eyes could better study her. After a tense moment, the Talyrian moved her head forward, sniffing the air between them and letting out a confused whine. Starshine could sense her mistress but did not recognize her through the glamour.

Not wanting to frighten or provoke her, Helena held out a hand for Starshine to sniff. The Talyrian bared her teeth in silent warning but pressed her muzzle into Helena's hand. As the moments passed, her hand grew warm from the humid puffs of air coming from the Talyrian's nose. Helena ran her other hand over the velvety fur, feeling tense muscles begin to relax as Starshine confirmed that the familiar scent was coming from the wrong person.

A soft buzzing filled the quiet space between them. Helena's body tingled as the feeling washed over her. Once it passed, Starshine let out an approving sound and pressed her head into Helena's hip. She raised a brow, about to tease the Talyrian for her odd behavior, when she realized what had just happened. Suddenly worried that Starshine had somehow managed to undo the disguise she had so carefully crafted, Helena quickly scanned herself. She was pleased, and more than a little relieved, to see that she still appeared to be Micha. Whatever the feline had done, it had only affected her ability to see Helena's true form, not interfered with Helena's glamour.

Helena was intrigued by this new display of magic. She had not realized that the Talyrian had powers outside of flight and fire, which she had always seen as being natural abilities versus magical ones. That said, no one could look at a Talyrian and not know that they were magical beings. Or be a little in awe of their overwhelming majesty.

Shaking her head ruefully, she gave Starshine another rub and asked, "What other secrets are you still hiding from me? Hmmm?"

Starshine just closed her eyes, rumbling in pleasure at the caress. Helena let out an amused snort, "It's a wonder I even bother talking to you at all. Not like you will answer me."

A slit of turquoise appeared, and Starshine shot Helena a glance that negated the comment. The Talyrian had no trouble communicating if one counted expressions and body language as forms of communication. Helena allowed herself a final moment of amusement, enjoying the quiet moment with Starshine before the smile started to fall from her face and her eyes moved back to the castle before them.

Setting her shoulders, Helena took a deep breath. "It's time."

HELENA MADE her way to the door, the howling wind making her cloak snap behind her. Walking in another person's body had been odd, at first, but the little time she had spent in Von's helped her quickly adapt.

This was absolute insanity. The others had known it, as had she, but there really was no other play available to them. The only way they were getting inside this castle without a full-on siege, which there was no guarantee they would win, was sneaking in. But without any real understanding of what they were walking into, it would be easier to enter as a welcomed guest rather than trying to remain hidden within the shadows. That didn't make it any less stupid. She was literally standing on her enemy's doorstep about to ask them to let her in. Insane didn't begin to cover it.

Offering a quick prayer to the Mother and sending a rush of love and longing to Von through the bond, Helena forced herself to push everything from her mind. Gripping the icy metal of the knocker, she lifted it and slammed it back down and onto the heavy wooden door.

There was a groan and a shudder as the sound of the knock reverberated in the room beyond the door. There was no answer. Helena had known, due to the utter stillness, that there were few people inhabiting the massive structure. She shouldn't have been surprised that there wasn't someone waiting for her at the door. But she was. Lifting her hand to knock again she flinched a little when there was a creak and the door slid back just enough for a familiar green eye to stare at her through the crack. The green eye widened as recognition dawned and the door pulled back further to reveal Gillian's thunderstruck expression.

"Micha!" she gasped. Joy filled her eyes but was immediately replaced by horror. "What are you doing here? You shouldn't be here. It's not safe!" she said furtively glancing around as if checking that they were, in fact, alone.

Rage and revulsion churned in her belly, and Helena had to force her expression into something more appropriate. Thankful she had spent the journey with Starshine planning for this moment and thinking about what she would say, Helena focused on the ruse and finally uttered the words that she committed to memory.

"Sister, is that any way to welcome your brother home?" Helena asked, using one of Micha's most troubled expressions. "I've been so worried about you. Rumors have been flying around the Palace since your disappearance. I hadn't given them any credence, knowing you couldn't have pulled off what they had been accusing you of. I mean, what reason could you possibly have for abducting Helena's mate?" Helena paused, letting some of the brotherly concern fade from her voice and replacing it with the annoyed tone she had heard so often from Darrin when he thought she was being stupid. "When you didn't return and put the rumors to rest, I realized that you were, in fact, absolutely irresponsible enough to kidnap Von. What I don't understand is why? What reason could you possibly have to be so stupid?"

Gillian's face had turned a bright red and she was clenching her teeth so hard, Helena could hear the grinding from where she stood. With another quick check over her shoulder, Gillian turned back and spat, "I did it for you! To protect you, you ungrateful ass!"

Helena allowed her eyes to widen, trying to convey shocked disbelief, "Me? How does stealing the Mate, help me? She had already soul-bonded with him; it's not like I had a chance at filling the position."

"No! Not to open up a spot for you," Gillian sputtered, "to save *you*. Mother had threatened—"

"Mother? Mother is dead, how could she be a threat to me?

"Mother is alive," Gillian hissed.

"I-I don't understand."

Gillian swallowed, her earlier fear at seeing Micha returning, "Mother faked her death. I-I helped her. But I had to Micha!" she protested, seeing the anger Helena wasn't quick enough to hide.

"Had to? Why?" Helena asked, trying to sound confused instead of enraged.

"She threatened to kill you if I didn't. She was tired of hearing about the prophecy, of the whispers that she was not a true Kiri as she had no Mate of her own. That another, more powerful than any we had seen, would replace her. It drove her mad, Micha. She snapped."

Helena shook her head, "So why didn't you tell me? I could have helped you, Gillian. You're my twin, you know I would do anything for you. We could have worked together to stop her."

Gillian reached out and grasped her brother's hand in her own, "And I would do anything for you. Micha, I was trying to protect you."

"I know," Helena forced herself to say softly.

Tears filled Gillian's eyes and she threw herself at Helena, holding the woman disguised as her brother as if her own life depended on it.

Helena swallowed back the bile and endured the embrace as long as possible before pushing Gillian back and asking earnestly, "Don't you see? This has gotten out of hand. You have to release Von before things go any further. I can help you."

Gillian was openly crying now. "It's too late," she whispered.

The bottom dropped out of Helena's stomach, and her knees almost buckled at the words. "What do you mean? What happened?"

Gillian shook her head, red pieces of hair falling from her braid, "I'm not sure, only that Mother no longer needs to keep Von alive. She has been…" Gillian trailed off looking sick.

"Has been what?" Helena snapped, barely restraining herself from shaking Gillian.

"Torturing him," Gillian whispered, her eyes still dripping with tears.

"Is she with him now?"

Gillian shook her head again, "No. She finally stopped about an hour ago. I think she got bored once he passed out. He's locked up in his room again."

"Take me to him. We've got to get him out of here."

"Micha, you don't understand. If she catches us, we're dead."

Helena could feel the rage burn through her as she snapped, "What good is our life if he dies? Do know what Helena will do if that happens? We will be on borrowed time as it is."

"We already are," Gillian admitted, sniffling back some tears.

"So wouldn't you rather your last acts on this earth be selfless ones? What are you going to say for yourself when you face the Great Mother and have to answer for your crimes?" Helena asked, infusing her words with tendrils of her compulsion magic.

Gillian's eyes seemed to glaze, Helena could tell that the thought had taken hold. Worry filled the girl's green eyes as she asked, "You don't think She would forgive me for my actions when they were to save you?"

The question gave Helena pause. Despite every disgusting thing this woman had done, she truly believed she had been saving someone she loved. Helena couldn't fault her for that, although she despised her for what she had done in the name of that misplaced belief.

"It is not for me to say," she said finally, "but I do know, that the more we can do now to repair the damage, the better it will go for us all."

Gillian chewed on her lower lip, before nodding finally. "Alright, Micha, if you are sure. But I do not think we will be able to get him out of here alone. Not without our Mother finding out."

"Leave that part to me. Just take me to him," Helena said firmly.

Nodding again, Gillian motioned for her to finally step inside. "Stay close," she whispered, as she pushed the heavy wooden door closed.

Helena nodded once to indicate that she understood. She walked quickly, adrenaline causing her heart to race as she followed the red-headed woman deeper into the darkness.

TIME CRAWLED as they made their way to the room where Von was being kept. Helena could feel the stiffness in her tense muscles, but could not seem to make herself relax. She kept waiting to run into someone, or for Gillian to realize that she was an imposter, but neither happened.

The twisting halls were completely empty and eerily silent. Helena followed closely behind Gillian, noting the general state of disuse throughout the castle. The rugs were faded and threadbare and the stone walls pitted and chipped. Where pictures had once hung, there were now squares of dust framing discolored stone. With each twist of the halls, it only grew more dank and dark, the flickering lights barely illuminating anything.

Helena tried to track the number of turns they had made, knowing she would need to move quickly once she had Von, but it was starting to feel more like a labyrinth than a castle. Not only that, but her mind was filled with images of finally getting her revenge on the red-haired schemer. The woman had been responsible for some of the worst pain she had ever endured, and she was finally going to be able to return the favor. The thought filled her with a grim giddiness that would have horrified her, had it been anyone else. But this was the woman that had taken Von, had been the impetus of every terrible thing he'd endured since. There was no punishment too great for that crime.

Realizing she was losing focus, Helena forced herself to think only of how many turns they had made since reaching this floor: seven. *Where was everyone?* Helena wondered again, *it wasn't just Gillian and her mother holed up here, was it?* She was just about to ask when Gillian stopped suddenly in front of a large wooden door. She turned to face Helena fully and asked in a hushed whisper, "Are you sure about this? It's not too late for you to leave before Mother sees you."

"Open the door, Gillian," she demanded. Helena could no longer remain patient, knowing that her Mate was only separated from her by a piece of wood and the woman that was quite literally standing between them. She could feel him now, had felt him as soon as she had stepped into that dark and empty castle. As they'd made their way down the winding halls to this part of the castle, the feeling had only grown in intensity. Helena had known that he was seriously hurt, which only frayed the already worn edges of her patience. But after Gillian confirmed he had been tortured; her need to see him could no longer be contained. It had become a living thing: wild and thrashing within her.

Gillian was clearly terrified. Helena didn't blame her; she should be. The girl's hand shook as she lifted it and pressed it against the door. Helena could feel a tremor of magic as the door's spell recognized Gillian and swung open. She made a move to step over the threshold, but Helena caught her arm, pulling her back, "Gillian, wait."

Confusion colored her face, and Helena studied it for a moment considering her next move. Now that the door was open, Gillian no longer served a purpose. The wait was over.

"Micha?" she asked in a quavering voice, sensing something was amiss.

"I'm not Micha," Helena said flatly, allowing the glamour to fade.

Gillian's eyes widened as Helena was revealed and she moaned in horror, "No! Oh no! What have I done?"

"Something useful, for once. Thanks for the idea, by the way," Helena said with a fierce smile, gesturing to her body.

Gillian struggled to break free from Helena's hold, but it only served to make Helena tighten her hold, using the power of Earth to make her grip unbreakable. As she bore down on the fragile bones of Gillian's wrist, she also allowed the sharp tips of her deadly black claws to appear, their razor-sharp points biting into tender flesh until pinpricks of blood appeared. Gillian went limp, deflating as she said, "She's going to kill you."

Helena leaned close, her aqua eyes glittering with promise, "Not if I get to her first. But that's not your problem, Gillian dear. You should be much more concerned with what I'm going to do to *you*."

Gillian swallowed, fear making her eyes large and her face pale. She still seemed too stricken to do more than stand there, waiting for Helena's to act. Not wanting to disappoint her, Helena called on her power, letting all of the rage and pain her separation to Von had caused feed it.

"Helena," Gillian implored, "please…"

Helena's iridescent eyes narrowed, and her hair flew around her as though wind was blowing around them, "I warned you, but you didn't listen. No one harms what is mine."

She let the magic go and Gillian flew back from the force of the blow, her head slamming back into the stone wall. She crumpled to the floor, blood beginning to flow freely from the impact. Gillian struggled to sit up, attempting to use her magic to stem the blood, but Helena was faster, already moving closer with another swirling ball of pulsing light in the palm of her hand. Left with no choice, Gillian lashed out, redirecting her magic into an attack. A blue-white orb shot through the air, but Helena easily intercepted it. Her own power vastly outmatched Gillian's and she was able to absorb the bolt of magic without injury.

"Now now, play nice," Helena sing-songed.

Gillian grit her teeth, blood staining them red. She called another swirling ball of magic and tried again, but Helena easily swatted it away, laughing when it hit the door, causing it to burst into thousands of jagged splinters. Helena was thankful for the shield she'd placed around herself, as she brushed the small flecks of wood off of her shoulder before looking back at Gillian. Her chest was rising and falling rapidly as she fought against the Air Helena was using to hold her in place.

Helena could almost read the girl's thoughts through the emotion that raced across her face. There was a flash of calculation in Gillian's green eyes as if she was weighing her options. It was obvious that she was sizing up her adversary and had just realized that this was not the naïve, powerless, girl she had met in Elysia. There was no way she could beat the woman standing over her. No way to beat the Vessel. With the realization, all remaining fight left Gillian.

"Finish it," she said bitterly, turning to spit a mouthful of blood onto the floor.

Helena tilted her head, studying the broken woman. The layered voice of her power seemingly devoid of emotion as she asked, "Where's the fun in that? We were only just getting started." She called twin balls of power into her hands. One flickered and danced like a living flame, while the other swirled like a miniature tornado. "What shall it be, Gillian dear? Should I purify your blackened soul with Fire or steal the very life from your lungs with Air?"

"Stop playing with me and finish it!" she shouted, staring up at her with shining green eyes.

"Why not both?" Helena crooned, ignoring the demand. Her brows lowered menacingly over iridescent eyes that had flickers of lightning in their depths. She fed the orbs of power until they swelled in her hands, becoming more erratic in their movements. Once they were as large as her head, she stopped, pinning Gillian with her gaze. There was no need for words as she released the Air storm. Gillian swallowed back a cry, slamming her eyes shut and muttering frantically under her breath.

"Mother forgive me," she whispered before Helena's magic stole the air from her lungs, causing her to sputter and choke. Her eyes began to bulge as she gasped for breath.

The girl's words finally sunk in, and Helena faltered as other, more cryptic, words rose unbidden:

'You have a choice before you.'

'Loyalty or love?'

'Mercy or vengeance?

'Life or death?'

Was this the choice the Keepers had alluded to? All three options could apply to this moment, she supposed. Choosing mercy and life over vengeance and death... Spending time meting out revenge under the guise of loyalty, while just beyond that door her love still suffered. Could the ramifications of this choice really lead to the slaughter in her vision? Helena shuddered at the memory of the carnage. It didn't seem possible, and yet...

Another whimper brought her focus back to Gillian. Helena could feel the shift in her magic. Her hair settled back around her shoulders while the ball of Fire snuffed out. When she'd arrived, Helena had every intention of making the woman pay for her actions with her life. Now that the moment had arrived, Helena realized that death would be too easy for Gillian. There was no punishment there.

"No, I don't think so," Helena said finally.

"Wh-what?" Gillian stuttered, her eyes flying open in shocked disbelief.

"Death is a kindness you do not deserve. You need to answer for what you have done." Any magic Helena used right now would have killed the girl. She was too amped up and fueled by rage for it not to. Thinking of Von, a dark smile grew across her face.

"Helena," Gillian whimpered, seeing the threat of violence that still remained in her eyes.

"Just because I'm not going to kill you, Gillian, doesn't mean I'm going to just let you go." With that, Helena closed the distance between them, pulled back her arm and slammed her fist straight into Gillian's nose. There was a wet crunch and blood sprayed everywhere as the girl's head flew back, slamming into the wall again. Helena couldn't help but think that Ronan would approve. By the time Gillian's head hit the floor, she was unconscious.

The need for revenge made it hard to step away but her need for Von was stronger. As she stood, a flicker of color caught her eye. Gillian was still wearing her necklace; the one that held the Kaelpas stone she'd used to help the Shadows find them and to take Von away.

Helena grasped it and yanked. The chain snapped and swung haphazardly from Helena's hand. "Perhaps you still had some use after all." Stuffing the broken necklace into her pocket, Helena quickly rose and ran into the room.

CHAPTER TWENTY-FIVE

*H*elena did not know what to expect when she stepped across the threshold and so there was no way for her to prepare for the onslaught of emotions that rose at the sight of Von, bloody and battered on the bed. Not that knowing would have made any difference. She was frozen in the doorway as her brain struggled to process each of the conflicting emotions... Anger at his mistreatment... Fear that she would not have time to heal him and also escape... Joy at the mere sight of him alive, at all. And love. More than anything, she felt a love so great it outshined all else.

Her eyes settled on his face completely blocking out his broken body for the moment. Matted strands of hair were stuck to pale golden skin. Dried blood was crusted everywhere while fresh blood was still trickling out of his mouth and nose. His bottom lip was split and swollen, as were his eyes, those beautiful eyes she was desperate to see. They were so bruised and swollen, she could hardly recognize them as eyes. It looked as though someone had used his face as a punching bag, for hours.

Rushing to his side, she pressed her hand to his face, pushing back blood and sweat-soaked strands, until her hand was resting against his neck. Beneath her fingers, his skin burned hot and she could feel the feeble, yet steady, throb of his pulse. Letting out a shuddering breath, she leaned down and pressed her lips against his, tasting the salt of her tears mingle with his blood as she did.

"Von," she whispered, her lips still touching his. *"I am here,"* she added when he did not stir. There was a flutter as his eyes shifted beneath their lids, but still they did not open.

"Mira?" he rasped along their bond, his psychic voice filled with pain.

"I need you to try and wake up, Mate."

She pulled back slightly, hoping to catch a glimpse of gray. She watched as he struggled to open his eyes, but they only cracked open before immediately closing again.

Moving her hand to rest above his heart, she closed her eyes and used her senses to assess his injuries. Her eyes snapped back open as a tidal wave of nausea caused her to gag.

"That bitch!" she seethed once she had recovered enough to speak. Rowena had not only tortured Von, she had used what magic she possessed to "heal" the wounds. It was clear the woman possessed none of Water's soothing magic. This was Fire and Earth fused into a cruel imitation of healing. Instead of using magic to repair the damage she had caused, she used it to lock it in and override the body's natural instinct to heal. No wonder Von could not break through to consciousness; his body was stuck in perpetual agony and his brain was trying to protect him in the only way it could.

Helena could feel the seconds slipping away. She needed to get him out of here now, but in his current state he was in no condition to be moved. To heal him fully would require more time and magic than she could spare since she could not risk being weakened or caught unaware. That left her the choice of doing just enough to get him mobile and stave off the pain. She would have to finish healing him once they were safely away.

She gave him another quick kiss, saying as she did, *"Try to stay with me; this may hurt."*

There was a vibration along the bond that she took to be acknowledgement before she let herself slip into the healing trance she'd last used with his brother. Allowing her magic to guide her, she reset bone and repaired tissue, doing only enough to help him walk and stop any bleeding. All of the bruising would have to remain. She moved quickly, using none of the care and finesse she had with Nial. There simply wasn't time.

Helena knew when she was finished because a harsh hiss greeted her ears, "Mother's Tits, Helena. I've known Daejaran wolves with a gentler touch than you." When she opened her eyes, Von was smiling up at her, albeit crookedly. His gray eyes had lost enough of the swelling that they could open, and they were currently shining with an emotion too vast to name. It was the most beautiful thing she had ever seen.

"You're lucky I love you. It could have been much worse," she muttered, settling for flippancy to keep herself from breaking down into gut-wrenching sobs.

He grimaced at the thought, and pushed himself up into a seated position, groaning a little with the movement. Helena couldn't keep herself from staring. He may still be covered in bruises and blood, but she was a starving woman and he was her feast.

Sensing her eyes on him, he looked at her from under thick lashes, "Darling, as much as I'd love to oblige you, I don't think there's time for that."

She blushed and made a face. That hadn't been her intention. Not really. It was just, he was here. He was alive. She reached out and touched his cheek, heart too full for words.

He pressed his face into her hand before brushing his lips against its center. They stayed there for a moment, enjoying the feeling of being with each other again, and knowing that the time for words would come later.

"Can you walk?" she asked, even though she knew that he could.

"Aye," he affirmed as he stood. He teetered a little, and she moved to quickly support his weight as he adjusted.

"Hold on to me," she murmured.

"Always, *Mira*. I'm just a little unsteady," he said gruffly, pressing his lips to the top of her head. She could feel him breathe her in, his ribs expanding under her hand.

Her heart contracted at the tender words, but before he could say anything else that would cause her to risk spending time they didn't have in this prison cell, she said quickly, "Then I think it's time we get you home."

"*Mira*, I told you, as long as I'm with you, I'm already home." Her breath hitched, tears thick in her throat. Von lifted a hand and caressed her cheek, turning her face up toward his. Leaning down, he pressed a kiss full of promise against her lips. Helena felt her knees go a bit weak when he finally pulled back and winked at her. With that he grasped her hand in his and pulled her toward the door.

THEY MOVED QUICKLY, hands still intertwined as they made their way through the halls back toward the exit. Von had snickered when he saw Gillian's inert body, approval radiating off him in waves. Helena had thought he might have been disappointed that she hadn't killed her outright, but he'd made no mention of it. He'd just brushed his lips against her knuckles and gestured for her to lead the way.

The halls were still empty, but there was something about the lack of security that caused her to move more cautiously. They were using Air to conceal the sound of their footsteps and would pause before making any turns, using their enhanced senses to check whether it was clear. The longer they went without seeing anyone, the more concerned she became. It seemed absolutely impossible to her that the woman who had orchestrated this whole scheme hadn't planned for this exact scenario.

"*Where are the others?*" Von asked suddenly across their bond.

"*If you're referring to Rowena's people, I am wondering the same thing myself,*" she replied, guessing that he might be thinking along the same lines.

"*No, I meant ours. How many fighters do we have? What is our plan?"* Von asked the questions one after another, his years as a Commander making him eager to hear the strategy.

Helena didn't bother to meet his gaze, choosing instead to scan for signs of Rowena's men as she listed, *"The rest of the Circle, Ronan, Serena, your brother, Micha, along with a couple of others I do not think you know. They were making their way to the castle when I left them. They should be here soon, if they aren't already."*

Von stopped short, halting her own forward movement. *"You came here alone?"* he asked in a voice filled with quiet thunder, *"and you plan on attacking with only two handfuls of men? Are you out of your mind?"*

Helena felt her hackles rise, and turned to face him with a frown, *"Are you really complaining about the manner in which I just rescued you, Mate? Do you doubt my ability? Or my judgment?"* She wasn't sure which part offended her most.

His brows lowered over darkening gray eyes, *"Helena, you have to know how foolish that was. What if she captured you as well? What are the rest of us supposed to do if something happened to you? How in the Mother's name are we supposed to defeat her with such a small force? You cannot think to win this fight so hamstrung."*

"I got to you, didn't I?" Exasperation filled her at his words; she was not some helpless farm girl any more. She was the Mother's Vessel, the strongest in history, if the prophecy was to be believed. If she wasn't capable of a rescue mission, then there wasn't much hope for her abilities at all.

"Do you have any idea what your absence has been doing to me?" she continued a bit desperately, *"The toll that each day of our separation took on me? I've been coming apart, Von. I couldn't wait any longer, not when I could feel you again. Not when she was hurting you and I could finally do something about it!"* Her words were hurried, reinforced with all of the emotion she'd had to bury the last few months in order to simply function.

Von's expression softened, and his lifted his free hand to caress her cheek. *"Mira—"* he started but she cut him off.

"You have to know that if there had been a better option available,

I would have used it. I would have done anything to get you free of this place. But this was the only way. No one else would have been able to get past her defenses without bloodshed."

"I wouldn't say you did either, Mate," he teased, his frustration with the choices she'd made in his absence evaporating with her words. He might be a Commander, but she was Kiri. Her will was law, and he lived to serve.

They exchanged tight, feral smiles, *"No, I suppose not. But better one deserving bitch than any of our men."*

A heartbeat passed and he squeezed her hand, indicating he was ready to continue. As she made to move forward, he stopped her again. *"Wait. Did you say my* brother *is with you?"*

This time Helena had no trouble meeting his eyes. Her smile shone with radiance as she nodded and said simply, *"I did."*

"You healed him," he said with no small bit of wonder.

"I did," she repeated.

She watched her strong warrior blink in stunned silence. When he spoke again, his voice was thick with emotion, *"Thank you, Helena. I cannot tell you what this means to me, to my family."*

"Hush, my love," she murmured, pressing her fingers to his lips as though he had spoken aloud. *"Nial has already thanked me more than enough. Healing him was my promise to you. I never intended to do otherwise."* She contemplated telling him that Serena would likely be thanking her in the near future, as well, but figured it was not the right time for that bombshell.

Happiness and awe made his eyes shine like silver. He shook his head, laughing a little, *"Of course you did. You have proven time and again that you are capable of performing miracles and showing compassion and mercy where others would, or could, not. You are the true miracle, my miracle."*

She rolled her eyes at his proclamation, but smiled despite herself, *"Worship and adore me later, Mate. We have an escape to finish."*

His smile was wolfish as he replied, *"Oh, I have every intention of making that my first priority once we are safely away."* Before she could respond he repeated his earlier question, *"So what's the plan?"*

Helena filled him in as they made their way carefully down the last hall. There was only one more turn until they reached the receiving room. Just as they were about to take the steps that would put them out in the open, they heard the soft rustling of footsteps. A lot of footsteps.

Exchanging glances, they froze, pressing their bodies into the wall. Even with his injuries, Von used his body to block hers, so that anyone who discovered them would see him first. There was a loud shout, and Helena panicked, certain that they had finally been spotted as the sound of footsteps grew louder. Von's hand squeezed hers, each of them bracing for an attack. It never came.

Helena peered over his shoulder, tentatively stepping away from the wall. Something was wrong. Something was very, very wrong. A searing pain in her side had her gasping. Von spun toward her, reaching out to hold her as she slumped against the wall.

"Helena? Mira, what's wrong?"

"My – my Jaka," she gasped. His eyes widened at her words, yet another unexpected discovery he did not have time to fully process. As she closed her eyes, trying to ride out the waves of pain, she was able to see the threads that tied her to the men in her Circle. Each flashed brilliantly, flickering and pulsing with light. Focusing on a strand that flared brilliantly once before dimming to a dull gray, Helena's eyes snapped back open. "Ronan!" she shouted, no longer concerned with being overheard.

Von's eyes bore into hers as he snapped to attention, "What about Ronan?"

"He's in trouble. They all are."

"How bad?" Von asked, every inch the warrior.

"As bad as it gets."

She could see Von scanning, anticipating the distance between them and the door, as she moved her hands off of her throbbing side. The movement caused her to run her hand over the small lump in her pocket. The Kaelpas. Pulling it out, she held the gleaming purple stone up for Von to see.

He glanced down at it and then back at her, "Do you know how to use that thing?"

"Has that ever once stopped me?" she retorted as they pressed themselves together. Closing her eyes, she took a shuddering breath and pictured the clearing she had been in with Starshine only an hour before. There was a small pop and then nothing. The spot where the couple once stood was now completely empty.

CHAPTER TWENTY-SIX

*M*icha stepped away from the others who were busy strapping the last of the weapons to their bodies. Serena's violet eyes caught the movement and froze him in place until she nodded once and refocused on her task.

This was where he left them. While they moved into place around the castle, he would go inside and try to reason with his mother. Perhaps if she and Gillian could hear him out, they would let go of this ludicrous idea to retake the throne. Although, Micha wasn't sure how happy Gillian would be to see him after Helena's trick, or that she'd even be alive to see him at all.

Micha frowned, not fond of any of the scenarios that awaited him. He was no fool and he was well aware that the likelihood of his success was slim, but if there was even the possibility he could end this without further lives being lost, he had to try. The others had only agreed to let him go off on his own because they hoped he would act as a further distraction for his mother, thereby giving Helena much-needed time to escape with Von and the rest of them an opportunity to get into place unannounced. Diversion or peacekeeper, Micha had a role to play, and he would see it through. That didn't mean he had to like it.

He was not like the others. The differences between them were glaringly obvious. Men and women alike, they all seemed eager at the promise of violence, whereas Micha shied away. He was not a fighter. Battle, and the resulting death, did not appeal to him in any capacity. He'd much rather hole up and get lost in a good book, a peaceful pastime he'd spent most of his life enjoying. Micha desperately wished he could leave the heroics to the others and go home to his library. But his place was with his family and his family was here. He needed to try and save them despite his vehement wish otherwise.

What had surprised Micha the most, was how easily Helena stepped into the role of warrior. It was not her need to protect the ones she loved that shocked him. That had been abundantly clear since she first set foot on the stage during her welcoming ceremony. It was how she did not cringe, or so much as flinch, at the thought of harming another. For one so nurturing and compassionate, she'd quickly embraced war and violence as a necessity. Helena had a warrior's soul and a mother's love, as deadly a combination as he'd ever seen. Micha was just glad he was on her side.

When he'd first met her, she had been so sweet. A lost little lamb in need of love and protection. He'd been enchanted at the first sight of those luminous aqua eyes. More than a part of him had hoped that she might choose him. Now he could see that he'd never even stood a chance. A woman like her deserved a man that could fight by her side without a second thought. A man who could see her thirst for blood and revel in her prowess on the battlefield, not one who would fear her when she stood surrounded by the bodies she had slain. She needed a man that understood and loved all the facets of her soul: the dark as well as the light. He was not that man; he had never been and never could be. It would not stop him from serving her though.

Micha took a steadying breath, letting his eyes briefly rest on the others and offering a quick prayer to the Mother that they would still be standing when the day was done. He may not be able to join them on this killing field, but he could fight in his own way. Without a word, he turned and started toward the place that had once been his home.

RONAN WATCHED Micha's retreating back, the calm that always preceded battle overtaking him.

Serena stepped up to his side, "Do you think he'll succeed?"

"Not a chance," Ronan said with derision.

"What about us?" she asked softly.

Ronan slanted a glance at her, uncertain which us she was referring to. "That's harder to say," he answered neutrally.

Serena let out a deep sigh, "I was afraid you'd say that. We've faced battles with worse odds and made it out relatively unscathed. At least we've got Helena on our side. That should help even the odds a little."

Well that answers that question, he thought without bitterness. "Indeed it will," he agreed.

"Ronan – I," she started hesitantly.

So they were going to have this conversation after all. "Serena, how long have we known each other?" he asked, wanting to make this easier for both of them.

Her eyes were warm as she replied, "It feels like our whole lives."

He nodded, returning her smile, "And in all of those years, have I ever given you any indication that I want anything other than your happiness?"

She blinked furiously and shook her head, silky blond strands flying wildly about her head.

Ronan gave her a sad smile, lifting his hand to gently brush a rogue tear off her cheek, "Then if we make it through this, know that you have my blessing to follow your heart, wherever it leads you. Not that you need it."

Serena pressed her hand over his, holding it against her cheek when he would have pulled away, "You know that I will always love you?"

He winked, pushing down the small pang her words caused, "And you know I will kill him if he hurts you. Being Von's brother won't save him."

Serena's laugh burst out and she threw her arms around his neck, holding him tightly. Ronan held her, his eyes closing as he savored the moment, knowing it was the last time she'd be in his arms.

There was a soft cough, and the two stepped away from one another. Nial stood there looking apologetic and determined in equal measure. "They are ready," he said, tipping his head to indicate the others.

Ronan nodded, squeezing Serena's shoulder a last time before walking toward Nial. He stopped when he was alongside him, the other man stiffening slightly. Ronan dipped his chin until his eyes were level with Nial's, forcing the other man to meet his icy gaze. "Treat her well, or you will deal with me. I don't care who you are puppy, if you hurt her, I will destroy you."

Nial swallowed, but did not flinch as he responded, "I am glad that she has you to look after her, but you will never need to worry about her with me."

Ronan narrowed his eyes, slapping his hand on Nial's shoulder, causing his knees to buckle under the force, "I'll be the judge of that." Ronan walked away, sucking in a harsh breath and letting his mind empty of everything but the fight ahead as he let it out.

KRAGEN STUDIED THE BARREN SCENE, not liking how little coverage there was for their approach.

"What are you thinking?" Darrin asked.

"No matter what we do, we'll be completely visible against the white of the snow. If she has any guards, they'll spot us at once," Kragen grumbled.

Darrin contemplated the castle, eyebrows furrowing as he tried to think of a solution. His eyes cleared and he turned to Kragen with some excitement, snapping his fingers as he did, "What if we were able to make it harder for them to see?"

Kragen lifted a brow, unimpressed with the words, "What do you think I'm trying to figure out over here? Which gift basket to send them?"

Darrin scowled, "No, asshole. What if we combine our powers to create a fog. One that would obscure the land between us and the castle enough to mask our approach."

He lifted his brows as he considered the suggestion, "It could definitely work, although it could hinder us as well."

The blond man shrugged, "We wouldn't need to see until we reached the castle, would we?"

"Not unless someone was able to sneak up on us through the same fog," Ronan interjected, having just reached them.

Kragen nodded, "My thoughts exactly. What say you Joquil? Is there a way to control the fog, so that we could release it once we've cleared the land?"

Joquil's amber eyes assessed the landscape, "Perhaps. It will take the combined efforts of many of us to create that kind of weather. It could weaken us."

"I have read about entire armies using such a strategy in the past. They had a dedicated force purely focused on controlling the weather. That amount of power definitely takes a toll," Timmins warned, having just joined them.

The men eyed each other carefully. They were not lacking for power, any one of them more powerful than a handful of other Chosen, but the idea of weakening themselves when they were uncertain what exactly they'd be facing was unappealing.

"Even still. It may be our best option," Kragen rumbled.

Ronan nodded his agreement while Serena pointed out, "We can always rely on our physical skills. We do train without our magic for a reason."

Joquil scratched his chin, "To create the type of fog you're speaking of will require the use of four of the five branches: Water to create the moisture, Fire to turn it to mist, Air to disperse it, and Earth to ground it and keep it from simply floating off."

Nial cleared his throat, his face reddening as he offered, "I am a master of all four branches."

"What are you proposing?" Timmins asked.

"I can make the elements work in harmony, while the rest of you are on the move. I—" he let out a soft chuckle, "I am the weakest fighter by far, I don't think any of us would deny it. I simply do not possess the same level of skill as the rest of you. But this I can do, and would do, gladly."

The Circle digested the words. "It could work," Joquil said, echoing Kragen's earlier words.

"It will require more power than you alone possess," Miranda said, placing her hand on Nial's shoulder, "but I can assist you."

Timmins' blue eyes widened in surprise as he turned to the Keeper. She felt the weight of his stare and shrugged prosaically, "What? I am hardly rushing head-first into a melee. I have my power to offer as well, and I will do so. From here," she added with a smirk.

Timmins shook his head, while Kragen grinned, "So we have our ranged team in place."

Effie stood quietly to the side, looking small surrounded by the others. Tilting her chin up, she squared her shoulders and declared, "I will go with the rest of you."

Darrin spun to her in surprise, opening his mouth to protest, but Effie kept talking, "I have been training with Helena when she works with Kragen and Ronan and have demonstrated some skill with the staff. I may have no power to offer, but I will fight in the way that I can. Just as the others are. I did not come with you all to sit on the sidelines and watch. I came to help."

Kragen placed his hand on her shoulder, squeezing in approval. Darrin looked like he had swallowed a lemon, but he did not argue.

"Alright, little warrior," Ronan said, "I will create a shield for you, it should protect you from most blows. If they get through it though, you run. No one will think less of you for staying alive."

Effie frowned, "I'm not a coward."

Ronan and Kragen turned to her with twin scowls. Ronan snapped, "Did you hear me say that you were? If you are going to be a part of the fighting force, when your Commander gives an order you obey it, or you don't fight. Going rogue in the midst of battle could lead to death. Yours or your cil'virga."

Effie flushed and ducked her head. "Sorry," she squeaked.

Ronan tilted her chin up, "No need to apologize, little warrior."

She grinned, posture relaxing as Ronan stepped back.

The group quieted, their eyes looking around as they mentally readied themselves. Ronan assessed his cil'virga, the Daejaran term for an elite military team. There was much to be desired in the way of their size, none of them expecting that this is where they would end up when they set out for Bael and the Keepers. They had gone in search of information, and at the time, it had made sense to have a smaller force for ease and speed while traveling. But the things that had been assets when they started could very well be what crippled them now; they may have started off on a rescue mission, but they were now heading into battle.

Luckily the men and women surrounding him were some of the Chosen's strongest and they were only facing off against one red-headed girl and her mother... And a potential army of Shadows. Ronan sighed. He'd faced off against worse enemies with less.

"Let's go," he said finally.

THE FOG WAS thick and completely blocked out the sky as they crept closer to the castle. It had an eerie effect, seeming to envelope them completely in a world of white. Ronan lost sight of all but those right next to him. As always Serena was at his right side, her silvery blonde hair now twisted in tight braids. Kragen took up the spot on the left, the spot that would have been his if they'd been following Von.

It was odd; he hadn't lead anyone into battle in years. Not since Von had been promoted to Commander and again when he broke from the military entirely to create his mercenary band. Von had always been the one to lead; he had been born for it. Ronan had no desire to lead. He was much more familiar with following orders than taking them, but that didn't mean he couldn't pick up the mantle with ease. There wasn't much Ronan wouldn't do to save the man that was the brother of his soul.

Seeing the black stone of the gate, he held up a fist. The others halted around him. He waited until he could hear the sound of footsteps fall silent around him before he opened his hand toward the sky, releasing the flare that would let Nial and Miranda know it was time to let go of the fog. It moved lazily, floating away from him in wisps until he could start to make out all of the others. Before long there was a cool breeze and the fog lifted completely.

Ronan let out a whispered "Fuck" when he saw what they had walked into. Spinning in a slow circle, he lost count of the Shadows that had surrounded them. The hunched and mottled gray bodies were completely still as they stared with dead white eyes, the black lines snaking through them all that was moving.

"To me!" he shouted. The others reacted immediately, moving in tight and turning so that their backs were toward each other as they faced their enemy.

There was a heartbeat of silence, each army assessing the other, until Ronan let out a fierce battle cry. Then there was nothing but chaos. Fire blasted out of his hand in an arc, setting four of the Shadows in front of him on fire. The rest of the Shadows moved inhumanly fast, the first of them jumping toward Serena. She swung her sword once he was airborne, the Fire and Earth enhanced weapon aiming true. There was a garbled groan and then a thump as the ghastly head flew from the body, covering them in its thick black ichor.

Ronan quickly lost track of the others as he began swinging his flaming axes, cutting heads from bodies with each swing. He kept moving, knowing if they caught him, they would take him down. With each turn he'd catch a glimpse of one of the others. Kragen, taking on multiple Shadows at once, ducking and spinning so fast they could not touch him. Darrin running and sliding beneath a grasping hand so that he came up behind a Shadow, slitting its throat so cleanly, the head teetered drunkenly on its neck before tumbling to the ground. Effie was expertly swinging her staff, stunning the Shadows with her blows while Serena worked to finish the kill. Even Timmins and Joquil had a swath of bodies around them. Joquil was weaving powerful Water magic, freezing the Shadows in place and allowing Timmins to swing his mace into their frozen heads making them shatter into small gray shards.

Around them, bodies continued to fall, but there was no end to the waves of mindless, soulless creatures. Ronan's hands were growing slick with the black blood, his grasp on his ax slipping. It was a minute movement, but it changed the angle just enough that his blow did not land at the neck but instead bit into the shoulder. The Shadow grinned at him as it launched itself at him. Ronan swung again, but the missed blow allowed another Shadow to reach him. He felt the nails and teeth scrape against him, piercing his shield.

Ronan grunted, pain flaring hot in his side as the poisonous blood made contact with his skin.

Then Serena was there, making quick work of the Shadow at his side so that he could dispatch the one before him. There was barely enough time for a hurried "Thanks" before more filled in the empty space.

Ronan couldn't miss the look in Serena's eyes as she braced for the next attack. It was impossible to say whether they had been fighting for hours or minutes, but the Shadows were relentless, and she wasn't sure how much longer they'd be able to hold them off.

There was a whimpered cry, and Ronan spun, seeing Effie go down under two of the brutes. Before he could move to assist her, Darrin was there, tackling them and knocking them to the ground. They were stunned just long enough for him to finish the kills. Effie blinked up at him with wide-eyed amazement. Darrin offered her a smug grin, before helping her stand and quickly dispatching three more.

Ronan lifted his eyes, seeing Nial and Miranda in the distance, using blasts of power to distract some of the Shadows. They were so focused on the ones in front of them, they did not notice the handful that had crept up behind them.

"Nial!" he shouted, using Air to reinforce the word so he would be able to hear it. Nial spun but went down under the combined attack. Serena had also spun at the word, and was already flying back across the field to his aid. Trying to buy her time, Ronan let out another blast of Fire, in an attempt to clear a path for her. It worked, at least long enough for her to get past them and start to make her way up the hill.

Unfortunately, the Shadows closest to him, now on fire, were still coming at him, trying to grasp him with their smoldering hands. Ronan continued his deadly dance, but there were too many, and his cil'virga was spread too thin. Kragen was trying to work his way back to him, but couldn't cover the distance in time. He knew he was in trouble when the searing heat of fire crept up his back.

The pain was fierce and immediate, but Ronan only shouted, "It will take more than that to stop me!" and spun around, axes slashing into the ring of bodies around him, severing limbs and knocking them down as he did. But the damage was done. The remaining Shadows smelt his blood and began flocking toward him, grasping and pulling at him until he stumbled, falling beneath the writhing mass of bodies.

CHAPTER TWENTY-SEVEN

*M*icha let himself into the castle, making his way down the familiar halls unimpeded. Despite spending most of his formative years here, the place felt foreign. If not in appearance, certainly in tone. What had once been a warm, welcoming home, richly decorated in vibrant fabrics and colors, was now dark and distinctly oppressive. Not a single fire burned in any of the large hearths, and Micha shivered at the chill that permeated through the thick stone walls.

His senses were screaming at him to get out, that this was not a safe place, but he forced himself to continue on. He was slowly working his way toward the back of the castle, toward the room his mother had often referred to as its center of power. Micha remembered loving the sound of that when he was young, as if the castle was alive and powerful, just like him. When he'd asked how she knew which room held the power, his mother had simply responded that there were certain places where the Great Mother was more present and if you were lucky you might find one. She told him it meant that they were very blessed indeed to have such a place in their own home. Given the recent turn of events, it seemed likely he would find her there.

Micha continued to wander, ghosts of childhood memories

haunting him with each step. He rounded a corner and stopped dead. "Gillian?" he whispered, staring in horror at the bloodied face of his twin.

Gillian had been taking stumbling steps toward him, using the wall to keep herself upright. Deep purple bruises anchored bloodshot eyes that were all but swollen closed. At the sound of her name, her eyes shot up wild with panic as she shrieked, "What are you still doing here? Changed your mind and come back to finish the job?" Her voice was completely distorted due to her injuries.

He frowned at her words and took a few steps toward her, holding up his hands in a placating way when she flinched. "Illy, it's me."

Tears filled her eyes at the nickname and she collapsed to the floor, "I-ika," she stammered.

Micha moved forward, going to his knees before her. "It's okay, I'm here now," he murmured soothingly, wrapping his arms around her and pressing her gently into his chest. He couldn't bear to see her suffering this way. Even though he'd been disappointed when he'd heard what she had been up to these past months, he couldn't bring himself to stay mad at her. This was his twin and he would love her regardless.

Gillian sobbed as he held her, whimpering over and over, "What have I done?"

"Shhh, Illy. It's alright. Everything will be alright," he promised.

"How can you say that?" she hiccupped, "The world is quite literally going to shit."

Micha chuckled at her words, "It just looks bad at the moment. You'll see, we will get through this together."

"How touching," an icy voice sneered from behind him.

The twins froze, moving away from each other and looking up at their mother. She stood just behind them, arms crossed with lips set in a severe frown. She looked impossibly young, as if the years had been going in reverse, erasing all of the smile lines that were once etched into her beautiful face.

Micha met her gaze and tensed. There was no recognition in her eyes. Nothing to indicate that she was pleased to see her son. This was not the woman he remembered. She was a cold, inhuman shell.

"Mother," Micha said formally, helping his sister stand. "It is good to see you well," he lied.

Rowena snorted, "I can't say the same."

He flinched as if he'd been struck, mouth falling open in shock. *Who was this imposter? This woman couldn't have actually given birth to him.*

Rowena turned coolly assessing eyes to Gillian, noting her injuries and stating, "It's a pity she didn't do me a favor and just kill you while she had the chance."

Gillian stiffened under his arm, chin trembling as she fought against further tears.

Micha opened his mouth to protest his mother's harsh words, but she lifted a hand before he could speak, cutting off his air supply and causing him to choke.

"That's quite enough out of you, traitor," she snapped, lifting her fisted hand higher and causing Micha's feet to scramble for purchase as he began to rise off of the floor.

"Mother please!" Gillian cried, "I've done everything you asked. You promised to spare him!"

"I have no use for a blood traitor. He led my enemy straight to me. As if that wasn't bad enough, you, my sorry excuse for a daughter, not only invite her in, you let her take the only leverage I had and walk back out! I've never seen a more worthless pair!" Rowena spat, her voice filled with venom.

Micha's face was red as he struggled against the invisible hands that held him. Rowena's eyes flashed with malice and she clenched her fist tighter before jerking it quickly to the right. A loud crack echoed off the stone walls as the bones in Micha's neck shattered and his body fell lifelessly to the floor.

"Micha!" Gillian wailed, staring aghast at her brother's crumpled form. Body shaking, Gillian moved to launch herself at her mother, calling what little bit of power she could to her hands.

Rowena laughed darkly, "Oh child, as if *you* could ever stand against *me*."

Gillian howled in rage.

Narrowing her eyes, Rowena lifted both her hands, palms facing Gillian. Black ropes of her insidious power snaked out, causing Gillian's eyes to widen in horrified recognition. She'd seen this spell before.

"No!" she shouted desperately, turning to run.

Rowena only laughed harder. Her power wrapped around Gillian, snaking into her still-screaming mouth. Gillian's green eyes turned milky white, black lines slowly forming within them, as her flailing limbs went still. Rowena did not stop, letting the full force of her power continue to seep into Gillian's body. Gillian's long limbs twisted, her body shrinking into itself as her skin turned a dull sickly gray. In opposition, Rowena seemed to swell. Her skin luminous with the power she was absorbing as she fed from her daughter's soul. When she was done, her daughter no longer stood before her. In her place was Rowena's newest Shadow.

Rowena beamed at her creation, "Perhaps now you won't have so much trouble following directions." With that, Rowena began walking, stepping over her son's corpse without pause. Behind her, Gillian's soulless body followed with slow, ambling steps.

CHAPTER TWENTY-EIGHT

*W*hen they arrived in the clearing, Helena staggered, bracing a hand against the rough bark of a tree to steady her while she gagged. She felt as though her body had tried to turn itself inside out. Von was beside her, looking much the same as she felt, although he'd at least managed to remain upright. He ran his hand along the length of her spine, the touch soothing, until she was clear-headed enough to stand on her own.

"Better?"

Her lips twisted in a grimace, "Definitely not my preferred method of travel, despite the convenience."

He chuckled and looked around. There was a thick fog rolling into the trees, blocking their view of the castle and surrounding them in a sparkling mist. Von paled at the sight, his eyes widening and darting over to her. Helena was quick to press her lips to his, letting the warmth of her body against his remind him that she was real and that this was not another of his horrific dreams.

Von rested his forehead against hers, sucking in a shaky breath. *"It would seem I am not as recovered as I'd hoped,"* he admitted, smoky gray eyes staring into hers.

"You will be," she promised as they straightened.

There was a searing pain in her side; the Jaka, reminding her that they needed to hurry. She moved away from her mate, although not far, shielding her eyes and using her power to help her see through the fog.

"What do you see?" he asked softly.

Helena shook her head, not having spotted anything of note, when her eyes finally found them. She let out a horrified gasp; the army of Shadows before her seemed endless as they swarmed her friends. Her eyes jumped from one to another, counting heads as she searched for one of fiery red. He wasn't there.

Panic began to claw at her, but she pushed it down, focusing instead on the psychic thread that told her he was there. She turned her head, thinking perhaps he'd been cut off from the others, when she saw a flash of red hidden beneath a mass of squirming limbs. They'd taken him down, she realized. Anger flared incandescent, causing her power to simmer and call her to the battle.

Before she could join them, she needed to find the rest of her friends. That was still only five. *Where were the others?* Her gaze continued to scan the field, noting the snapping jaws of the wolves as they too took down Rowena's monstrosities, but only stopping her frantic search once she spotted the last of her friends. Nial was beside Miranda, colorful orbs flying from their hands and into a wall of approaching Shadows. Serena was just about to reach them, her ax alight with fire as her mouth opened on a war-cry that had the others ducking. She let go of her weapon. It flew in tight circles, until it made contact and neatly lopped off the head of the nearest Shadow, before returning to her open hand.

Helena's rage grew with each passing second. These were her people, the ones she'd vowed to protect. She could not let them continue to fight alone. Especially not when they were so clearly outnumbered.

She spun to Von, her voice urgent, "I need to go."

"Not without me," he countered, thick arms crossed over his broad chest.

Helena eyed him. He was barely pieced together, but there was no way he'd willingly stand back while the others were under attack; it went against everything he believed in. Helena should know; it was the same for her. "I don't have time to argue with you about all the reasons that's a bad idea. Please stay safe, my love. I just got you back." She leaned up and pressed a kiss, hot and fierce, against his lips before taking a few steps back.

His eyes smoldered, love and desire swirling in their depths, "You as well, Mate."

She nodded, and let out the low whistle that would bring Starshine to her.

When she spoke again, her eyes had begun to swirl with iridescent fire, and her voice was thick with power. "Your brother is to the west, it looks like he could use you. I will clear the field."

Von looked up as dark roiling clouds began to amass in the early morning sky before nodding and taking off in the direction she had indicated, using his power to cover the distance via a series of blinks. Helena watched him go, hating that he was entering a battle when he was already weakened. She would just have to ensure it was a short one.

Determination filled her as her Talyrian came into view. Starshine had barely landed when Helena launched herself onto her back.

"Fly, girl," she shouted, drawing her power, every churning drop, to the surface.

Starshine took two running steps and flung them into the air, gaining height quickly. Once airborne, they were surrounded by heavy black clouds and Starshine streaked through them like a falling star. Thunder growled and lightning cracked as the pair approached the place where her friends were fighting.

Helena let out an inarticulate cry which caused the others to look up in raw panic. Their reassurance at the sight of her was palpable, their cheers turning to battle cries that spurred them to fight with renewed vigor. Holding out her hands, now glowing with her power, she let out one savage word, "Burn!"

Starshine roared, letting out a pure beam of fire that caused an entire row of Shadows to turn to ash. Helena threw her hands up, releasing her power into the clouds. Her hair flew behind her, the ends looking like living flame as they floated on the air. There was another roll of thunder as fiery comets began to streak through the storming sky. The world was on fire.

Everywhere she turned, Shadows were alight. Helena channeled her power to create shields for each of her friends, using her connection through the Jaka to help isolate where they were, and using proximity to locate the others. She did the same for herself and Starshine, allowing them to fly unscathed through the sky.

Catching Kragen's eye, Helena pointed to where Ronan had fallen. Her Sword made his way over, easily dispatching the few lingering Shadows, until he was able to pull Ronan up. The man was covered in thick black blood, and it seemed he'd acquired several new injuries that would scar. Helena watched as long as she could, waiting to ensure he was alright before refocusing on the fight. She finally moved on, once he'd pulled his weapon out of a dead body and swung it into another Shadow.

They continued circling the field as Helena's power fueled the firestorm. The air was thick with ash, floating up from the charred bodies and spiraling into the air. It was getting hard to see clearly, but it looked like they were finally making a dent in Rowena's army. Helena could sense someone watching her. The hair on the back of her neck lifted as she risked a glance toward the castle. That was when she saw her.

It was the scene from the Keepers' warning, but not. A blonde woman was standing on a balcony, but she was not alone. Unlike her vision, she was flanked by six others and they were nothing like the hairless, skeletal creatures fighting below. These beings still appeared mostly human, having only the same white eyes shot through with black that indicated they were some form of Shadow. All of them were clearly male, except one.

Helena gasped, recognition shooting through her at the red-haired female at Rowena's side. The bitch queen had turned her own daughter into a monster, taking her soul and feeding on her power until there was nothing left but an abomination. Disgust caused her stomach to roll and Helena launched a ball of Fire toward the balcony.

Rowena's lips curled in amusement as her own mouth opened. Two things happened at once: a large creak, like the sound of a gate being lowered, echoed over the field just as Helena's fireball froze and began to plummet. The glittering ball smashed into the stone of the balcony, missing its mark entirely. Starshine shot jets of fire at Rowena, but they hit an invisible barrier and turned to smoke. Helena fumed while Rowena laughed.

It was then that the second thing Rowena had done became apparent. Row after row of shadows made their way through a now open gate and onto the killing field; their mindless bodies stumbling over the corpses of the fallen. There were not mere hundreds of new Shadows, there were thousands of the creatures marching toward her friends.

Comprehension dawned. This was where everyone had gone, why she hadn't seen a single person when she made her way to the castle. All of the people that should have been needed to keep a castle such as this running, all of the villagers that would have helped work the land and feed them; Rowena had turned every single one of them into one of her Shadows.

It was no wonder she had not bothered them these last months, she has been building her army. With every Shadow Rowena created, she also added to her own power, not just her fighting force.

Helena looked at where her friends were still fighting, clearly losing ground under the new assault. They'd been making progress, had almost completely eliminated all the Shadows that remained, but they would not be able to fend off a couple thousand more. Each one of them was already showing signs of fatigue. She watched as Darrin slipped, his weapon lopping off an arm instead of the creature's head. The Shadow did not stop, slashing at Darrin with its remaining hand, causing thin ribbons of blood to appear.

They were outmatched. Her stomach dropped, she alone would not be enough to save them. There were just too many, and if Rowena added her power to the fight, she could destroy them all. Helena needed to get them out. Now.

Sensing her need, Starshine dove, eradicating the entire front line of the Shadows with a long torrent of flame. It was enough of a break for her to be able to shout to the others, "Back! Get back!"

Helena watched as her friends ran, Effie stumbling and falling to her hands and knees. Darrin was already beside her, lifting her into his arms and running. Timmins and Joquil continued to fend off the remaining Shadows that were closest, keeping an open path for Kragen and Ronan to run through. Once together, the four men followed after the other two.

She fed the storm, fire flying through the sky until there was a wall of flame between her people and Rowena's army. It should be enough to buy them the time they needed to escape. Starshine made one last turn, ready to head back, when a blast of power hit her.

Helena and Starshine let out twin shrieks of rage at the impact that rocked Helena so hard she was almost hanging off the side. Starshine righted, allowing Helena to climb back into place, but her wing had been damaged and each flap of her great wings was an obvious struggle. The blast of power must have obliterated the shield that had been protecting the Talyrian. Releasing some of the Fire she was still channeling, Helena pressed her hand into Starshine's fur, assessing the injury and pouring Water's healing magic into her. Bone and flesh knit itself back together, allowing Starshine to continue flying them to safety.

They landed and Helena slid off, running toward the others. They were all there, some in better shape than others, but all alive. There was no time to explain what she intended.

"Go!" She screamed to Starshine, who let out a roar and took to the sky.

"Everyone grab onto each other!" she barked the orders, trusting they would follow without question.

Von moved to stand beside her, wrapping his arm around her waist, his eyes never straying from his brother. Helena hastily scanned her Mate, checking for new injuries, but while he was covered in foul black ichor, there were none. She allowed herself a brief instant of relief before shifting her focus.

Ronan was at her other side, his hand clasping and squeezing hers.

The others pulled in. Serena and Nial holding each other, while Darrin still carried Effie. Timmins had hauled Miranda to him, and Joquil and Kragen filled in the spaces between them. Even Karma and the rest of the bloodied, battle-worn Daejaran wolves drew close, sensing the urgency in her order.

"Where's Micha?" she asked, just now realizing his red head was not among them.

Ronan frowned and shook his head. There wasn't time for Helena to feel more than a pang at the news, the need to get away overriding every other emotion. She pulled the small purple stone once more from her pocket.

"Helena," Von said tersely, "are you sure that's possible?"

She wasn't. Knowing that the stones worked off charge, and not knowing how much remained, she could only hope. Safe; they needed to get somewhere safe. Her mind scrambled to think of a place she could transport them.

"Hold on!" she shouted, squeezing her eyes shut and focusing on the image of a campsite they'd had near the border. Helena used every last vestige of power that remained to reinforce her intention as the world went black.

CHAPTER TWENTY-NINE

*S*everal days had passed since they had made it back to the Palace. Their injuries had been relatively minor. Surprisingly, Ronan suffered the worst out of all of them, if you discounted Von. Helena couldn't help the small snort of laughter that escaped at his reaction when she'd healed him.

Unable to distinguish between new and old injuries, or perhaps it was because she was simply too tired to try, Helena had flooded his body with her healing magic. When Ronan had looked in the mirror he'd scowled darkly and shouted, "Put it back!"

Her magic had repaired *all* the damage, meaning that the scar that had bisected his face for so long was gone. The rest of them had been greatly amused to see the amount of female attention he was now receiving, but it only annoyed Ronan further; a testament to the fierce reputation he'd worked so hard to foster having vanished along with the marks of battles fought and won.

"I hope that smile is for me, Mate," Von whispered in her ear, large hands kneading into the muscles of her back.

"Mmm," she murmured, eyes closing, "all of my smiles are for you."

He nipped at her ear playfully before moving to stand before her.

247

Helena looked up into eyes that were anything but playful, her cheeks flooding with color as his desire rolled over her. The air between them was charged as Von held out a hand, helping her out of her chair and pulling her into his arms.

They had spent the past few nights tangled together, whispering until the sky began to lighten, not wanting to close their eyes and find that being together again was a dream. It had been a time of tenderness, letting bodies and hearts heal from their separation, their need to simply hear and touch each other surpassing any other physical need. But no longer. Her Mate's intention was clear.

He dropped his head to kiss the fingers grasping his, looking up at her through thick black lashes and grinning wickedly, "It's time for bed, Mate."

Helena felt her mouth go dry, only capable of nodding. Von led her to their bed, stopping to pull back the thick purple blanket before facing her again. He let his fingers trace the edges of her dress, dipping them into the valley between her breasts briefly, before continuing his exploration.

She could feel her breath hitch, the gentle caresses at complete odds with the hunger she could see in his eyes. The same hunger she was feeling. Von lifted his other hand, both grasping the thin cotton before rending it in two.

Helena looked down, shocked. Large aqua eyes looked back into his, "I liked that dress!"

Von chuckled, "I'll get you a new one. We're now even for the time you ruined the one I liked." He peeled the dress away, his hands continuing their exploration of her body. His touched faltered when he caught the subtle shimmer of her Jaka in the soft light. He was silent as he traced the tattoo along her side, his touch sending flickers of electricity throughout her body. His thumb brushed the underside of her breast as he followed the swirling marks that represented their bond.

"I'd be lying if I said it didn't bring me great pride to see you wearing the mark of my people." Von's low growl was as sensual as his touch. His eyes were molten silver as they bore into hers, "But I hate that you were marked by another."

Helena tried to bite back her smile, "I knew you would say that."

A corner of Von's mouth curled as he purred, "Did you now?"

She tilted her head to the side as she teased, "I would have to be an utter fool not to." He chuckled at that, his eyes dropping to her lips as she continued, "But even you cannot deny that you are more than adequately represented in the mark."

His eyes filled with pleasure as they swept over the Jaka again, "Aye."

The possessive pleasure she heard in the word also reverberated through their bond and she felt her lips tip in delight. This was her Mate. The man who, with only a look, had her soul cry out *'Mine.'*

Von knew the instant her mood shifted from amusement to arousal, his nostrils flaring as his eyes darkened in response. He bent to kiss her, pressing his body against hers until there was not even a sliver of space between them. The kiss was a fierce claiming, his mouth and tongue moving against hers in an erotic prelude to what their bodies would do. Helena shivered at the contact, feeling her nipples contract into tight points while heat flooded her core.

He pulled back to rest his forehead against hers, chest rising and falling with his harsh breaths. *"I do not think I can be gentle,"* he warned her, cherishing the added intimacy of speaking to her through their bond.

"Then don't be," she responded, wrapping her arms around his neck and pushing up onto her toes. Her fingers threaded through his silky black hair as she kissed him with all of the pent-up desire she'd been feeling. Von's hands gripped at her hips, fingers digging in deeply as he took a step back and sat down hard on the bed, pulling her body on top of his.

Helena straddled his lap, rubbing herself against the straining bulge beneath his pants, "I need you," she whispered hotly against his lips, biting and sucking on them as he ran his hands along the sides of her body.

Von growled low in his throat, twisting so that Helena fell onto her back and he was kneeling between her spread legs. He moved his hands up her thighs, stretching her wider.

"Please," she whispered, wanting the feeling of completion that would come when he slid into her.

He let his fingers slip through the slickness at her center, smiling at the harsh gasp and lift of her hips the movement caused. His eyes bore into hers when he slipped a finger inside of her, "Is this what you want?"

Helena shook her head from side to side, "N-no," she moaned.

"No?" he asked, lifting a dark brow, his fingers stilling inside her.

"M-more," she panted, pressing down around the finger that was curling inside her.

Von slid another finger in, working her slowly as his other hand released the binding of his pants. "Better?" he asked in a carnal rumble.

"No," she whimpered, eying the flesh now exposed and hanging thick and heavy between his legs.

Von grinned, tracking her eyes, "Feeling greedy, Mate?"

Helena nodded, her tongue darting out to wet her lips, "Very."

His eyes darkened at the sight of her tongue and he let out a low grunt. Von pulled his fingers slowly out of her, rubbing her wetness into the small bundle of nerves and causing her to groan. He removed his pants and returned to her, grasping her around the knees and pulling her toward where he was standing. He used his power to create the phantom hands that continued to run over her body as he took his thick length into his hand and ran it along her center.

"Is this what you want?" he asked again, his voice harsh with need.

"Yes," she moaned, trying to press the tip of him deeper inside her.

"Good," he growled, slamming into her in one long thrust while his fingers, real and phantom, rubbed and plucked at her.

"Von!" she cried, arching off the bed and coming apart around him.

"Mine," he snarled, bending over to capture her lips with his.

He began pushing into her, thrusting hard and fast. Her heart raced in time with his, each of them reveling in the feeling of being joined again. Helena met him thrust for thrust, nails digging into his back as she held him.

She could feel him all around her: his smell, his body, his love. It was overwhelming. Her need began to spiral again. Sensing it, Von bit down on the skin between her neck and shoulder, hips driving faster. Helena broke, crying out his name. He followed, stealing her cries with his lips as he emptied himself inside her.

They lay there, wrapped around each other, hearts still pounding and bodies slick with sweat. "Now I'm home," he whispered.

Her heart was too full for words, so she held him tighter, not letting him move away from the cocoon of her body. She let her hand continue to run up and down his back, tugging on the strands of hair that had grown long while he was away.

He chuckled, and looked down at her, "Enjoying yourself?"

"Aye," she responded, hands now squeezing the firm muscles of his butt.

His smile fell and his eyes glittered, "Keep it up."

The sexual warning had languid muscles tensing with desire. "Like this?" she whispered, hands cupping the heavy weight of him.

Von flexed into her, hard once more.

"Already?" she teased.

He gave her a look, equal parts adoration and arousal, "Always. I will always be ready for you, *Mira*. To remind you that you belong to me," he whispered, taking her lower lip between his teeth and running his tongue along the length of it.

"Mmm," she murmured in approval.

"Besides, Mate, we have barely begun to make up for the time we lost."

She smiled, fingers running up his back and into his hair, "If you insist."

"I do," he said fiercely, his body reinforcing the promise of his words.

Helena's eyes rolled back, feeling whole once again as a broken part of her soul finally fell back in place.

CHAPTER THIRTY

*H*elena woke up slowly, enjoying the feeling of being curled around Von. He ran his hands over her hair, pressing his lips into the top of her head, "Good morning, Mate."

"Morning, my love," she whispered, snuggling deeper into him.

"Timmins has already sent word. The Circle is meeting to discuss the formal steps of declaring war against the traitor Rowena."

Helena scowled, annoyed that the bitch had found a way to sour her morning already.

"We cannot put it off much longer, *Mira*," Von said with soft understanding, "her army is vast already. We need to call on our allies if we are to have any hope of defeating her."

She pressed her face into his neck and muttered inaudibly.

"What was that?" he laughed, pulling away to see her face.

"I know," she sighed, rolling her eyes and sitting up.

Von's gaze darkened as he took in the sight of her naked body, his hands moving to trace over the sparkling swirls of her Jaka. He replaced his fingers with his lips, pressing a lingering kiss over the central mark between her ribs before looking up at her with hopeful eyes.

She slapped his hand away with a breathless laugh, "You're the one that said we had to go."

He frowned, looking like a child that had been denied his favorite toy, "What's five more minutes? We're late already."

Helena smirked, "Only five minutes?"

Von grinned lasciviously and made to move on top of her when a knock sounded on the door.

They each let out annoyed sighs and pulled the discarded remnants of clothing up to quickly dress. Helena laughed when she found the torn dress she'd worn the night before, Von winking as she used her magic to repair the damage.

Alina popped her head in, her smile radiant as she took in her mistress slapping away the hands of her Mate. "They are calling for you, Kiri," she announced once she caught their attention, trying not to laugh at Helena's flustered expression.

"We're on our way," Helena informed her maid.

With a quick nod, Alina disappeared back through the door.

Once they were both dressed, and appeared mostly unrumpled, Von grasped Helena's hand in his and led her down toward the Circle's Chambers.

THE MEN WERE MILLING around the hallway, chatting in quiet but jovial voices when they rounded the corner. Helena smiled when she saw that Ronan had been invited to join them. Still an unofficial member of the Circle, he had more than proven that he deserved a place as one of her trusted advisors. Helena had briefly contemplated asking if he would consider being the leader of the Rasmiri, but his loyalty to Von and the people of Daejara had held her back. Perhaps it was something she and Von could discuss later.

A sense of peace greeted her at the sight of the ones she had come to love; safe and whole at home. There had been a moment, when Helena had considered unleashing everything she had at Rowena, but the energy required for such an attack would have left the rest of them vulnerable. She'd had to choose between eliminating her enemy and protecting thousands of nameless others, or saving the lives of the ones she'd already sworn to protect and letting Rowena go. It had not been an easy choice, but she'd made it gladly. Seeing them here, now, laughing and joking with one another, only reinforced that she'd made the right choice. They would deal with Rowena together.

Kragen saw her first, lifting an arm to wave, "There they are! We were about to draw straws to see which of us was going to have to haul you two lovebirds out of bed."

From the glower on Darrin's face, Helena could already tell who had drawn the short straw.

"Lucky for all of you, none of you were foolish enough to try," Von drawled as he punched Ronan on the arm by way of greeting.

Ronan frowned and rubbed his shoulder, "What was that for? I wasn't the one that was going to interrupt you..." he trailed off, smirking smugly as he added, "this time."

Von grinned, "That would have earned you a punch in the balls instead."

Ronan gave Von a skeptical sidelong glance as he protectively placed his hands in front of his crotch; years of friendship and familiarity causing him to doubt such a blow wasn't about to be delivered anyway.

Noting the stance, Von snickered, "At ease, bastard. I was only paying you back for touching my Mate."

Ronan looked confused for a moment, trying to ascertain when he'd inappropriately touched Helena, before his knitted brows lifted and he laughed with understanding.

"It was beautifully done," Von added in a more subdued tone, referring to the Jaka he'd so lovingly traced earlier that morning, "I could not have done better myself."

The red-haired warrior shrugged in a show of dismissal, but Helena noted the way his cheeks tinged red at the compliment.

"It was also incredibly useful," Helena added, offering her own appreciative smile.

The two men made murmurs of agreement, although Von's lips

twitched with laughter as he threatened, "Don't think that means you can do it again."

Ronan winked at Helena, "Only if the lady asks me to."

"Dream on," Von sneered, punching his friend again.

Ronan's shoulders shook with laughter and Helena shook her head in amusement at their antics before kissing Von's cheek and stepping past them toward the others. "Shall we get started?" The men nodded and followed her as she made her way into the familiar room.

A black lacquered box sat unopened in the middle of the table shining in the soft glow of the firelight. "What's this?" she asked with delighted surprise as she stepped into the room. "A present? It's not my name day."

She stepped toward it quickly, filled with giddy anticipation. Her hands eagerly reached for the lid, lifting a cream piece of parchment. It had been sealed with a deep purple wax; a knot of thorns its emblem.

Helena looked up from the box and back toward her Circle. The smile began to fade from her face as she took in the expressions of confusion and unease. The same feelings grated against her mind's inner barrier through her connection to each of them.

Her blood turned to ice and her brows knit together.

"Helena," Joquil cautioned. Her aqua eyes were transitioning to iridescent as she scanned the box for any lingering sense of magic, something that would indicate who it was from or what was inside it. There was nothing.

Using a nail to peel back the seal, Helena unfolded the small piece of parchment. Two words were scrawled in a feminine hand: *Your move.* The note fell from Helena's trembling fingers. Kragen moved quickly to snatch it before it hit the ground. She struggled to open the box's latch until it finally came free with a soft click.

"Helena!" Von shouted, realizing who the package was from after reading the words over Kragen's shoulder. Her name also reverberated within her mind as he reinforced the cry through their bond.

He blinked, crossing the distance between them with his power, but he was still too late. Helena had already opened the box. Her face drained of all color and her mouth opened on a keening wail that amplified the men's fear tenfold. The Circle closed in around her.

Von looked into the box and felt his stomach lurch. He made a move to grab Helena when her knees buckled and she fell to the floor. He caught her and fell with her so that they both knelt on the floor. He tried to comfort her by tucking her into his body.

"No," she sobbed, seeming to gasp for air. All traces of the happiness she'd felt just moments ago completely vanished and were replaced by bone-deep terror. Von tried again to wrap his arms around his shaking Mate, but she pushed him off. On her hands and knees she panted, struggling to breathe.

Darrin peered into the box before staggering back. Horror and revulsion stole across his handsome face. He heaved and barely made it to the window before becoming violently ill.

"Breathe. Breathe, my love," Von murmured, stroking her back and adding through their bond, *"Please, Mira. You've got to try."*

Helena took a deep shuddering breath, her entire body shaking. Von winced as he felt her nails crack and break as she scraped them along the ground. He watched as she grasped and crumpled the forgotten piece of parchment that Kragen had let slip through his fingers, blood smearing along its creamy surface. Watched as she slowly sat back on her heels, threw her head back, and screamed.

The scream shattered every piece of glass in the Palace, and echoed through the grounds and beyond. Birds scattered from their perches in the trees, taking flight in an attempt to flee the pain and rage that created that sound.

In her fist, the note began to smoke and caught fire. It burned quickly until all that remained was a smoldering pile of ash. The men paled as they took in the sight of her. Her hair flew around her like flame and her eyes glowed with swirling light as she stared past them, unseeing, and snarled the words that were both promise and verdict.

"My turn."

To be continued in Crown of Embers

FROM THE AUTHOR

If you enjoyed this book, please consider writing a short review and posting it on Amazon, Goodreads and/or anywhere else you share your love of books. Reviews are very helpful to other readers and are greatly appreciated by authors (especially this one!) When you post a review, send me an email and let me know! I might feature part, or all, of it on my blog or social media sites.

XOXO

Meg Anne

Meg@MegAnneWrites.com
Want to know when I have a new release or get exclusive access to my works in progress?
Join my mailing list: MegAnneWrites.com/Newsletter

ACKNOWLEDGMENTS

I can't believe it's already time to sit down again and thank the people that helped make this book possible. From the bottom of my heart, thank you for your patience, kind words, and encouragement. I continue to write because of you.

Grandpa: The safest place I've ever known was curled in your lap. You inspire me even now. I miss you. See you in my dreams.

Maggiepants: You're not even a reader and you love my books. I can't tell you what that means to me. You continue to be the strongest woman I know, no matter what the world throws at you. I still want to be like you when I grow up: dancing my way down the halls and eating ice cream for dinner.

To the Lady that Borne Me: Hearing you pimp my book to literally everyone makes my heart want to explode. I'll never forget being at book signings (as a reader) and having other authors come over and tell me they are looking forward to reading *my* book. I am so lucky I get to call you Mom. I love you forever.

Bruce: You love unconditionally. People will never understand what true love is until they see the way you look at mom. Thank you for feeding me <3

Lil Bit: I promise if I ever write about you, I'll do you justice.

She'll be just as strong, passionate, and independent as you. A true unicorn in the midst of a bunch of horses. And her hair will change color regularly. Love you alotta bit.

Brother: I am so proud of the man you are turning into. Your kindness and humor never cease to make me laugh. I love that I can be a geek with you, and that you continue to indulge my massive nerd moments. Love you.

Auntie Stacy: This year has been a rough one for you. There have been way too many close calls. You continue to show me what a strong woman can accomplish when she believes in herself (and that nothing else matters if she does). We are all better for having you in our lives.

Fran: We made it through another book without you cutting me off! Thank you for being a shoulder to cry on, my safe place, the person I can be my ugliest self with and still know that I am loved. You keep me honest. I can only hope I am ½ the friend to you that you have been, and continue to be, for me.

Gabe: You are my person. I am the luckiest girl in the world to have someone who supports me the way that you do. You are my alpha reader, critique partner, cheerleader, big spoon, and favorite Canadian in the entire world (sorry Karma – you're a close second). Love you all of the muches.

BFB: Thank you for your unflappable faith in my words and me. You make me laugh and you are beyond generous with your time and support. I appreciate everything you continue to do for me.

J. Mill & Gypsy: My unicorn sisters!!! The universe was feeling generous the day he brought you into my life. Your friendship and support (of each other and for me) is sacred. Everyone should have a friendship as amazing as yours. I am thankful you let me bask in it for awhile.

#Squadpod: There are no words. Thank you for the support, dirty GIFs, naughty jokes, and endless epic stories. Your talent inspires me to do better. Jess, Ava, Jane, Liv, JL, Paige, Nicole, CL, Kim, Brooke & Harloe I love you!

The Future Mrs. Pratt (sorry Biceps): Girl… I fudging love you. You are AMAZEBALLS. Seriously. I think you might be the kindest, sweetest, most cheerful ball of sunshine in the entire world. You make everything better. When I feel like no one else gets it, you do. You and I are going to take over the world. God help them.

Becks & AlphaBeta: You girls rock! I am so thankful to have you as friends. I value your opinions and appreciate all of the support and demand for my words. You kept me going when I got too in my head. I can't wait for next year!

Hanleigh: Thank you again for helping my words shine. You are incredible and I'm so happy I found you!

Lori: Your covers are simply glorious. On top of that, you are simply a top-notch human being. Thank you for bringing my words to life via your art. I can't wait to see what we come up with next. #tarotcards

Chosen: Thank you for bringing light and laughter to each of my days. You sure know how to make a girl feel loved. I've enjoyed getting to share the journey of this book with you. I hope that it was worth the wait!

Hellscream Peeps: I really miss our raid nights. You guys are some of the best friends a girl can have. Ser, Paul, NRN, Dunosaur, Jhinnx, Rub, Sonic, Adrianne, Aset, Red, Marvae #Megglebites #Mountup #ImUncomfortable #thatmeanstwothangs #54321 #Flove

Henry <3 You might be my cat son, but you bring me so much joy. Your little kitty purrs and all of your cat fails make my days complete. You are the bestest cat that ever catted. Now if you would only let me cuddle you…

ALSO BY MEG ANNE

FANTASY ROMANCE

THE CHOSEN UNIVERSE

THE CHOSEN
MOTHER OF SHADOWS

REIGN OF ASH

CROWN OF EMBERS

QUEEN OF LIGHT

THE KEEPERS
THE KEEPER'S LEGACY

THE KEEPER'S RETRIBUTION (COMING 2019)

THE KEEPER'S VOW (COMING 2019)

PARANORMAL ROMANCE

CURSED HEARTS
CO-WRITTEN WITH JESSICA WAYNE

STAR CROSSED

AMRIA

SUPERNOVA

ABOUT MEG ANNE

Meg Anne has always had stories running on a loop in her head. They started off as daydreams about how the evil queen (aka Mom) had her slaving away doing chores; and more recently shifted into creating backgrounds about the people stuck beside her during rush hour. The stories have been there, they were just waiting for her to tell them.

Like any true SoCal native, Meg enjoys staying inside curled up with a good book and her cat Henry... or maybe that's just her; sunburns hurt! You can convince Meg to buy just about anything if it's covered in glitter or rhinestones, or make her laugh by sharing your favorite bad joke. She also accepts bribes in the form of baked goods and Mexican food.

Meg loves to write about sassy heroines and the men that love them. She is best known for her fantasy romance series The Chosen, which can be found on Amazon.

CPSIA information can be obtained
at www.ICGtesting.com
Printed in the USA
LVHW030722140721
692648LV00006B/820